CRICS

EDWARD J. MCFADDEN III

SEVEREDPRESS

CRICS

"Citizenship is an attitude, a state of mind, an emotional conviction that the whole is greater than the part... and that the part should be humbly proud to sacrifice itself that the whole may live."

— Robert A. Heinlein, Starship Troopers

PROLOGUE

Bright Spring Lab, Staten Island, New York, 8:19 PM EST, *present day*

The night sky glowed with flames, and the acrid scent of burning chemicals filled the air. Thick clouds billowed across the complex, a relentless wind driving the smoke east.

At the center of the thriving scientific campus, the state-of-the-art biological laboratory stands as a bastion of innovation and discovery, and even as the structure burned, its majestic beauty of glass and dull metal remained. The facility hosted groundbreaking research that promised to revolutionize cellular biology and genomics via DNA and RNA splicing, cell-renewal, and deep gene sequencing. It was well known that the researchers who worked at the center created unique life and then killed it as part of their experiments.

The once-pristine corridors flickered with red and white flames, and panic and chaos reigned as researchers and staff burning the midnight oil fought to escape the blaze. In the distance, sirens wailed, and campus emergency services were doing their best, but it was like trying to take the salt out of the sea.

As the flames grew hotter the laboratory's safety protocols were compromised, and hazardous substances were released into the air. Contaminated smoke filled the sky and was carried east with the gusting wind. Sparks shot into the darkness like fireworks, and black specks of ash twisted and eddied like ethereal snow.

Despite the firefighters' best efforts and the laboratory's advanced emergency protection system, the building burned through the night, and when the sun rose over Long Island the Gene Katz Center for Molecular Biology and Genomics was nothing but a smoking skeleton of steel and blackened bricks.

Firefighters poured water, sprayed foam, and spread dry powder on the remnants of the building, but it would take days to fully douse the smoldering remains. Smoke twisted and swirled in a mesmerizing ballet, ghostly tendrils caressing the air, and in this dance, the smoke and wind became one.

The Atlantic Ocean to the east and south, and the Long Island Sound to the north, created a maritime climate, and as the sun heated the island, the temperature rose faster over the land than over the water. This difference caused cooler air from the ocean to flow inland, and this resulted in easterly winds that could carry a candy wrapper from the top of the Empire State Building to the Montauk Lighthouse.

As Long Islanders went to work, many noticed nothing more than the faint scent of smoke and the astringent smell of burning plastic. Newscasters did stories about the Canadian wildfires and preached safety and lectured about the Air Quality Index, a numerical scale used to communicate the quality of the air in a specific location at a given time. The AQI formula measures various air pollutants, including ground-level ozone, particulate matter, carbon monoxide, sulfur dioxide, and nitrogen dioxide, but it was the unknowns that kept the conspiracy theorists and the employees of the Centers for Disease Control and Prevention awake at night.

The smoke plume carried over Long Island and dispersed, and the AQI maxed out at a hundred and seventy-nine on a scale of zero to five hundred. The government urged Long Islanders to stay indoors and avoid outdoor activities, especially sensitive groups like children, the elderly, and those with respiratory conditions. If one had to go out, an N-95 mask or equivalent was recommended.

There was a pile-up on the expressway, a shooting at the Davis Park Casino, and a famous pop star was found passed out on a beach in the Hamptons. The hot sun burned away the morning mist, and by evening rush the smoke plume had passed the lighthouse, where it was scattered on the ocean and within its swirling mists and thick spray.

Saltwater possesses unique properties, and it is often hazardous to tender biological organisms. The toxic smoke was neutralized as it dispersed, the seawater and its briny wind transforming its composition.

What was for a brief time was no more, but the ecology of Long Island was forever altered.

1

Stones Throw, Long Island, New York, 12:27 AM EST, *six days later*

Scott Ward couldn't sleep, and he stared at his bedroom ceiling, trying to piece together his life and figure out what had gone wrong and when.

Jenni ripped a snore, and Ward looked over at his new wife. It wasn't so much that things had gone wrong as much as things hadn't gone as he'd expected. At thirty-one, he'd just enjoyed what he liked to refer to as his second shot at being a teenager. One with some cheese. College graduation led to his job at the firm, and after he passed the bar and got his license he was promoted and was making good money. The problem was that he hated family law, but when he met Jenni, everything had been fresh and new, and the job receded into the background.

A spider crawled across the ceiling and Ward fixed his gaze on it.

The chaos of the engagement, the challenges of COVID-19, then the wedding planning, the event, and the honeymoon period that followed all masked the fact that Jenni and Ward didn't know each other very well and lately, he felt their relationship floundering. He loved her. That he knew, but depression constantly gnawed at the edges of his happiness, and he couldn't seem to shake it.

Beep. Beep. Beep.

Ward's hand shot out and he silenced his phone before it woke his wife. The last thing he needed at two in the morning was a series of questions he didn't have the answers to yet. He couldn't recall hearing the foreign beep before, but the phone showed an alarm from the water sensor in the basement.

Ward sighed as he leaned off the bed, lifted a window shade, and peered outside.

The streetlight cast wavering light over the dark road, but he saw no rain. He'd installed the sensor because the basement leaked sometimes, and pain knifed down his spine as he tried to think of another reason why the sensor was triggered. A malfunction? Then he remembered the old water heater and vaulted from bed.

Jenni stirred and said, "What is it?"

"Nothing." Ward closed the door behind him.

As he padded downstairs, he heard Muffin mewing and crying. When he reached the bottom of the steps he peered through the windows at the top of the front door. No rain.

Ward found the orange and white tabby house cat pressed to the carpet staring under the basement door. Muffin's coat shimmered in the darkness, silvery white whorls and stripes glowing in the half-light.

"Everything alright, Buddy?"

The cat clawed at the carpet as if trying to squeeze under the basement door, then looked up at Ward and meowed.

He bent and stroked the animal. "Easy, sweetie. Easy."

As if Ward hadn't believed her explicit warning, Muffin arched her back, turned, and lifted her tail to give Ward a view of her undercarriage. The cat meowed once more, then sprang away into the darkness.

The house went still. A clock ticked in the kitchen, a fan whirred in the living room, the refrigerator hummed, and he caught the faint scent of garbage. Pale moonlight leaked through the windows, shadows frolicking with the darkness.

An unease crawled just beneath his skin that he couldn't explain. An itch he couldn't scratch, and a warning light flashed on his mental dashboard. Ward considered grabbing one of his guns. The pistol, the Benelli M2 tactical, and the double barrel were secured in the gun locker mounted to the wall in his bedroom's walk-in closet, but he kept a single-shot crack barrel shotgun loaded in the downstairs closet secured with a combination trigger lock.

He rolled his shoulders and shook off the anxiety. What he probably needed was a mop and bucket.

The basement door creaked open, and Ward flicked on the light. An LED dome at the bottom of the steps came to life, illuminating the stairwell. An odd smell wafted up and tickled his nose, and it wasn't the stale odor of soaked carpet. Ward sniffed. The air was oily and musty, and he didn't think he'd ever smelled anything like it.

Ward rubbed sleep from his eyes as he descended the steps, the wall to his right giving way to a half-wall. Moonlight streamed through two egress windows and painted the basement ghostly black and white. He turned on the lights, and old fluorescent fixtures tinkled and snapped as they came to life.

The newlyweds had done nothing to the basement since they'd purchased the house, and green and orange carpet circa 1960 covered the concrete slab floor. There was a series of shelves holding household items, exercise equipment, and a stack of boxes that contained items that hadn't made the cut when he and Jenni had combined their lives. Most of the boxes had his name on them. An old bumper pool table that he and Jenni had never used sat at the center of the space, a rack holding pool cues mounted to the wall by the staircase.

In the far corner was the washer and dryer, and an old wooden table that held supplies and a mound of dirty clothes. On the opposite wall, a door led to the unfinished section of the basement that housed the boiler, the water heater, and an old workbench he hadn't touched.

The musky scent grew stronger, but still Ward saw no signs of water.

He threaded through the basement and inched open the boiler room door. Nothing moved in the pale light leaking in through the egress windows, and he wandered into darkness until he found the chain hanging from the light fixture. He pulled the cord and the space filled with light.

Everything was exactly where he'd left it. There was no water on the floor, and the boiler and water heater looked fine. He breathed a sigh of relief. The sensor was malfunctioning, and that was a hell of a lot cheaper than bringing in a plumber. Not that he had to worry about money, but nobody liked paying for home repairs. There were uneven decks, leaky roofs, puddle-ridden walkways, and ugly paint jobs all over the world that proved this

The sensor was in the far corner of the room under the workbench, because that was where the water usually found its way in. Stones Throw was just north of Montauk Highway, which meant the Ward Casa was only a couple of miles from the Great South Bay. If Ward dug a hole in his backyard, which he had yet to do, he would hit water at around eight feet. That meant the house's basement floor was only a foot or so above the water table.

Ward got down on his hands and knees, the concrete digging into his kneecaps because there was no carpet in the utility room. He reached under the workbench, his hand searching for the sensor, but he couldn't find it. He got low and used his cellphone light, and he jumped when a camelback cricket caught on a glue trap bucked and heaved as it fought to escape. The fat spider-like beasts gave him the willies, even though they were harmless, and he avoided touching the traps as he grabbed the sensor.

He wasn't a tech genius, but he knew his way around a cellphone, and it only took a couple of minutes for Ward to determine that the sensor was functioning properly. With a sigh of frustration, he reset the device, put it back in its place, and made a mental note to hire the kid across the street to replace the glue traps.

With a potential problem averted, Ward straightened and cracked his back.

The sound of a box hitting the floor carried into the boiler room.

His thoughts went to the shotgun. Ward pulled the light cord and killed the lights as he went to investigate, all the bugs in his stomach that had just nodded off to sleep fully awake and stirring the spaghetti and meatballs he'd had for dinner.

At first, he saw nothing unusual, the fluorescent light pushing away the darkness, deep shadows filling every hollow and gap.

Ward's breath caught in his throat, cold terror rooting his feet to the floor.

Beneath the bumper pool table sat a creature that looked like a camelback cricket, better known as a spider-cric, but this was no ordinary house pest. The thing was black and larger than a cat, the upper portion of its hind legs the size of turkey drumsticks, its forelegs arced well above its humped back, which was crisscrossed with white stripes. The vicious thing looked to be half mouth, its jaws lined with transparent icicle-like teeth. Two long antennas wavered above its bulbous eyes, but it was the pinchers at the ends of its front legs that drew Ward's eye.

He stepped back and the Cric inched out from under the pool table, its bulbous eyes locked on Ward. The Cric hopped forward, and Ward pressed himself to the wall and felt the rack holding the pool cues.

The Cric hopped again, this time three feet in the air, and it landed five feet away.

Ward grabbed a pool cue, flipped it so he was holding the thin end, and brandished it like a bat. Sweat trickled down his back, his head pounding as he struggled to wrap his noodle around what he was seeing.

The thing hissed as it pressed itself to the carpet and hopped forward.

Ward swung away with the pool cue but missed.

With a deftness and speed that made Ward's vision go blurry, the Cric sprang at him, jaws flexed open, pinchers snapping and out front in attack position.

He swung again, and this time he made contact.

The thick end of the cue stick smacked the Cric's humped back, and the sound of the cracking carapace and the beast's squeal echoed through the basement. Black blood-like fluid leaked from the cracked shell, and the creature's legs cycled wildly as it tried to right itself.

Ward swung again, and again. He was lost in his fear as he pounded the Cric. When the cue snapped there was nothing but a broken pile of thin bones and black ooze.

He looked around, certain there must be more of the beasts because he felt them, but he didn't see any. With his heart pounding so hard his chest hurt, Ward knelt and examined the Cric's remains.

Without a doubt the creature was some type of camel cricket. A freak of nature, a crossbreed monstrosity that shouldn't be. Crics shouldn't have teeth, and he'd never seen any with pinchers, but what did he know? He'd only had a damp basement for a year. What he did know was the things his mom had called sprickets weren't supposed to be bigger than cats. His thoughts shifted to Jenni.

"Shit," he said to the dead Cric. If Jenni saw this she would want to move, and not just to another house. But what she didn't know wouldn't hurt her. And what did it matter? This mutant was surely one of a kind, an anomaly, and until he saw another one, he saw no reason to worry his wife.

Ward searched the basement and saw no signs of more super Crics. Nor did he see any openings big enough that the monster Cric could've gotten through, even though he knew normal Crics could squeeze through very small cracks, and their eggs were almost microscopic. He used a piece of cardboard to shovel the remains of the dead Cric into a laundry bag and buried the evidence under a pile of empty detergent and fabric softener bottles in the trash can.

With that done, he hid the broken cue stick and did his best to clean the carpet of the Cric's spilled guts with a dirty towel before heading upstairs.

The house was quiet, as if the events in the basement had occurred on another plane of existence. He took a deep breath and let it out slowly before he set out to search the first floor.

Shadows danced in the moonlight that slanted through the windows, and the hum of the house soothed Ward's nerves. The kitchen was clear, the den, his office, the dining room, the living room.

The bathroom door flew open and crashed back against the wall.

Ward no longer had his pool cue, so he threw up his arms to shield his face, his mind's eye painting a picture of bulbous eyes sitting above a mouth full of crystal teeth.

Muffin bolted from the bathroom with a scream of frustration.

Ward fell back and yelled at the cat as it scampered away. "Thanks, Muffin. I really needed that."

With his nerves still tap-dancing on his spine, Ward went up to bed.

"Are you O.K.?" Jenni asked as Ward slipped under the sheets. "You were gone a long time."

"Everything is fine. Go back to sleep." That was what Ward tried to do, but every time he closed his eyes, he saw the Cric, its claws and teeth. Couldn't be, he told himself. Not possible. But his mind just couldn't deny what he'd seen, and he lay still for over two hours staring at the ceiling before he finally fell into a fitful sleep.

2

When the sun came up the next morning the mutant spider-crics were everywhere.

Crics ranging in size from a dime to a basketball covered the house, the lawn, every exterior surface, whether vertical, horizontal, or in-between.

Muffin was the alarm. The cat's incessant meowing drove Ward from bed, and he found the feline sitting on the back of the couch staring out the front bay window. The glass was covered in Crics of various sizes, their pinchers scratching at the glass, antennas waving, bulbous eyes vacant yet shifting in tune with all movement.

"What the hell?" Jenni said as she arrived at the bottom of the stairs.

Ward told her of his adventures the prior night but slipped in the white lie that he'd planned to tell her when she woke.

"What are they? They look like..." She came forward and touched the window and the insects on the glass beneath her fingers stirred. "They look like spider-crics, but..."

"Yeah, but..." he said.

"Turn on the TV and I'll check my phone," she said.

The next hour was spent checking in with family and discovering that the phenomena was localized, and only Long Island had been affected so far. The bridges and tunnels were closed, and until further notice Long Island was, for all intents and purposes, quarantined. The talking heads went on and on about the Crics' growth rate and their amazing ability to replicate, but they had no information about why the creatures had metamorphosized, nor did they know what had caused the predatory modifications to what appeared to be camelback crickets.

It was speculated that the explosion of predatory life was tied to incubation periods and species alignment. No other lifeforms on the island had shown contamination, and the scientists said samples of the creatures needed to be studied before any explanations or remedies could be explored.

To nobody's surprise, the internet had even fewer facts. There were theories galore, most of which centered around mutations caused by the recent smoke plume that had engulfed the island. But the most disturbing thing the newlyweds learned about was the growing segment of opinions, even in these infant stages of the crisis, that wanted to wipe Long Island off the map before the problem broke containment and extended beyond the island.

Not everything they learned was useless.

Ward and Jenni went to work sealing the house. They locked all the windows and used cut-up garbage bags and duct tape to seal every crack, no matter how small.

"What are we going to do when the air runs out?" Jenni asked.

That was a great question and Ward didn't have an answer. He pulled his phone and asked. The net was sluggish. That was to be expected with every connection point currently in use. Nobody had gone to work, and everyone was home like on March 12, 2020, when most of the United States shut down for COVID-19, and people lived on their couches before their TVs like they were adrift in lifeboats.

"It looks like we're O.K.," he said. "The estimates are all over the place, but based on our square footage we've got a minimum of months and a maximum of years."

"With no fresh air intake?"

Ward nodded. "That's what the math says. We'll run out of food way before we run out of oxygen."

Jenni's eyes went wide, and she went into the kitchen and checked that the water was still flowing, and it was. So they filled the bathtub and every vessel in the house and took stock of all sustenance, including cat food, bird seed, and peanuts for the squirrels.

Seeing the animal food made Ward think about the other creatures of the island, the ones who didn't have sealed houses. It was difficult to see out the windows with them covered with Crics, but no squirrels, chipmunks, or other animals could be seen, and no bird song could be heard above the incessant tittering and clicking of the creatures.

When the couple set out to have breakfast, the first survival disagreement occurred.

"I think we should conserve as much food as possible, and eat only when we're really hungry," he said.

"On the surface that may make sense, and it might in the long run, but how long do you think it will be before we lose power, and all the perishables start to go bad?"

"We've got the generator," Ward said, then quickly added, "And gas."

"I know, but where is it?" Her face was free of emotion, but her voice carried the 'know-it-all' tone.

"In the garage." Damn. She had a point. He had envisioned improvised biohazard-type suits, but then he'd remember the pinchers, the mouths full of transparent teeth.

"And even if you could get there, if you opened the garage door the place would be inundated in moments. And would the Crics leave the extension cord alone?"

"Point taken," he said. "I'm not even sure how I'd get out of the house without letting the things in." If the situation stretched out, he'd have to figure out a way to create a makeshift airlock.

With that, the conversation died a natural death, and the partners were subdued as they ate a breakfast of eggs and bacon.

Muffin sat dutifully beside the table, hoping and whining for a piece of bacon.

When they were done a new issue presented itself.

As Jenni scraped congealed egg and stray pieces of toast into the trash, she said, "What should we do with the garbage? It's going to pile up in here and start to stink."

Ward nodded. "I'll clean out the storage cabinet in the basement. We can seal it in there. Let's make sure we tie the bags up tight. They might be down there for a bit."

Jenni glanced toward the hallway and the cellar door. "What did you do with... it?"

At first, Ward didn't understand, then he said, "I used a laundry bag and disposed of it."

"Outside?"

"No, in the basement pail."

The kitchen clock ticked, the refrigerator hummed, and the static of the droning Crics filled the silence.

Ward hadn't been down the cellar, and truth be told he was scared to open the basement door.

Camel crickets were known by many names, one of which was cave cricket because the creatures were commonly found in caves or old mines. In recent times the bugs had proliferated in the basements of homes in suburban areas, drains, sewers, wells, and firewood stacks. All that, combined with the newscasters' assertions about fabulous growth rates, made Ward wonder what waited beyond the basement door.

Jenni said, "Can I see it?"

He said nothing.

She lifted her eyebrows.

Ward sighed and said, "I figure the Cric I killed last night entered the basement when it was small, or it was born down there and its mother was infected, or changed, whatever. I know the things lay eggs, but beyond that, I only know how to catch them."

"So... you think there might be more down there?"

He shrugged.

"If there are, don't we want to know so we can deal with it?"

His wife had a point. Fleeing the house was the worst possible outcome, and if the beasts took over the cellar, it was only a matter of time before they broke through to the upstairs.

This time there was no internal debate about whether to bring a gun with him on his subterranean exploration. Ward left the single-shot shotgun in the downstairs closet and fetched the keys for the gun safe. As Jenni finished with the breakfast cleanup, he retrieved the double-barrel shotgun and the Benelli M2. He loaded the double barrel with one shell of buckshot and one bird, then pumped five shells of buckshot into the Benelli, and slipped a sixth into the firing chamber. The M2 tactical had a pistol grip, double sights, and was semi-automatic after the first load.

Back downstairs, Jenni gripping the double barrel and Ward the Benelli, the couple stood behind the closed cellar door as if it opened on the vacuum of space.

Ward felt the tension poking at his skin and his wife's face was tight with stress.

Meow. Meow.

Jenni jumped and said, "I forgot about Muffin." She leaned her gun against the wall and scooped up the cat.

"Lock her in the spare bedroom," he said.

Jenni complied and said, "How do you want to do this?"

"I'm going to put my back to the wall. You throw open the door and stay out of the way. If there's anything on the stairs, I'll blast it."

His wife smiled. "I think I like this new Rambo you."

Ward licked his lips. They hadn't had sex in weeks, so perhaps he would clean his guns more.

Jenni threw open the door and nothing moved in the shadowy darkness of the stairwell.

Ward turned on the lights. Nothing.

Down in the basement, there were no signs of his previous night's adventure except for the faint black stain on the green and orange carpet, and the spilled box the creature had knocked over. Old Star Wars collectibles were scattered about, and a Han Solo action figure holding a blaster stood upright in the pile of toys.

The couple searched the entire basement, Ward with the tactical shotgun to his shoulder, Jenni bracing the double barrel on her hip. The dead mutant Cric was where Ward had left it, and the stink when he opened the garbage can made the duo cover their noses, but it didn't help.

Jenni stared into the bag, her eyes wide, her lips pressed together, her cheeks taut as her jaws tightened. "It doesn't look like much, but those legs... the teeth and pinchers..."

"You know how cave crickets look huge until you smash them? Sometimes all that's left is legs and it's hard to see the deflated torso. Do you remember the time I—"

The rata-tat of gunfire leaked into the basement, and the titter and whine of the Crics ceased for an instant before resuming louder.

"That can't be good," Ward said.

With the basement cleared, the partners headed back upstairs to investigate.

The sound of more cackling gunshots came from the front of the house.

There was a rumor going around in the local social media groups that claimed the creatures didn't like intense heat, and one could use a hairdryer to heat window glass to chase the creatures away.

"Grab your hairdryer. Fast," said Ward as he pulled the couch away from the front window.

When Jenni returned with her turbo max ionic dryer, Ward cranked it up and played its heat across the bay window. He moved the heat gun in a steady circle and expanded outward from the center of the window.

The Crics squeaked and scuttled over one another as the glass slowly cleared.

Someone walked down Southwood Street, an AR-15 pressed to a shoulder as the person picked off larger targets. The bug soldier wore black hip waders, a leather motorcycle jacket, gloves, and a full crash helmet with its reflective face shield down.

A Cric the size of a poodle leaped at the person from behind a bush, and the bug soldier swung the AR-15 and splattered the bug over its smaller brethren which the person was stomping into oblivion with each step.

All the beasts trilled like a flock of geese protecting one of their own, and Crics big and small hurried to surround and protect their fallen companion.

The bug soldier fired methodically, the rifle barking each time the marksman shifted aim.

But there were too many Crics, and the bug soldier was overcome. The person flailed about as the creatures burrowed and clawed into the neckline of the leather jacket and the motorcycle helmet.

The unfortunate soul fell to a knee, the AR-15 barking and firing into the sky. A shrill wail paused the creatures for a heartbeat, but as the person fell forward, and the rifle clicked empty, the Crics swarmed the fallen body and soon the bug soldier was nothing but a mound of writhing mutants.

Ward shut off the hairdryer, and the window filled with wriggling Crics.

3

Sundown was stressful so Ward and Jenni agreed to sleep in shifts and keep watch. When darkness fell the Crics screeched and argued, mounding over each other in a frenzy as they fought for food. Ward didn't want to think about what would happen when there were no insects left, no rodents, birds, and other small game for the big boys. Most animals—including humans —become increasingly aggressive and violent as food gets scarcer. If the crisis wasn't resolved quickly, humanity would turn on itself. There were far too many examples strewn throughout history to deny the idea.

He sat in the living room, shards of moonlight cutting through the layer of Crics blanketing the windows. To avoid attracting attention, Ward had decided to keep the lights off. He listened to the hum and wheeze of his wife's snoring from the upstairs bedroom. Ward didn't know how he'd missed that warning sign during their courtship. The woman sounded like a steam engine when she slept.

There was a hollow thump from above as a large Cric jumped onto the roof.

Ward stood, heart hammering as he aimed the Benelli at the ceiling, then lowered it. Even if his M2 could make it through the ceiling, a hardwood floor, and the roof, the last thing he needed was a hole in the roof. He sighed and rolled his shoulders, pain leeching through his extremities, the tips of his fingers and toes stinging with stress.

A thump, a long suction-like hiss, then tapping and scraping.

He followed the eerie melody into the den where his phone's light dissolved the darkness.

Ward jumped back, hit the wall, and knocked a picture of Jenni in her softball uniform from its hook. The picture crashed to the floor and the frame's glass front shattered.

A huge Cric was pasted on the outside of the room's large window, its legs cycling, antennas swaying. The creature's underside was ribbed, its hard shell tapping the glass as the Cric gyrated up and down. Pinchers twice the size of any lobster claw Ward had ever seen snapped, the creature's mandibles clicking. He couldn't see the beast's bulbous eyes or its jaws full of clear teeth, but he took note of the spikes on the tips of the second set of legs behind the pincer legs.

He turned off the cell's light and gathered his nerves, which were tap-dancing on his spine in tune with the tittering of the Crics. Ward listened hard, trying to hear if his wife's snoring had stopped.

The static of the Crics moving about outside, the hum of the kitchen, and... yes, he heard his wife's labored wheezing.

To settle his nerves Ward dug out a bottle of Jonny Walker Blue label he'd been saving for a special occasion that never seemed to arrive. Being inundated with mutant bugs wasn't exactly a special occasion, but at a minimum it was justification. No way he was getting eaten alive without having at least tasted the best scotch Jonny Walker produced.

Ward planted himself on the living room couch, bottle in hand. He would only take a nip because he needed to be alert and on his game, not asleep and drunk.

Drinking fine whiskey was a process. It was supposed to be decanted, allowed to breathe, etc., but at a minimum a fine-cut crystal glass was needed. Ward ignored scotch etiquette, broke the seal, twisted off the top, and took a hit straight from the bottle. Velvety heat leaked down his throat, the scotch's smoky essence infused with notes of peat and a blend of dried fruit, honey, and vanilla. He closed his eyes, enjoying the scotch's lingering nutty aftertaste, then took another pull and capped the bottle. The last twenty-four hours had stretched every nerve in Ward's body, and if he wasn't careful, half the bottle would be gone before he realized he'd made himself useless.

He pulled out his phone and called up the two exterior house cameras.

In the white glow of the cameras, the Crics gyrated and swayed as they were massaged by the gentle breeze that carried through the night. Bulbous eyes glowed under the cameras' glare, and Ward felt their stares. Internet research had revealed that camelback crickets had very poor eyesight—some none at all, because most lived in dark environments and many species never saw the light of day in their lifetimes, which was roughly one to two years.

That little fact had knocked most of the hope out of Ward. While he knew the creatures covering his house weren't sprickets, but a mutant bastardization of the species, still certain assumptions could be made based on the genus of spider-cric. Many insects don't live long, and Ward had hoped the current crisis would resolve itself as the mutants died off within twenty-four hours of their birth like mayflies.

Ward took another pull of scotch as one of the cameras was obscured by a black, white-striped carapace. Bile inched up his throat as his mind spun back to the person getting devoured in the street. He tried to guess which one of his neighbors had been so stupid, but couldn't come up with anyone. The people that lived on the block were a decent lot for the most part, but when crisis strikes folks circle their wagons, and he didn't think he could count on much help from his neighbors.

The way the Crics had covered the guy like ants on a fallen lollipop drained all Ward's energy, and the final nip of Jonny Blue sat in his stomach like a shot of gasoline. Was that how things would end for him? Jenni? Everyone? What might the government do if the powers that be felt the situation was getting out of hand? The good of the many outweighs the good of the few.

His vision was a bit sluggish around the edges, and the warmth of a gentle buzz wrapped him in its warm cocoon. What if he lived and Jenni didn't make it? The idea of being single again was terrifying, yet… How much of his current stagnation and unhappiness could be attributed to his marriage? He didn't know, but he hadn't been married very long, so he knew there was much more to it, but still…

Ward's imagination went to work alongside the scotch, and soon Jenni's flawless face was covered in writhing mutant Crics, their pinchers digging into her skin, pulling her hair, and cycling chunks of her flesh into their tooth-filled maws. She didn't scream, or struggle, but simply stared at Ward with a crooked smiled that asked, "Is this what you want?"

For the briefest of instants, he thought maybe he did. Ward sucked his lips and rocked back. The stress of the situation was getting to him. He lifted the bottle of Jonny Walker, intending to take another pull, but left the cap on and leaned back into the deep couch cushions, trying to clear his mental slate.

Hissing, then mewing from the kitchen snapped him from his musings.

Ward scooped up the M2 and surged to his feet. Shadows danced along the hallway, his heart pounding in rhythm with his head, the stock of the tactical shotgun pressed to his shoulder as he stared through the double sight. Muffin wasn't in the hall, and nothing moved within the syrupy darkness.

Muffin's mewing grew louder, but as Ward swung into the kitchen, ranging around the Benelli, he didn't see the cat. The refrigerator hummed and thin rays of moonlight leaked through the writhing Crics and painted the room dusky gray.

Meow. Meow. Meow. The calls were fast and frenzied now, and Ward turned on the kitchen light.

The Crics on the windows pulsed and shifted, their legs tapping the glass, their odd titter and squeal static-like. He moved around the counter island at the center of the room but still didn't see Muffin. There was a table and chairs before the triple windows at the back of the room, and cabinetry lined the walls. The sink faucet dripped, and the clock ticked.

Sometimes Muffin slept on the kitchen table chairs hidden by the tablecloth, so Ward lifted the white linen and peered beneath the table. Nothing.

Meow. Meow. Meow.

Muffin was crouched low, underside pressed to the floor in attack position, staring into the corner by the back door like she was being punished. Her tail was rigid and out straight, the hair on her back standing on end.

"What is it, sweet—"

A Cric hopped, its quarter-sized form appearing for an instant above Muffin's head. The cat screeched and pawed at the air as she backed off.

Ward turned on his cell light to get a better view and see if he was dealing with a regular spider-Cric or a mutant.

Muffin clawed at the Cric, and it jumped again.

It was a mutant. Ward couldn't see teeth in the tiny beast's mouth, but there was no missing the pinchers.

"Leave it be, Muffin."

The cat hissed, but backed off.

Ward remembered he was holding the M2 but searched for a more practical weapon. Though he was itching to fire the Benelli, blowing the little bug to smithereens would waste a shell, and most likely make a hole in the wall.

He opened the utensil drawer and fished out his BBQ spatula. It had a long wooden handle and a large stainless-steel flipper.

With the spatula in hand, Ward shooed Muffin away and moved in for the kill, but the tiny Cric had different ideas. The spider-like beast hopped and jumped in a random pattern that kept the Cric in basically the same area. It wasn't coming at him, or trying to get away, it was just bouncing around in an awkward dance that was hard for the eye to follow.

It landed and didn't move. It was five feet away.

Ward lunged, spatula out like a sword, his back on fire with pain as muscles tensed. He brought the spatula down and it hit the tile floor with a *clang*.

The Cric sprang toward him.

Ward batted it out of the air and brought the flat steel head of the spatula down on the Cric.

An epic crunch echoed through the kitchen, and though he couldn't be certain, Ward thought the Crics on the window undulated and shifted with extra ferocity upon hearing their brethren flattened.

Nasty ooze sprayed across the floor, and a musty scent carried through the room and tickled his nose.

Ward got the uneasy feeling that he was being watched, and he spun around as he brandished the spatula.

Muffin sat staring at him, her eyes dark wet pits.

"That the only one?" Ward asked the cat.

Meow.

"Thanks." He got the cat treats from the cabinet, but before rewarding the furball, Ward made the cat trail after him, mewing and rubbing his legs as he searched the house. He found no more Crics, nor did Muffin sense any because the feline made no sign.

A thud echoed up through the floor, and Ward gripped the Benelli so tight his fingers hurt. He grabbed a towel from the bathroom and stuffed it under the cellar door. With that done he surfed the web looking for ways to kill infant sprickets. When very young, spider-crics appear translucent and the creatures are almost impossible to see, especially on carpets or colored tiles.

One trick he learned was to place bowls of soapy water around the area infested with camelbacks. The Crics were drawn to the water and drank the poison. Seemed easy enough.

He filled twenty salad bowls with water and soap and placed several in the area around the squished Cric as well as other strategic locations around the outer walls of the house. When he was done, he cleaned up the Cric splatter and tossed the tiny pile of bones and black skin in the trash. There was no internal debate this time about telling Jenni. She needed to know because now they needed to keep a constant watch within the house.

Ward's time was up, and it was Jenni's turn to stand watch, but he decided against waking his wife. He could sleep during the day when the Crics were less active. That was another fact that seemed to jive with the general physiology of sprickets; they were nocturnal and often were disoriented by light.

After two rounds of searching, he picked a spot at the end of the hallway by the living room where he could see a good chunk of the house. Ward sat with his back pressed to the wall, his phone resting against the base molding showing the exterior cameras. With the M2 laid across his arms he watched Crics cover the camera lenses as they scuttled about, the rhythmic movement like a rolling ocean.

His eyes drooped as his skin itched with nervous energy, but that didn't stop him from falling asleep.

4

"Honey. Honey, wake up."

Ward came awake to find Jenni standing over him, her face etched with concern. Drool ran from his mouth onto his cheek and the shotgun lay on the floor. Morning sunlight fought through the Crics covering the windows, the new day reduced to a gray dawn. He stiffened, his eyes darting around as he searched for tiny Crics. When he saw none, he said, "I must have dozed off."

"No harm, no foul," she said. "Looks the same out there. Are you hungry?"

"I could eat."

Jenni helped him to his feet. "What are you in the mood for? We should use the milk," she said as she headed for the kitchen.

Ward's hand shot out and he gripped her arm. "Wait," he said. As he checked the kitchen, he told her what happened the previous night

"That's not good, Scott."

"No. No, it isn't." He told her about all the precautions he'd taken and when they checked the soapy water traps, they found two dead Crics and one of them was a mutant. Both were very small.

When the lenses weren't covered by mutants, the exterior cameras showed every surface covered with Crics of all sizes.

"Are there more of them than yesterday?" Jenni asked.

It sure looked like it, so Ward said nothing.

As the duo ate, they scanned their phones, and from the inside looking out, Ward thought their situation was precarious at best.

Long Island had slipped into chaos, and emergency services were stretched to the breaking point as they tried to help those stranded in their homes. The hospitals were mostly out of commission because they'd been overrun with Crics, and panic had caused the citizenry to crank up their drawbridges and close the shutters.

County, state, and federal authorities were considering several options as the bigheads rushed to learn anything they could about the creatures and what exactly had transformed them.

There were only two camps in Ward's opinion. You were either on the inside or outside, and it was only a matter of time before the goals of those two factions conflicted. The folks on the outside were afraid the Crics would escape containment and those on the island saw escape as their only hope, and every islander over the age of twenty knew the U.S. government wasn't above sacrificing a few of its own to save the world.

In the meantime, while the bureaucratic dance occurred and the immediate major emergencies were dealt with, the rest of the population waited and did their best to survive.

The morning news was a sobering experience.

Opportunistic politicians stoked the fires of panic inside and outside the Containment Zone, as Long Island had come to be known. There were online interviews with islanders pleading for help and telling horrific stories of mutilation and death, and the fact that the military had yet to make an appearance inside the Containment Zone both eased the fears of islanders, but also brought worries of nonresponse.

Confusion reigned, and there was already a group of hardline Red Hats at the federal level advocating for a gassing plan that would wipe out all unprotected life on the island. Puppet heads jousted and pontificated, and finally, the president made a statement that a plan would be in place and communicated to the public by sundown. The seas, East River, and bridges were sealed by the military, and as of 8:49 AM EST, there had been no reported incidents of the creatures outside the Containment Zone.

With the hard news completed, the second-rate attention seekers took over, and the conversation degenerated to a low during which a FOX news anchor asked, "What's the problem? In other countries, they eat these things."

That's when Jenni turned off the T.V. in frustration and Ward was happy for it.

"That stuff about the water could be useful," Jenni said as she tried to put lipstick on a pig.

Ward nodded. "I can't see how a little rain wouldn't help, but you heard them, water doesn't hurt the things, but lucky for the world they can't swim and drown easily."

He called his brother Tim who lived further out on the island, but his parents were in Florida and his sister in Texas, so he had no local worries.

Jenni's situation was more complicated. Her mother was a widow, and she was in an apartment building in Queens. That was good in that there were other people in the building to help her, but though he didn't say anything to his wife, Ward couldn't envision an old apartment building being sealed adequately, so it was only a matter of time before the Crics got in or matured from contaminated eggs. Then it was every human for themselves, and her mother wouldn't be able to keep up.

In all the ranting about the creatures, there had been nothing about the mutation being passed on to the new generation of Crics, or if their tremendous growth and higher birthrate would continue until the Crics were two feet deep. Ward didn't see how—

The house phone rang.

Jenni vaulted to her feet and grabbed the double barrel.

Ward simply stared at the cordless phone in its cradle. He couldn't recall the last time he'd used it. Shoot, he couldn't remember the last time it rang. The elimination of the landline was a regular debate during the household budget meetings. Ward always argued that having hardwired communication could be useful during times of emergency, but they'd become obsolete, and he just hadn't gotten around to canceling it.

The phone rang seven times before Ward answered it. He'd fully expected to hear a computerized voice giving him instructions, but that wasn't what it was.

"Scott. Scott? Are you there?"

It was an old woman's voice that he didn't recognize. His mother's voice was timid, and Jenni's Mom's was smoke-ridden. He licked his lips, and said, "This is Scott Ward. Who am I speaking with?"

"Oh, dear, I'm so sorry. It's Ruth from next door. Ruth Drazen."

Relief spread through Ward, and he said, "It's Ruth." He pointed south.

"I don't know what to do, Scott," Ruth said. "I'm so scared."

"Here, let me put Jenni on," Ward said. His wife was much more patient and understanding and would do a better job soothing the old woman's angst.

"No. No. I need to talk to you."

The saliva in Ward's mouth migrated to his armpits, and he said nothing.

"You know I had that heart attack last year?"

"Yes." He didn't like where this was going. If Ruth was in a bad way, she was screwed because there were currently no emergency services.

"Well, I've been on oxygen, and…"

His heart sank as he stared at Jenni. He didn't have any spare canisters of oxygen around, and getting one in the current climate would be next to impossible. That made him think of all the elderly in their houses alone, waiting on homecare workers, food, and drug deliveries that might never arrive. It all made him sick to his stomach. He said, "I don't know how I can get you a fresh tank, I—"

"No, I've got two spare tanks that will last a while. But… I feel so stupid…"

"What is it, Ruth?" Ward was starting to get frustrated.

"Terry or Tom always changes the tank for me because I'm not strong enough. I tried, but I think I broke something. I've reduced the flow and I'm taking the smallest percentage I can, but I only have a couple of hours left."

"Then what happens?"

Ruth said nothing.

Ward let a long stream of air escape his lips. "O.K., Ruth, I need you to tell me what the gauge on top of the cylinder says. We need to—"

Static filled the line, a beep, and the line went dead.

"Ruth? Ruth!" he screamed into his cellphone. No signal. He turned on the TV. Nothing.

"Great," Jenni said. "Just great. Communications are down."

"Hopefully it's temporary."

"Is that what you think?" Jenni said, the edge in her voice unmistakable.

Ward said nothing.

In stressful situations it was always best to focus on what one can control, having an impact where possible while not wasting time and resources. He needed to get to Ruth, but how? Her house to the south was forty feet from his, but it might as well have been four thousand miles. "Let's clear the side window in the den," he said. "Maybe we can communicate with signs."

"Communicate what?"

That was a good question.

The sound of a revving engine leaked through the titter of the Crics into the house. There was a vehicle coming down Southwood Street.

Jenni went to work on the front bay window with the hair dryer and she was able to clear a spot just in time to see an army green armored personnel carrier rolling through the Crics like a snowplow, the popping and cracking of crushed carapaces and broken bones rising above the squeal of the dying mutants. The M113 had six wheels, with an armored turret on its roof, but no mounted gun. The vehicle rolled by, and its tracks were soon filled with writhing Crics.

"And so it begins," Jenni said.

"My guess is that was local national guard, but yeah."

The hairdryer fell silent, and Jenni asked, "Showing us we haven't been forgotten?"

"Yup. It's all about presence. Make us think things are going to be fine so we don't do anything stupid."

"Like?"

"Oh, I don't know, try and get to a boat?" he said, and as soon as the words escaped his lips, he wished he could have them back. Just putting that idea out in the universe was a bad thing. It brought hope, and hope was deadly.

"Do you really think there's a single boat left?"

"You asked for stupid, so I gave you stupid."

The rumble of the armored carrier faded, and Jenni set about clearing the den window, which was opposite Ruth's house. It only took a few minutes because as the sun moved to its zenith, Ward saw there was a higher density of Crics in the shade areas.

A patch of grass, a three-foot high fence, and a line of small shrubs separated the Ward Casa from Ruth's place. The northern side of her house was in the shade, and the light blue of her asbestos shingle facade was fully covered with Crics mounding and climbing over one another.

Ward saw the outline of windows, but it didn't appear that any of them were being cleared using heat.

"Now what?" Jenni asked.

"Got any ideas? I knew the odds of her clearing the windows were slim—she might not even know about the hack."

"Or what a hack is."

He said nothing.

"Do you think she called anyone else?"

Ward shrugged. "I'd think so, but who would be closer than us?"

"What can we do? You saw what happens to anyone who goes out there."

He had, but since he'd seen the person torn apart in the road an idea had been fermenting in his head. "I need to go to the garage," he said.

She rocked back like she'd been punched. "What? How? You can't even get out of the house."

"Have some faith."

"Even if you can get out of the house, there's no way to keep them from taking the garage if you open the door," she pressed.

Ward said, "True, but who cares? I grab what I need, clear them out the best I can, close the door, and consider the garage taken. What can the things do in there?"

Jenni chuckled. "Can I help?"

Twenty minutes later Ward was stuffed into his 5/6 MM wetsuit with the hood pulled up, his booties and gloves on, but that was only the first layer. Over the wetsuit, he donned thick work pants and high winter boots. Then he added his jacket, his ski helmet, a full hood, and goggles.

Two seconds after completing his ensemble he was so hot a river of sweat ran down his back and covered his face.

He carried the Benelli on his back via its shoulder strap, clipped his grandfather's Colt Government .45 to his belt, a bullet in the firing chamber, and brandished a large broom. The plan was to use the broom, when possible, to clear his path and only use ammo on the big ones. In the garage, there was gasoline, a kickass leaf blower, a lawn mower, and other useful items that could chew the Crics to dust.

"While you're waiting on me, pack a couple of backpacks. Clothes, some food," Ward said as he checked his gear one last time.

She nodded, but didn't meet his eye.

Ward didn't blame his wife for not wanting to think about what would happen if the house was breached, but it was always better to be safe than sorry.

As Jenni had predicted, getting out of the house proved to be the biggest challenge.

"Bring up the back exterior camera on your phone so I can see what's happening out there," Ward said.

"No internet, remember?"

He hadn't. Jenni used the dryer to clear a back window, and when there was nothing bigger than a mouse visible in the backyard the couple took up positions by the sliding glass doors that opened onto the house's rear patio.

"Ready to do this?" he said.

Jenni stood ready with the hairdryer and a large can of bug spray. "As ready as I'll ever be. You've got the key to the garage, right?"

He nodded as he unlocked the slider, the snap of the lock disengaging one of the loudest sounds Ward had ever heard. Deep breaths. Deep breaths.

The screen door was closed, and as Ward opened the slider a couple of feet and pressed through the gap, he drove himself into the screen door and the flimsy aluminum frame tore from its track.

Ward hit the ground, the screen door beneath him flattening a field of Crics, their nasty life blood oozing through the screen. As Ward pressed to his feet he heard the sliding glass door slam home behind him, its lock falling into place with a clang.

5

Though he knew it was only his mind messing with him, Ward felt the creatures crawling over him as he got to his feet. Crics hopped and bounced all around and Ward went to work with his broom. He spun in a circle as he swept away Crics like leaves. The creatures weighed nothing, and they flew through the air, their legs flailing, pinchers snapping.

Ward started for the detached garage which was forty feet away. Crics crunched beneath his boots as he ran... waddled quickly was more like it because his protective suit made it hard to move.

Crics attached themselves to the broom's whiskers, so he pressed extra hard, pasting the beasts to the ground. Several of the creatures crawled up his legs, but their tiny pinchers and teeth were making no progress getting through his makeshift safety suit.

His goggles were fogging, and it was hard to see, but Ward was just starting to believe he was going to make it unscathed when two dog-sized Crics hopped around the corner of the garage. They bounced across the driveway coming straight at him.

The larger creatures appeared less bothered by the daylight, their bulbous eyes black under the light of day. Foot-long pinchers cracked, antennas as long as fishing poles swayed, the beasts' rear turkey leg femurs thick as a bodybuilder's forearm.

The appearance of the big boys stirred the smaller Crics, and they mounded and climbed over one another to get to Ward.

The heat inside his suit was unbearable, and Ward's breaths came in ragged bursts, his vision going blurry as his goggles clouded over.

Camel crickets normally make no sounds, but the two big boys screeched as they stopped ten feet from Ward. The Crics appraised him, their legs cycling around, jaws sliding open and revealing sharp crooked transparent teeth.

Ward drew down his grandfather's .45 and blew both creatures back to hell.

Black slimy goo sprayed the side of the garage and the Crics, the rancid fluid scattering the smaller creatures. A musty smell leaked through his face mask, and tiny white pinpricks of light spun across Ward's vision as he overheated.

Too late to turn back.

He holstered the .45 and resumed sweeping as he worked his way to the garage. The path ended at the blacktop driveway, and Ward spent a couple of minutes doing his best to clear away the Crics clinging to the rollup garage door. The creatures jumped onto his legs and climbed for his head.

Loud clicking and popping and the Crics all around Ward undulated with extra coordination and intensity. A Cric the size of a deer had paused on the road at the end of the driveway. The thing was a hundred feet away, but still Ward's nerves crawled with terror. He had his guns and could defend himself, but still... To see something so surreal, so unbelievable, it was hard to focus.

Ward stood watching the beast, smaller Crics creeping up his legs, the area he'd cleared on the garage door clouding over with Crics.

The big guy at the end of the driveway lurched into motion, and it hopped onto and over Ward and Jenni's cars where they sat at the end of the driveway, the crunch and pop as it crushed the smaller of its kind echoing over the bug-encrusted blacktop.

He tore his gaze from the beast and fumbled in his pocket for the garage key, but the heavy gloves made the search difficult, and when he pulled his hand free the key fell to the blacktop and disappeared under a layer of Crics.

The large Cric was halfway up the driveway, bouncing like a rubber ball as it approached, antennas swaying, legs churning.

Ward thought the .45 might not pack enough of a punch, so he leaned the broom against the garage and swung the Benelli off his back. There was a round in the firing chamber and he leveled the weapon at the approaching beast.

When the Cric was twenty feet away Ward opened up, three shots, the booms of the shotgun like distant thunder. The first shot blew off a back leg, and the next two reduced the jumbo Cric to a nasty pile of flesh and bones. The smaller creatures fled as the beast's innards splattered the driveway.

Ward swung the Benelli onto his back as he bent, found the key, fumbled it for an instant, then managed to fit it into the lock.

Crics crawled up his legs, dropped onto his head, and alighted on his arms and shoulders.

Ward shook himself like a dog as he used the broom to clear Crics from the garage door. He was losing the battle, so he pulled the garage door open two feet, dropped and rolled, then slammed the door closed behind him.

Crics clung to his safety suit, and he brushed them away as he grabbed a shovel from its holding rack. With a fury and relentlessness he'd never experienced, he flattened every Cric he saw, the smack of the metal shovel head hitting concrete and the crackling of exoskeletons filling the garage.

Several of the beasts escaped and disappeared within the accumulated stuff that hadn't made it into the basement. He brushed himself off, and when he was sure he was free of clinging beasts, he pulled off his helmet, goggles, and hood.

Jenni had insisted on him bringing a bottle of water, and if his wife had been there, he would have gotten on his knees to show thanks. He gobbled down the H2O, his eyes ranging around for Crics, the creaking and scraping as the beasts crawled over the garage constant background static.

Refreshed, he went to work.

Ward stripped off his gloves, adjusted the fuel flow on the leaf blower, and pulled the starter cord. Rumbling pops, but it didn't start. Three pulls later the Echo 1110 CFM leaf blower roared to life, and Ward smiled. The Echo would have no problem clearing away any Cric smaller than a fieldmouse. He shut the unit down and searched the garage.

There was a large rubber storage bin that served as the vortex of the Ward family camping gear. He emptied it and went about filling it with anything useful he could find. There was the Honda 2000i lightweight, long-running generator, a bottle of weed killer with a spray head, and an old pair of two-way radios that he and Jenni had used to communicate while skiing before the advent of cellphones. There were two gas cans, both half full, so he combined them into one and put it in the bin along with rat and ant poison, rope, and a few other odds and ends. With the container full he searched for the parts he needed to make his flame stick.

Ward dug out the portable gas grill and fished out three green sixteen-ounce propane cylinders. With those in hand, he went in search of his Fire in a Can. He bought the unit for a camping trip in a national park where wood fires weren't permitted, and the thing was nothing more than a metal bucket with a large gas burner, ceramic logs, and a ten-foot pressure hose used to connect the unit to a propane tank.

A Cric the size of a tarantula inched out from behind the lawn mower, and Ward crushed it under his bootheel. He'd forgotten about the mower. It would be useful for clearing a path through Crics.

Using an adjustable wrench, he took apart the Fire in a Can and affixed its burner to the end of a pole he used to clean the gutters. Then he secured the burner's hose to the pole with duct tape, fit a gas cylinder to the regulator at the end of the hose, and taped the can to the pole. Now all he had to do was figure out how to ignite the device while on the move.

There was a lighter in the box with the tiki candles, and he fetched it and tested the device. The small gas cans wouldn't last long, so he only opened the regulator a little, and then using the lighter he ignited the burner at the end of the pole. It flickered to life with blue flame, and as he twisted the regulator knob the flames grew. The fire stick was no flamethrower, but it would serve.

Ward's legs ached, and he felt sick to his stomach from drinking the water too fast. He took deep breaths as he put his hood back on, the helmet, goggles, gloves, and made sure the .45 was secure in its holster and the shotgun was still on his back. He fashioned a strap for his flame stick using twine and hung it over the Benelli. The weight of everything was wearing him out, but there was no way he could rest. Ruth needed him, and courageous Crics were starting to venture out from cover, inching over the garage floor, watching him from afar as they waited for an opportunity to advance.

It was difficult with the gloves on and all the weight hanging on him, but Ward managed to get the blower going again, and as he opened the garage door, he used it like a machine gun to clear a path.

The blower roared as Ward swept it back and forth, clearing the garage entrance of Crics. He worked until he was comfortable he'd wiped away enough of the creatures, then nudged the storage container out of the garage onto the driveway.

Heart racing so fast it hurt his chest, Ward released the blower's trigger and placed the running machine atop the lawn mower's catch-bag as he pumped the mower's handle and primed its motor. He yanked on the starter cord and the mower roared to life.

Ward pressed forward, out of the garage and into a field of Crics. The diced beasts clinked and clanged off the inside of the lawn mower housing as legs, skin, and goo spewed into the catch-bag. He pulled the garage door down, but as he did so he saw Crics scuttle inside.

The mower coughed and choked as Ward pushed it forward, blazing a trail over Crics. Back-and-forth he went, and it was easy work because the Crics didn't appear to like the loud noise of the mower or the splatter of their compatriots' guts and many fled before the machine. When he had a decent path cleared, he left the blower by the back door and worked his way back to the garage with the mower. Once there, he balanced the rubber container on the mower's housing and brought it to the house where he left it by the back door.

While the smaller Crics appeared to be afraid of Ward's new weapons, several larger Crics came to investigate. Bigger mutants appeared along the fence line in the backyard and behind him on the driveway. A Cric the size of a cat inched over the lip of the house's roof, its bulbous eyes fixed on Ward as he retrieved the blower.

The Cric coiled to jump, and Ward drew the .45 and blew the creature off the roof.

Ward straightened and rolled his shoulders, weariness threatening to unhinge his knees, the temperature within his suit reaching critical levels. Sweat stung his eyes as he shook his head to clear the cobwebs.

Jenni stared at him through the back door window. She held the hairdryer in her hand, her eyes wet with tears. She gave him a thumbs up and the newlyweds reached out and touched fingers, the glass and Ward's glove separating them.

The lawn mower still roared, and the leaf blower gurgled, but the Crics were beginning to get over their fear and pressed in closer.

Ward had done well so far, so he saw no reason not to continue to Ruth's. The plan had been to regroup in the house, but the thought of getting into the house, clearing out the Crics, and stripping off his suit only to have to put it back on made little sense. He got his wife's attention and pointed toward Ruth's place.

A sorrowful smile spread over her face, and she nodded with understanding. She blew him a kiss, but the stress was evident in his wife's tight features and the dark bags under her eyes.

Ward turned to leave and saw Muffin watching him from an upstairs window, the cat's tail swishing back and forth as though she didn't have a care in the world. He mock saluted the feline and took inventory of his weapons. Everything was where he'd left it.

Two large Crics were inching across the backyard and Ward figured it was as good a time as any to test his fire stick.

To save gasoline he shut down the mower and the leaf blower, then used the lighter to ignite the fire stick. The gas burner at the end of the pole came to life with white and blue flames before orange fire jetted three feet from the burner.

He worked his way across the yard like he was using a metal detector and searching for gold. Back and forth as he burned Crics to cinders and the beasts fled before him. The larger creatures wanted no part of the fire, and he cackled as they ran. Ward was burning through a field of mutant Crics with a gas burner taped to the end of a pole. He could have been given a thousand guesses... a million... and there was no way he would have envisioned doing this today.

6

Ward killed the fire stick and slung it over his back, taking particular care not to touch the hot burner. With Jenni watching and cheering him on, he cranked up the mower and pressed forward, his skin crawling as Crics hopped all around him.

Ruth's backyard wasn't far. A four-foot wooden fence separated the yards, and beyond that, he had another thirty feet to her back door. A raised deck shot off the back of her house, so when he reached it, Ward would be forced to change weapons. No matter. He felt like Rambo, and there—

He was knocked to the side, and he let go of the mower's handle as a black claw snapped inches from his face.

The safety lever shot up, and the mower's engine sputtered and stalled.

Ward managed to stay on his feet as he slid on crushed Crics and came to a stop, staggering for an instant before regaining his balance. He cross-drew the .45 as he spun and aimed.

A Cric the size of an easy chair flexed its jaws and displayed its pinchers as the spikes at the tips of its second pair of legs stabbed the ground. The beast was all black, with no stripes or blotches of white or brown, and its eyes glowed with an ethereal paleness.

He double-tapped the thing right between the eyes and half the creature's body disappeared in a spray of black mist.

The wind gusted and the Crics swayed and heaved. Ward caught his breath and tried to settle his nerves, but his emotions were dancing on a wire, and he was so hot he felt his strength draining away with his sweat. He holstered the .45, started the mower, and continued blazing a trail to Ruth's place.

He plowed through the fence, knocking a panel free of its poles. When he reached the deck, Ward abandoned the mower and cranked up the leaf blower. Crics fled before him, but a few brave souls the size of rats stood their ground only to be punted across the yard.

Ruth's back door was covered in Crics. Between the asbestos shingles and the door, there were thick strips of wood molding painted white. Ward let go of the mower handle and the machine shut down as he wielded the leaf blower.

The blower snarled and Crics scattered. Ward cleared the area as he considered how to get into Ruth's house, and determined it was time for the fire stick again.

He knocked on the back door to get Ruth's attention, but no face appeared in the window.

Tension tugging at his nerves, Ward killed the blower, ignited the fire stick, and played its flame around the door. Crics scattered and burnt to ash as he charred the house, and paint bubbled on the asbestos shingles, the white molding turned black, and the door window cleared.

Ruth stared at him, oxygen tube sticking from her nose, eyes wide as quarters, freckled skin hanging loose around her face and neck.

He motioned for her to step back, and she did.

Crics probed the burnt area.

Ward threw open the screen door and twisted the doorknob.

Locked.

He kicked the door and twisted the knob.

Nothing.

Ward put his back to the door and waved the fire stick around as he kicked the door over and over with the bottom of his foot. He gave the knob another twist before abandoning his effort and the knob turned. The door opened, and as he spilled through, he killed the fire stick with a quick twist of the regulator control knob.

The door slammed shut, Ruth crunched several Crics with a pizza board, and then everything settled. Crics rumbled and tittered as they crawled over the house, and Ward noticed the static was much louder than back home.

Ward struggled to his feet, swatting at himself, trying to clear away brave Crics.

Two hopped off him and scuttled across the kitchen.

Ruth got them with bug spray, the can's long stream arcing across the kitchen and catching the beasts as they tried to get away.

"You have to get the buggers when they're small," the old woman said.

Understatement of the year.

"Sorry about the locked door," she said. "My mind isn't what it once was."

"No worries. First order of business is stripping out of this suit," Ward said. When he was down to shorts and a t-shirt, he had to go in the bathroom and wring both out. He checked the weapons, cleaned everything up, reloaded, and put the .45 in the waistband of his shorts.

"Are there any areas… you no longer have access to?" he asked.

She shook her head no.

Ward drank down a sixteen-ounce water in one pull and set about checking Ruth's house from top to bottom. She'd done an excellent job Cric-proofing the place in the same manner he and Jenni had, and after declaring the place safe, he went to work on the oxygen tank.

Ruth bombarded him with thanks. "I don't know what I would have done... well, I would have died. You saved me, Scott."

"We'll see."

The 1602E aluminum oxygen cylinder sat on a stainless steel cart. Most of its long hose was coiled around the cart's handle, the pressure gauge was in the red zone, and the mix rate was set below its normal setting as Ruth attempted to conserve oxygen by depriving her body of it.

Ruth showed Ward what she had done, but as far as he could tell, she hadn't damaged anything. The valve post was askew, but that was an easy fix, and he had no issues replacing the tank.

Ten minutes after his arrival Ruth was breathing freely again, her oxygen percentage down just a hair to conserve. Nobody knew how long it would be before she could get her replacement cylinders.

Ruth said, "I called the company, and I'm on their emergency list, whatever that means."

Ward drank another water as he sat at the kitchen table to reset. Ruth offered cold chicken, and though he would've normally turned it down, he sucked down two drumsticks, the hind legs of the bigger Crics flashing through his mind as he ate.

"I can't thank you enough, Scott." She put a hand on his arm. "You're my savior."

He said nothing. Ward felt good about what he'd done, but what other choice did he have? Self-preservation was a building block of his psyche, but there was no way he could stand by and watch someone die. Not when there was something he could do about it.

"How's Jenni? I haven't se—"

A loud thump from the basement and the kitchen light went out.

Ward vaulted to his feet and ran to the window intending to check if the houses around Ruth's were also dark, but Crics covered the glass.

"Do you have a hairdryer?" he asked.

Ruth's face scrunched and she licked her lips, confusion spreading over her features.

"They don't like heat, and when you use the dryer on the window glass they scatter."

She nodded and said, "Under the bathroom sink, but I'm embarrassed to say I haven't used it in years, so I have no idea if it works."

Ward double-timed it to the bathroom, and as he ran through the living room, he saw the TV's red indicator light was out, as was the digital clock on the DVD/VHS player. He abandoned his mission to the bathroom. Without power the hairdryer was useless.

Back in the kitchen, he said, "Looks like the power is out in the entire house." He lit the fire stick, let it blaze for a few seconds, then turned it off. Then he used the hot burner to clear a window and he saw no lights of any kind within the houses behind Ruth's place.

Ruth said, "It's going to be dark soon."

"Speaking of dark," Ward said as he leaned the fire stick against a wall. He was going to say he needed to get home before dark, but he didn't because he couldn't drop that on the woman just yet.

Another loud boom from below.

He checked the house again. "I think it's a large Cric bouncing off the exterior of the house or trying to work its way through a basement egress window," he said.

Ruth sat at the table when he returned to the kitchen, and he dropped into the chair beside her. Ward wanted to set off for home, but Ruth was alone and scared, and the last thing he wanted to do was run out on her. So he ate more chicken and drank more water.

Ward tapped his leg with impatience as he ate.

The old woman picked up on his discomfort because she said, "Go home to your wife. She'll need you tonight."

He said nothing.

"Scott, you've done more for me than I could have wished. Go."

"Just leave you here?"

She lifted her eyebrows and smiled. "Leave me here? I've been here by myself since Oscar died. I'll be fine."

Even though he hadn't lived on Southwood Street long, a wave of guilt broke over him, and he tried to think of a way to bring Ruth with him, but it wasn't possible. Could he bring Jenni to Ruth's place? Maybe, but it just didn't make sense to take the risk.

"I left the wrench on the counter in case…"

Ruth stared at the orange and white linoleum floor that was installed before Jimmy Carter was elected president.

Ward got back into his suit, which was no small feat given the inside of the wetsuit was soaked with his sweat. Ditto the gloves, but when he was wrapped once again in his protective clothing, the pistol on his hip, the Benelli on his back, he was ready to leave.

He cleared the back door window and Ward saw that the leaf blower and mower were covered in Crics. No matter, they were all small and it appeared no damage had been done to the units… yet.

The screen door was ajar and smaller Crics had worked their way through the gap.

"This is going to be fast," he said. "A few are going to get through. Make sure you don't hit me in the face with the bug spray."

She nodded.

He cranked up the fire stick and adjusted the flow so that the blue flame was hardly visible. "Ready?"

Ruth nodded again.

Ward took a deep breath, inched the door open a crack, and sprayed the poison through the gap. When white foam filled the space, he drew back the door and pushed outside, holding the flame stick out before him.

The door slammed as he slid on dead Crics. Intense heat and flames drove the beasts away, the fire stick charring the braver mutants to black dust. Ward started the mower, the leaf blower balanced on its catch-bag, and he extinguished the fire stick and slung it onto his back by the weapon's makeshift strap. Then he was mowing his way home, the field of Crics parting before him as the mutants scuttled out of the way.

In the failing light of the dying day, the Crics became more animated, and even the meekest left their hiding spots in search of prey.

Ward ran, frantically pushing the lawn mower, his field of vision speckled with jumping Crics and tiny starbursts of white light. The heat of the suit was dragging him down, but he saw his back door and Jenni's face as she watched him.

His mind spun with darkness, his chest hot with the guilt of leaving Ruth behind. Ward knew he had no reason to feel responsible for the woman's situation. He had saved Ruth's life, after all, but leaving her still didn't sit well with him. No matter how the crisis played out, he vowed to stop over and visit with the woman, maybe help her out a little.

There was nothing left of the sun except a bruised sky, and Ward's thoughts strayed to the night as he ran. He'd killed that little bugger in the kitchen, and there were more of the things today than there was yesterday. Ward's heart sank as he considered what the night would bring.

7

A fighter jet streaked overhead, and the mutants froze for a heartbeat as Ward hit the gap in the fence at a full run, the mower sucking in and dicing slower-moving Crics. When the mower hit the patio, he saw Jenni frantically waving around a torch, its flickering flame dancing beyond the sliding glass doors.

Thoughts of protecting the mower and leaf blower scampered through his mind as he reached the house, but he was tired, practically staggering on his feet, and he needed to get out of the suit again. The second time in the wetsuit, boots, jeans, jacket, full hood, helmet, and goggles had been brutal. Ward felt like he'd run a mile, even though it had only been seventy feet.

He wasted no time lighting the candle and clearing the sliding doors. The storage container was right where he'd left it, but it was covered in Crics. He played the fire stick around, and the Crics fled before its flame as the last light of the day flickered out and darkness fell.

With Jenni's help, ten seconds later the slider was open just enough for the storage container to squeeze through, and Ward threw the running leaf blower into the house before working his way through the gap.

A huge Cric the size of a small dog jumped from the roof, landed on the patio, spun, and hopped at Ward as he slid the door closed.

The Cric wedged a claw into the gap and Ward slammed the door on the pincher, its shell cracking, the beast wailing as its other legs cycled over the glass.

Ward pulled back the door and drove it into the claw again, and again, his rage bubbling over, his vision frayed black at the edges.

The beast's second set of legs stabbed at Ward, and he fell back to avoid getting impaled.

Metal shrieked as the sliding glass door was pushed open on its track and Crics spilled into the house.

With a squeal and hiss that sent a shiver through Ward, Muffin launched herself at the large Cric, claws out, two-inch fangs bared. The cat landed on the monster's back, and the Cric spun and bucked as Muffin clawed at the creature's back. Dark goo sprayed from the Cric, its body deflating as Muffin's jaws clamped onto the beast's face and crunched it to mush. The cat thrashed its head and when the Cric was ripped into several pieces the feline went after the smaller creatures that were swarming over the floor and up the walls.

Ward rolled to his feet and brought up the flame stick, but there were too many of the creatures, and he was concerned he would set the house on fire.

"Jenni! Take this!" He handed off the fire stick and his wife threw her flaming torch of rolled-up cut carpet through the open door onto the Cric-encrusted patio beyond.

Ward wielded the leaf blower, pressing the trigger and driving the horde of Crics back, but there were too many. The creatures swirled in the air and darted away in every direction when they hit the floor. He was still in his suit, and Jenni was unprotected, and he needed to get her to safety.

"Go to the living room. I'll be right behind you! Make sure Muffin goes with you," he yelled, and thankfully there was no debate, no "I'm not leaving you behind", and his wife darted through the archway that led from the den to the living room.

In the intervening seconds as Ward dealt with his wife, four larger Crics pressed through the open door into the house.

So much for trying to get the door shut. Ward dropped the leaf blower, swung the Benelli M2 off his back, and fired. He'd reloaded at Ruth's and the six blasts turned the Crics to skin, bone, and goo, but he'd also blown out the sliding glass doors and obliterated part of the frame.

"Shit!" he screamed. Now there was no way to seal the house.

As he ran for the living room, he scooped up the leaf blower and considered what room to hole up in. With darkness blanketing the island, abandoning the house wasn't an option. The best bet was to hole up and wait for morning. There would probably be more Crics, but at least they'd be more docile, and he'd be able to see what was happening. By morning, perhaps there would be a rescue plan in place, some type of support.

Crics scuttled behind him as he ran, and he pressed them back with the blower. When he reached his wife and saw the stairs leading to the second floor, he considered which was a better place to hide, upstairs or down.

Up. No doubts. It's where the gun cabinet with the ammo was, and higher ground was always better. The only issue was there was no egress, but that wasn't true. He and Jenni could climb out onto the roof and shimmy down the gutter downspout to the ground if necessary.

"Upstairs!" Ward yelled.

Muffin wasted no time. She darted across the room, leaped onto the couch, slipped through the stair railing, and disappeared upstairs.

The fire stick sputtered out, so Jenni left it behind and wielded the double barrel as she and Ward bolted for the steps. Behind them, the room was overrun by hungry Crics big and small.

The Benelli still hung across Ward's back, but it was empty.

Jenni's double barrel wasn't. She fired and splattered two larger beasts onto the chartreuse walls she'd just painted, the tiny round copper pellets peppering the sheetrock.

"Here!" Ward tossed Jenni the leaf blower and drew the .45 as he held his ground at the center of the room.

Jenni fled upstairs, the blower roaring.

Ward methodically shot larger Crics as the smaller beasts climbed up his legs and launched at him from the walls.

He held the .45 in a double-handed grip the way he did at the range, and Ward's senses danced with pleasure as he blew the creatures away like he was playing a video game.

When the gun clicked empty, the larger Crics were nothing but deflated piles of legs and cracked carapaces. Ward holstered the pistol, grabbed a cushion from the couch, and began beating his legs. As he cleared the Crics, more swarmed into the room, the walls filling with churning legs, snapping pinchers, swaying antennas, and chomping jaws.

Ward mounted the steps at a full run, and when he reached the second floor, he found Jenni holding open their bedroom door, the leaf blower roaring in her hand, her eyes aflame with fright and survival.

Instead of bolting into his bedroom, he made a left and ran down the hallway that led to the bathroom and a second bedroom.

"Scott!" Jenni screamed, and then she was trailing after him.

The upstairs hall closet had a tool kit for hanging pictures and such, a roll of masking tape, as well as a cleaning bucket that could serve as a commode. Ward grabbed the items as Jenni gathered towels, Muffin watching with eager eyes.

Crics swarmed up the staircase, covering the steps, walls, and banister. Jenni used the blower to drive them back as the newlyweds took the supplies back to their bedroom.

Ward slammed the door home as Jenni went to work sealing the gap beneath the door with a towel. When she was done, she shut down the leaf blower.

Small strays had hopped into the bedroom, and Ward and Jenni quickly pounded them to dust before sitting on the floor, adrenaline fleeing, their harsh breathing filling the room.

Ward's legs and arms felt like they were filled with cement, and he was exhausted, angry, hungry, thirsty, and scared. "I've got to get out of this suit," he said.

As Jenni helped him, Ward noticed there were several bites on his wife's legs.

"Do those hurt?" He knew they must. Blood dripped down her legs, the bites snake-like.

Jenni had wasted no time while Ward was helping Ruth, and she'd loaded two backpacks with water and food, and she'd gathered items for her safety suit. Laid out on the bed was an ensemble of spandex workout pants, a snowsuit, boots, ski gloves, a hood, and goggles. The improvised suit would be hot, but not as bad as the wetsuit and less restrictive.

Ward changed into fresh undergarments, shorts, and a Jets t-shirt before going to work breaking apart their pressboard T.V. stand. The cheap piece of furniture came apart easily, and he used the wood, screws, and nails from the unit to board up the room's two windows.

Ward and Jenni used the roll of masking tape to seal the windows and doorframe, the sounds of the night leaking into the house.

Syrupy darkness filled the room as Ward drank water and ate a power bar. Then under the light of Jenni's phone he cleaned and reloaded the guns.

Jenni stowed the remainder of the ammunition, and Ward was upset to see they only had four boxes of buckshot, two bird, and two cartons of .45 ACP rounds, which was only forty bullets. He rarely shot the pistol, and he couldn't recall the last time he'd gone skeet shooting with the Benelli, so most of the ammo was old. Even though all the ammunition was well within the parameters of its useful life, he inspected each bullet anyway.

When he was done with the guns Jenni killed the cell's light. Ward had no idea where his phone was, and with the supply chest lost there was no generator, no power, and no way to recharge the only source of communication available to them. Still, Ward felt much better with the M2 loaded and ready, as well as the pistol and double barrel.

Ward sensed something else in the room. "Turn on your phone light."

Jenni complied and harsh white light pushed away the darkness.

A Cric the size of a regular house spider jumped out from under the bed. It hopped around, its claws barely visible, its hair-like antennas swaying.

It took Ward three strikes, but he took extra pleasure in crushing the thing with his boot, and he didn't stop pounding the Cric until it was nothing more than a stain on the carpet.

Crics clawed and scraped and banged on the house as mutants scratched at the bedroom door. When a small one worked its way into the room via the floor penetration for the baseboard heating pipe a debate about the need for a night watch became unnecessary.

"I'll take the first one," Jenni said.

"That's O.K.," he said. "I don't think…" Ward yawned.

"You don't think you'll be able to fall asleep?" She chuckled, and the sound was like fine music for his stress-ravaged soul. "You caught a catnap last night. And after what you've been through today, you need the rest. Don't worry. I got this."

Ward nodded. She had a point, and he would be a foot away.

A loud thump from above and imaginary ants marched up Ward's spine. "Are you sure you can stay awake?" He'd fallen asleep on watch the prior night, and in some quarters that was an unforgivable sin. Luckily, it hadn't cost them, but tonight it very well could.

"I'll wake you in four hours," she said.

He didn't argue, and she nuzzled up to him where he sat on the bed, the .45 beside him, the M2 on his lap. "Wake me if anything happens," he said. "Anything."

"Got it."

Ward closed his eyes and was assailed by memories. His body tingled as imaginary legs cycled over him, pinchers tearing at him, teeth breaking skin and drawing blood. The brain is an amazing deception machine, and as he kept his eyes pressed closed and fought off the memories, he saw something he hadn't seen before. Many of the thick oak trees that were prevalent in the neighborhood had been stripped of leaves as though a swarm of locusts had mowed through them. If the mutants were omnivores that meant there was much more food available for them. Could the things eat cardboard? Sheetrock? Rats and other pests dined on those materials regularly.

He fought to keep his eyes closed and not stare at the sheetrock walls that had a thin piece of plywood and some installation and plastic separating it from the Crics. He stayed still, not moving at all, but it was a long time before the sound of the Crics and the thump of his heart lulled him into a dream-torn sleep.

8

There was no dawn, not in a traditional sense.

The sun came up, and its bright rays baked the island, but most of that light failed to make its way into the bedroom where Ward and Jenni were hunkered-down. A battery-powered shell clock on the wall told the couple what time it was, but otherwise, the Cric-packed windows gave little sign.

With the mutants hammering on the roof, the newlyweds ate a breakfast of water and peanut butter and jelly sandwiches.

Jenni looked exhausted. He'd seen her sleep, but like him, Jenni's dreams had been overrun with Crics, blood, and terrible ideas. The first thing she'd done when she woke was to fashion a chest harness and safety suit for Muffin. When Ward asked what had given her the idea, she refused to describe the dream.

Ward felt like he hadn't slept a wink, and he had that horrible feeling upon waking that he'd just fallen asleep and hadn't slept at all. His muscles ached and cramped from dehydration, and he'd only been half joking when he'd suggested now might be a good time to weigh in. He'd been dieting and what could produce better weight loss results than running around like a nut in a wetsuit and work clothes?

Getting Muffin into the modified rash guard and sweatshirt was easier than Ward anticipated. The feline seemed to understand it was necessary, and the cat watched Ward with eager eyes as he arrayed his wetsuit and the rest of his ensemble for easy access.

The leaf blower sat by the door, all the guns were loaded and ready to fire, and the backpacks were good to go. Ward made a mental list of the supplies lost to the Crics. The fire stick with its empty canister was in the living room, the supply chest was theoretically still by the sliding glass doors, and unless the Crics liked to eat rubber, steel, and gasoline, the mower should be where he left it and might be in useable condition. Problem was, the fastest way out of the house was the front door at the bottom of the stairs. Plus, the loud engine noise seemed to bring the larger creatures.

"We never talked last night about…" Jenni looked at the floor as she finished with Muffin and the cat scampered away to probe the limits of her protective suit.

"About the plan?" he said.

She nodded as she tested Muffin's chest harness that she'd made from a leather jacket. "Where are we going and why should we leave?"

The crash of a light fixture shattering downstairs silenced the hum and tinkle of the Crics for a heartbeat.

"Hole up here and wait," Jenni said, but he could tell by the tone of her voice that she didn't believe her suggestion was the right thing to do.

Ward didn't know what to do. He said, "Wait for what?"

She hiked her shoulders.

"It's not like this is a hurricane, and we know when it will be over and when we can expect help," Ward said. He didn't know what he was advocating for, but he did know that when stuff like this happened in movies and books, staying in one place usually led to disaster.

Jenni licked her lips and opened her mouth to say something, but instead, her eyes grew wide. "You might have something there, Scott."

His wife often joked that Ward was puzzled by his own genius, so he said nothing.

"What would we do if a really bad hurricane came through? Where would we go?"

Ward searched his memory. When he was a boy, the family had gone to the local firehouse, and when he was older the old elementary school. "The firehouse," he said. "If people are gathering and standing their ground anywhere it will be there."

Jenni nodded and smiled.

Loud thumps and grunt-like shrieks filtered into the room as a large Cric... or Crics... climbed the stairs to the second floor.

Ward and Jenni stayed motionless in semi-darkness.

"There are probably many more in the house now because they're trying to get out of the sun," Ward said.

"Great."

"We better get in our suits and button up Muffin," he said.

"We're going now? Don't we—"

Jenni's cellphone chimed and vibrated as its screen came to life.

Ward and his wife stared at the device. Jenni had turned it off to conserve its battery.

The couple gave the device the hairy-eyeball until a knock on the bedroom door brought them back to the here and now.

Jenni grabbed her phone and said, "It's an Emergency Broadcast Notice."

"They can turn our phones on?" Ward knew a car could be shut down from space, and he was careful what he said when his phone was in earshot to avoid unwanted ads about multiple-ply toilet paper, food apps, and political advocacy groups.

"They can because it's on." She scanned the phone and read, "This is an announcement via the Emergency Broadcast System. The situation within the Containment Zone worsened overnight. Avoid going outside. If you are forced to leave shelter, seek out brick structures that contain supplies and sustenance. The creatures dislike water, though it doesn't harm them. It has been reported that water guns, hoses, and other water delivery devices have been effective in driving back the smaller Crics. If possible, head to a shoreline where rescue boats are waiting to assist residents in their evacuation. TEXT back at this address with your location and situation and the health emergencies of the youngest citizens will be put in property order. Check back here at sundown when the President is due to address the nation."

The continuous tapping on the bedroom door grated Ward's nerves and he drew the .45 and aimed it at the door. He had no intention of firing the weapon, but he wanted to. Badly. The chatter of the Crics was like sandpaper being dragged through his anus, and his sense of urgency hit high gear.

"Get into your suit. Fast!" he shrieked as he went to work suiting up.

Jenni finished first, then she helped him. When they were both in their makeshift battle armor, Ward grabbed an unhappy Muffin and stuffed her into the leather jacket harness that hung across Jenni's chest.

The cat screeched and wailed, its legs and arms flailing wildly inside the modified leather jacket. Jenni put a knit cap on the feline, which left only her face exposed. Muffin bared her teeth, her long whiskers bent back and captured within the hat. Jenni tried to soothe the beast, but the growing chaos in the hallway beyond the bedroom door had the cat in a near frenzy.

Jenni stowed her phone and Ward handed her the double barrel.

He checked the Benelli. Fully loaded with five shells and a sixth in the firing chamber. Ward clipped the .45 on his hip and pulled on his hood, helmet, goggles, and gloves. In seconds he was sweating profusely, the heavy suit sucking the water from his body like salt as he cranked up the leaf blower.

A black spike pierced the bedroom door and stuck there like a nail before retracting. The door flexed and shook as a large Cric pounded on it. As the spike repeatedly drove through the wood, the door cracked and buckled.

Crics funneled through the cracks into the bedroom and cycled over the walls and carpet.

Ward turned the blower on the beasts, but there was nowhere for them to go, and all he accomplished was moving them around.

Jenni positioned herself behind Ward, Muffin screaming like she was trying to give the feline a bath.

A huge pincher claw pushed through the growing hole in the door, snapping and searching for prey.

Ward drew down the .45 and fired, the blower still roaring in his other hand.

The ACP round thumped into the pincer, and it pulled back as the creature shrieked and drove its bulk into the door.

With a crash of breaking wood and rending metal, the door was torn from its hinges, and a Cric the size of a man filled the doorway.

Ward and Jenni fired, the deafening blasts filling the room. Four shots hammered the creature's midsection, and its carapace shattered, shell shrapnel and tender innards splattering the hallway walls. Huge legs caved-in on one another like a collapsing structure as the mutant's torso deflated, and the beast's dying wail fell to a low rumble before going still.

"Let's go!" Ward said as he holstered the .45 and swung out into the hallway, blower raging as he stepped around the giant mutant's remains which were covered in smaller Crics.

Muffin screeched and Jenni fell in behind Ward as he inched down the steps with the leaf blower out before him, clearing the Crics away.

A huge Cric sat at the bottom of the steps staring at the partners. Crics the size of rats cycled around the big boy, their antennas swaying, legs churning, bulbous eyes shining in the half-light.

The rat-sized Crics paid no attention to the smaller beasts, and they scuttled up the steps as if on an advance mission for the big boy. The blower wasn't strong enough to clear the rat-Crics away, and when the first one reached Ward, he stomped it to oblivion.

Big-boy squealed and mounted the steps.

Ward put down the blower, swung the Benelli off his back, and pasted the huge Cric onto the front door with two fast shots.

But another, larger Cric took its place, and Ward saw more big boys pressing in from behind, the *snap* and *pop* of tiny carapaces getting crushed carrying over the chaos.

"Retreat!" Ward yelled. "Back up."

"But Ward, I—"

Ward grabbed the blower and drove his wife back up the steps.

Behind them Crics climbed over the walls, steps, and up his legs. The rat-sized Crics had stronger jaws, and Ward felt their sharp bites through the wetsuit and protective clothing, but as far as he could tell none of the bites had gotten through or broken skin.

A rat-sized Cric launched at Muffin from its perch atop the banister, and the cat batted it away like an overzealous display of affection. Even with her claws covered in leather, the Cric thumped into the wall, fell to the steps, and disappeared within the swirling mass of mutants.

Ward made a left and headed for the spare bedroom when the couple reached the second floor. Though it wouldn't buy them much time, the room still had a functioning door and the climb over the roof on that side of the house was easier than from the master bedroom, and it was on the southern side of the house in full sun.

The partners ran down the hallway, Muffin crying and whimpering. Ward bolted into the spare bedroom, followed by Jenni and Muffin, and he slammed the door behind them.

Crics covered every surface, but Ward didn't turn the blower on them because there was nowhere for the creatures to go. Instead, he let the rumble of the unit's engine do the work, and the Crics backed off as he strode across the room.

Ward threw open the window on the southern side of the house.

Crics poured through, but Ward used the blower to drive them back and clear the roof outside the window.

Jenni and Muffin went first, the reloaded double barrel out before her, Jenni's face covered with a ski hood and goggles. Crics crawled up her legs and jumped and hopped all around her as she inched over the slanted roof.

Ward went to work with the blower as he pressed through the window, and the air was filled with swirling Crics, the chatter of their pincers echoing over the devastation.

All the trees had been stripped bare except the evergreens, and Ward figured the Crics were deterred by their strong scent. Every flower, shrub, and weed had been picked clean of greenery, and the scent of must was so strong Ward coughed.

Jenni reached the edge of the roof and waited.

The yard below was inundated with mutants of all sizes, but there were only a few bigger than a cat.

Ward used the blower to clear his way before dropping onto his stomach, dangling the blower over the roof's edge by the end of its tube before dropping it to the ground. Then he shimmied down the gutter's downspout to the Cric-coated ground.

Jenni lay on her side, Muffin wailing and clawing at the roof singles with her leather-covered paws. She swung her legs out over the edge of the roof and started down, but she'd only gone a couple of feet before she slipped.

Muffin screeched.

Ward gripped the downspout and Jenni used his shoulders as a stepladder. Pain rocketed through him as Ward took the weight of his wife. He went to his knees as she climbed off, and when her boots were crunching Crics, he picked up the blower and went back to work.

The plan had been to go out the front door, but the plan hadn't survived implementation. Since he was already halfway around the house, he figured it would be easy to get to the lawn mower.

"Stay close!" he yelled.

Jenni didn't need to be told twice, and Ward felt her right behind him as he swung the blower back and forth, clearing a path to the backyard. He saw where he'd plowed through the fence and as he came around the corner of the house he found the mower sitting beside the blown-out sliding glass doors, the destroyed doorframe packed with Crics as they cycled into the house to avoid the morning sun.

Ward handed the blower off to his wife when the crew reached the mower. He pulled the starter cord and the motor rumbled and popped, but didn't start. He jerked the cord five times, pain knotting his arm. When he gave up and inspected the machine, he discovered its wires had been chewed.

The mower was dead.

9

Frustration boiled in Ward, sweat streamed down his back, and the rage that climbed through him knotted his muscles and made his head pound. In that moment he wanted the government to nuke the island and send every last Cric to the bone pile. In the absence of that, he would burn the nasty bugs to cinders.

Ward saw the storage container just inside the sliders where he'd left it. It was covered in Crics, but if he could get the gasoline…

"Cover me!" Ward yelled and pointed at the blower.

Jenni nodded.

Ward inched his way into the house, Crics filling the air and crunching under his feet, the blower screaming as Jenni cleared his way. He pulled the top off the container, the warm wind of the blower keeping most of the Crics off him. As he searched the storage box a rat-sized Cric hopped onto his ski goggles, and he crushed it against the thin plastic, the beast's innards sliding down the goggle's lens and hampering his vision.

There was the generator, spare mini propane tanks, the gasoline tank, the weed killer with a spray nozzle…

With a cackle that made Jenni look at him askance, he pulled the weed killer free and began dousing the Crics with the poison.

Crics screeched and cried as they fled, the toxic brew burning away the creatures' exoskeletons. Like in the past, the shrill cries of the smaller creatures stirred the interest of the larger beasts, and jumbo Crics appeared along the back fence line and in Ruth's backyard.

When the weed killer ran out, and dead Crics littered the ground, Ward pulled the gas can free. He had a moment of panic when he couldn't find the lighter, but then he remembered he'd used it to light the fire stick. It was difficult with the gloves on, but relief flooded through him as he felt the device in a front pocket.

The larger beasts watched from afar, and Ward figured the monsters might be smarter than they looked. He really wanted to light his backyard on fire.

Wielding the leaf blower and a shotgun was difficult, so Ward decided to make use of the broken lawn mower.

"Here, let me have that." Ward took the blower from his wife, and she let the double barrel fall into her hands from where it hung from her shoulder.

Ward tied the leaf blower to the top of the mower using the machine's starter cord and locked the trigger in the ON position. Then he topped off the blower's small tank and wedged the gas can between the mower's handle mounts and the engine.

"Here," he said, and traded off the M2 for the double barrel. Ward still had the .45 on his belt, and now the firepower was better dispersed.

As Ward gathered his strength, a heatwave washing over him, the wetsuit chafing his skin, he met his wife's eye.

Jenni looked scared; her eyes were bloodshot, and thin red lines ran away from her eye sockets like laugh lines. Concern churned through him, love, loss, and regret stirring him into motion. Jenni was fine. She had to be.

Though the mower didn't run, it was still effective in clearing Crics. Ward pushed the mower in a zigzag pattern, the blower clearing away most of the mutants. He headed for the driveway, and when he reached it, Muffin shrieked a squeal of warning.

Ward turned, but the cat was buried within her leather jacket harness, and he couldn't see her.

A group of six beaver-sized Crics bounced across the backyard towards the driveway. They were still fifty yards distant, so Ward didn't waste ammo.

The first swarm hit the couple as they came around the corner of the house and headed up their blacktop driveway.

Crics crawled and mounded over each other like a black wave closing out on the driveway. The roiling knot of pincers, legs, and dagger-like teeth surged forward, the creatures moving as if controlled by one mind.

Normal Crics weren't like bees and ants. They served no queen and had no discernable allegiance to any living thing except themselves. But the mutants... Was it possible they possessed a collective cognition? Were there queens out there? In one way that might be a good thing. Kill the queens and the hives fail, but the idea of a giant Cric spewing eggs made the peanut butter and jelly sandwich he'd eaten just one short hour ago attempt a curtain call.

In the dark the prior night, with the creatures scraping on the house, the newlyweds discussed their strategy for dealing with the mutants, and Jenni had agreed that in this one rare instance size did matter. The plan had been to prioritize based on size and avoid larger Crics, but with the swarm bearing down on them that plan was scrapped.

Ward wasn't that concerned because now he had gasoline.

The wave of Crics broke, tiny bugs spilling over the driveway and climbing over the Ward Casa.

From the frothing mass of clear teeth, pincers, and legs emerged a colossal Cric. Its body was the size of an elephant, and the creature's back legs arced halfway to the house's roofline, its forelegs churning, the spikes on the second pair of legs stabbing the blacktop. Pincers wavered in the air, searching for targets, and the claws moved so fast it was hard to see them, but their *crack* and *snap* were unmistakable. The beast's mouth hung open like a ragged wound, rows of crooked transparent teeth rivaling those of any shark.

Time slowed, and Ward looked on the scene like a spectator at a car race that was about to get killed by a rogue broken wheel.

There had been no time to think about how the mutants' teeth could be so pronounced. He was no scientist, but he knew Lemon sharks grew an entirely new set of teeth every two weeks, and rats were born with their permanent teeth.

His mind spun as the blower roared. Who would be trying to kill rats? Lab rats? The thoughts scampered through his head so fast they were gone.

Smaller Crics fled before the behemoth, and the driveway cleared like two gunslingers were about to square off.

The massive Cric stopped, pressed itself to the ground, and let loose with a thin, wheezing, whistle-like wail that went through Ward like a puppy squealing.

He let go of the mower and sighted the double barrel, but his wife stepped in front of him.

Jenni leveled the Benelli and aimed at the beast's mouth using the double-sight the way she'd been taught at the range. She fired, two quick shots that blew out the back of the creature's head, the sound of exploding shotgun shells and cracking exoskeleton echoing off the houses.

The behemoth staggered forward, legs still churning, inky black eyes bulging, gray-black goo speckled blue and pink spilling from the beast. A rush of foul air pushed up the driveway as the creature's torso deflated and the Cric crashed to the ground.

Muffin shrieked, the tip of her winter hat sticking out from the top of her leather cocoon.

With the alpha dead, the smaller Crics were regaining their mojo, and Ward slung the double barrel over a shoulder and danced around with the mower, spinning it on its rear wheels as he cleared a circle.

The house to the north was only forty feet away, but a tall fence between the driveways created a narrow tunnel that led from Ward's garage to the road. Vegetation ran along the fence on both sides, but there was nothing substantial enough to climb.

Crics dined on the fallen big boy, but most of the mutants were forming-up for a second swarm.

A flood of Crics surged up the driveway. There were thousands... millions of them, and there weren't enough bullets on Long Island to kill them all.

He pointed the mower and its blower cannon at the Crics and went to work fishing the lighter from his pocket. Brave Crics crawled up his legs, hopped off bushes onto his head, and pinched and stabbed at him as they searched for any crack in his improvised armor.

Crics fled as he twisted off the gas can's cap, the beasts scattering at the mere scent of gasoline.

Ward found that he was laughing again.

Stress wreaked havoc with the human body, and Ward's knees wouldn't bend. His feet were cemented to the blacktop as he stared at the mountain of Crics heaving toward him. It was an impressive sight, and in the swirling mass of Crics he saw his death. What the hell were he and Jenni doing? There was no way they would survive this.

"Scott!" screamed Jenni.

He shook out the cobwebs as he ran a thick line of gasoline across the driveway.

The swarm of Crics was fifteen feet away.

Ward dropped to a knee, closed his eyes, took a deep breath, and scraped his glove-covered thumb over the lighter.

No *womp* of the gasoline igniting.

Panic caused needles of pain to poke his extremities and Ward opened his eyes to find no flame at the end of the lighter. He flicked it over and over, the cloud of Crics closing in at astonishing speed.

The lighter sparked, a flame appeared, and Ward brushed it over the gas-soaked blacktop.

An explosion of fire knocked Ward back as intense heat washed over him.

The advancing army of Crics was unable to stop its collective momentum and the first line of the swarm was vaporized as it drove into the wall of flame. The sound of Crics popping in the flames made Ward laugh louder, but when he saw Jenni staring at him, he shut it down. Was he losing it? Naw. There was nothing wrong with taking a bit of pleasure from killing your enemies. Especially when said adversaries were bugs with icicle-like teeth.

Crics scattered, and the swarm broke up as flaming mutants hopped and scuttled away from the heat.

Gasoline consists mostly of organic compounds obtained by the fractional distillation of petroleum and enhanced by additives. It ignites easily and burns hot, but without fuel to sustain it a gasoline fire doesn't last long.

The gasoline burned off the driveway, the live vegetation burnt away, and with nothing to sustain the flames the fire withered, Cric bodies *popping* and *snapping* in the cinders like popcorn.

But the wind forced dying flames onto a bush next to the house and it crackled and smoked as it caught fire. In seconds the corner of Scott and Jenni's house was on fire, and flames licked the plastic siding and climbed up the wooden trim. Clouds of toxic black smoke poured into the sky and rolled across the lawn, and to Ward's delight, the Crics scattered before it.

The wind chose that moment to gust and shift, and the smoke eddied and was pushed west as the driveway cleared.

Out on the road, another huge Cric peered up the driveway, its surfcasting pole-sized antennas swaying, huge black eyes wet with focus, claws snapping. The creature lurched forward, climbing over the cars, and coming up the driveway, another swarm of Crics forming around the beast.

It was too late to escape around the front of the house, and helplessness spread through Ward like sewage through clear water. All at once the heat of the suit and his hunger and weariness consumed him and he couldn't breathe. This was over. Done. He needed out of this suit. Now!

Ward turned to retreat, but his wife grabbed him.

"No going backward," she yelled.

"We can't keep this up!" he screamed. "We're already low on ammo."

"I know," she said. Then she turned and leveled the Benelli at the oncoming storm.

10

Crics poured from the smoke-filled house as flames consumed Ward and Jenni's home. Ward had no cares for the house as he pushed the mower with its blower cannon. The newlyweds had three hundred and thirty-nine more payments on the place they wouldn't be making, and that idea was somehow refreshing.

Losing all his belongings was another matter.

The smaller Crics burned away like paper butterflies, but the bigger beasts hopped and jumped from the burning building, terrible flames engulfing the creatures, their legs, pincers, and antennas on fire. Crics popped balloons as their internal organs cooked and their lifeblood boiled. The creatures spilled from every crack and hole as the fire spread across the house's roof and spilled down its front.

When Jenni reached her car she stopped and looked back, and though he couldn't see her face, Ward thought he saw the pain in his wife's eyes through the yellow lens of her ski goggles. Sorrow and shame washed over him as Ward skidded to a stop, the blower roaring. Jenni had worked hard to make a nice home for him. She'd spent endless hours picking colors, furniture, artwork, and antiques.

The newlyweds watched charred Crics flee in every direction as the flames reached higher and became hotter. He felt the heat of the fire on his face despite the hood and goggles, and most of the Crics backed away from the burning house.

Muffin screeched and pushed her tiny head from her protective leather cocoon, her orange and white fur tinged black with soot, her head still covered in the winter cap. The feline gazed at what was left of the Ward Casa, then turned her narrow eyes on Jenni, bared her teeth, hissed, and disappeared back into the jacket harness.

Ward felt eyes on him and found his neighbor Jessica staring at him from a side window of her house. He waved, and she waved back. She appeared to be holding a candle, and when she moved away from the window it was again covered in Crics. As he'd figured, it wasn't fair to expect much help from his neighbors.

The flames raged and the entire house was engulfed. No more Crics spilled out as the bushes in the flowerbeds burned and ash and pieces of house shrapnel littered the air. Many of the sparks and shards of flaming plastic and wood landed on the lawn and were caught in the defoliated vegetation. Bare trees caught fire, bushes chewed clean of leaves burned, and the evergreens still lush with life but dry from the lack of summer rains went up like torches. Dark clouds of smoke rolled across the neighborhood, further disturbing the Crics, but the beasts didn't flee.

A gust of wind tore away the smoke and a sunray illuminated the two family vehicles at the end of the driveway. Ward had given little thought to the vehicles since they'd decided to make a run for the firehouse because it was less than a mile away. As the couple worked their way around the vehicles, Ward confirmed what he'd seen from inside the house.

The windshield of Ward's Tahoe was smashed, as was a side window, and the car was inundated with Crics. Jenni's Honda no longer had a back window, all four of its door windows were gone, and the car's footwells were filled with heaving Crics hiding from the sun.

He had brought the keys to both vehicles because desperate times sometimes required desperate measures. There was gasoline in the tanks and both the cars would start. If need be, the vehicles could be cleared out and shored up, but that wasn't his current intention. It would take too long to put one of the cars in usable condition, and the engines were sure to attract the attention of the bigger Crics. So for now the cars would stay where they were.

Ward wished he had the play wagon which was in the garage. He was overloaded. Dealing with the guns, wearing the backpacks, pushing the mower with its blower canon while trying to keep the gas can from toppling off, all in his heavy safety suit, made each step an effort. They hadn't even made it to the road, and he was so exhausted Ward didn't know how much farther he could go. He considered retreating to the garage.

But what solace would be found there? It was overrun from the supply mission and who knew what size the Crics in the garage were now? Just opening the rollup door would be a challenge, and he didn't need any more of those.

Jenni was right. There was only one way to go, forward, and going down just wasn't an option. Could Jenni leave him behind if he could go no farther? Would she? He would tell her to, but... She was in better shape and didn't appear affected by the heat in her spandex, snow pants, ski jacket, and the rest.

A loud *crack*, followed by an explosive *pop*, reverberated across the lawn like a shockwave. The main support beam of Ward's house gave up the ghost, and the roof collapsed, feeding the flames, which now reached sixty feet into the sky above the smoking ruins.

Ash, sparks, and debris fell like rain, and thick waves of nasty smoke swirled, driving back the Crics.

Jenni jerked into motion and Ward followed as she led the way down the street.

The fire crackled and snapped behind them, and Ward could still feel the heat of the destruction, his safety suit cooking him like an egg on hot pavement as he pushed the mower.

Three Crics the size of dogs sprayed out from underneath Jenni's car and were upon the partners so fast Ward slipped as he drew the .45.

He used the mower handle to stay on his feet and managed to snap off two shots.

The first blew the lead Cric from the air in mid-jump, its legs and guts splattering the hood of Jenni's car and the driveway. Ward's second shot missed and thumped into an oak tree on the front lawn that was burned to a tall cinder. The trunk was all that was left, a dark spire of burning wood that stood over fifty feet tall, its flames licking the sky like a beacon.

Hope surged through him. Would the fire bring help? Even as the idea flashed across his subconscious, he knew it was a pipedream. People were dying everywhere, and he didn't believe for a second that his house was even on the priority list, let alone at its top.

Jenni was too slow to act. One of the dog-Crics slammed into her chest and she was knocked to the ground. She flipped onto her butt, and crab-walked backward, putting space between her and her attacker, Muffin whining the entire time.

Ward pivoted and fired three times.

All three shots struck home. The first pierced Jenni's attacker in its humped carapace, and the shell broke apart like a lobster tail smacked with a hammer. The second took off a rear turkey leg, and the third hit the creature dead in its face and splattered the Cric onto Jenni where she lay sprawled on the driveway, pellets peppering the ground all around her.

Muffin screeched and Ward saw that the leather jacket harness was bulging and stretching as the cat clawed and fought to get out.

Jenni hugged herself, protecting Muffin as she rolled and pressed to her feet.

The third jumbo beast was hanging back. Watching. Appraising.

Ward sighted the .45 but didn't have time to pull the trigger.

With the leaf blower raging beside her, Jenni leveled the Benelli and fired twice, the thunder of the shots still echoing in Ward's ears as he watched the Cric get reduced to ground beef and bloody chopsticks.

Jenni let loose with a battle cry that sounded nothing like her, and she bolted forward, M2 at the ready. As she moved, she reloaded with shells from a pocket, never taking her eyes off the large Cric that had been watching the festivities at the base of the driveway.

Ward's patience was gone, and in that moment of blind rage and anger, he wondered if he'd ever had any. He aimed the .45 at the large Cric at the end of the driveway and opened up, his grandfather's old Colt government bucking in his hand.

The gun clicked empty, and from the looks of it, all the .45 caliber bullets had done was aggravate the beast.

Jenni fired the M2, and Ward fell in beside her as he holstered the .45 and swung the double barrel off his shoulder. He fired, pulling both triggers, and the blasts of gunpowder expanding, the screech as the pellets left the gun barrels, and the shriek as the copper pellets zipped through the air was all Ward heard.

The shots obliterated the massive mutant. Blue-gray blood and innards leaked onto the blacktop as the Cric's torso deflated and its tall legs stood straight, then toppled over with nothing left to hold them in place.

Ward cracked open the shotgun, let the two empty shells fall from its barrels, and grabbed two fresh shells from the ammo holder on the side of the gun's stock. He thumbed the shells into the weapon and with a flick of his wrist, snapped the gun closed, and continued down the driveway, pushing the mower with one hand while holding onto the gun with the other.

There were more .45 rounds in the backpack, but reloading would have to wait.

The fire had drawn spectators, and Crics of all sizes inched up the street. Unlike their normal state of frenzy, the beasts approached with caution. The beasts didn't mound or climb over each other, and a calmness pervaded them that made Ward's stomach hurt.

When the couple reached the road, they both saw the remains of the person who had been devoured the prior day. Bloody bones covered in gristle filled the empty clothes, and Ward jumped when he saw the man's eyes had been eaten along with most of the rest of him.

Beyond what remained of the corpse, two tracks of squashed Crics caused by the military vehicle trailed down the center of the road.

Ward was getting dizzy and weak from the heat. Spacesuits and the like had fans, life support systems, and were made of special materials, all designed to regulate temperature. The wetsuit, while it had kept him free of bites, was designed to contain his body heat, and with all the rest of the protective gear on he was drowning in his sweat.

The Ward family house was fully ablaze, the .45 empty, and he'd barely made it off the property. A debilitating wave of loss and futility washed over him, and Ward reckoned he was in the worst position of his life. Wasn't even close. He was going to die. There was no hope of help or rescue, and it appeared that nature itself had conspired to eradicate him from the planet.

He couldn't have felt sorrier for himself if he tried, but as the fickle bitch of fate rearranged destiny, Ward realized he'd had no idea how screwed he was. He wasn't a bullet to the head or a fast decapitation lucky. No, he would be slowly consumed and pecked apart by buzzards like a carcass in the desert.

The Crics fell still, and that silence caused a wave of nausea to wash through Ward. A dog barked, the wind whispered and bitched, and it seemed as though some god somewhere had pressed the pause button on reality.

A shrill wail pierced the day, followed by a low tittering chorus, and everything jerked into motion. Crics ranging in size from a normal cave cricket to a horse squirmed and jumped with such intensity they tricked the eye and gave the impression there were no stationary objects.

Two gigantic swarms surged up Southwood Street from both directions. They gathered like bees on a honeycomb, and the swarms whined as the sea of Crics spilled down the road.

A fast survey of the houses on both sides of the road showed masses of Crics climbing and hopping through backyards and across lawns, though the beasts stayed clear of the fire. Smoke filled the air, the scent of singed musk working its way through Ward's hood.

The fire? Go back and toast some marshmallows? Use the flames and heat from his burning life to keep the mutants away?

Jenni turned three hundred and sixty degrees, the Benelli's stock to her shoulder, Muffin shrieking from inside her leather cocoon.

Ward didn't know what to do. They were surrounded and the U S. Army didn't have enough bullets.

A bright light blazed through the haze of Crics and there came a burning flame. Crics sizzled and popped as a modified Ford cargo van with a giant mouse painted on its side surged through the smoke, Crics of all sizes bouncing off its protected grill, the sound of crunching carapaces music to Ward's ears.

11

The modified Ford Cargo van had a matte black exterior, and its grill and all its windows, including the windshield, were covered with plating that looked to be recycled sheet metal. A man wearing a gas mask and wielding a flamethrower stuck from the van's roof, and Crics burnt and fled before him.

It looked like the shielding covering the wheels would hinder the vehicle's turn radius, but at least the tires were protected. The giant rat on the side of the van told Ward who owned... or who *had* owned... the van. Bill the Bugman lived a few houses up the street, and he ran his own exterminator business. Talk about a man with a plan.

Ward spared a brief moment to ask himself how the pilot of the van was driving the vehicle without being able to see the road. Though it was hard to see through the smoke, raining ash, and charred Cric parts, he saw a Plexiglass box mounted on the van's hood with a camera inside it, and that gave him his answer.

With a screech of tearing rubber and the crunch of exoskeletons getting crushed, the van came to a swaying halt twenty feet from where Jenni and Ward stood rooted to the road. Sensing help, maybe even rescue, Ward abandoned the mower, and snatched up the gas can and the leaf blower.

Jenni was picking off larger Crics with the Benelli, and when she ran dry, Ward covered her with the blower as she reloaded.

The person using the flamethrower wore a leather jacket and a gas mask with a leather executioner-like hood that Ward recognized as modified beekeeper headgear. Flames cleared the area around the van, and no instructions were necessary.

Ward and Jenni beelined for the back of the van, Muffin whining inside her leather cocoon.

Jenni squeezed off shots selectively, taking out anything bigger than a cat. But there were too many, and soon the M2 was empty and there was no time to reload. Jenni fell in behind Ward, who worked the blower as best he could. The .45 was dry, but he had two fresh shells in the double barrel that he planned to save as a last resort.

As Ward and Jenni rounded the back of the van he saw another Plexiglass camera enclosure, and next to it a speaker.

"Stand away from the doors!" shrieked a voice from the speaker.

Jenni and Ward complied, and they took up positions on either side of the double doors.

One of the van's rear doors flew open, and a gust of mist and foam sprayed from the vehicle as the Bugman's weapons deployed.

Any Crics unlucky enough to be in the firing line of the spray dissolved as the chemicals consumed them, their high-pitched squeals almost pitiable. Almost.

When the shooting white foam ceased, Ward and Jenni rounded the van and slipped through the open door. Ward couldn't think of a happier sound than the van door slamming home.

The person sticking from the van's roof dropped into the vehicle with the flamethrower and dogged down the roof hatch. Through the large eyes of the gas mask, Ward saw it was Bill.

Ward put a hand on the man's shoulder and said, "Thank you."

Bill nodded and said, "We're not out of this yet. Take us home, Desmond."

The driver slammed the van in reverse as he stared at the display screen mounted to the dashboard, the rear camera guiding him back down the street the way they'd come.

Muffin screeched and everyone jumped, their nerves stretched beyond their recommended design parameters. The harness undulated as the cat fought to claw its way free.

In addition to Bill and Desmond, a third person sat wrapped in headgear and wore tinted goggles.

Jenni unzipped Muffin's harness, and the feline leaped from within her leather cocoon. The cat saw the newcomers with the gas masks and hissed as she backed into a corner. Muffin looked like a drowned rat; her hat was gone, and she was soaked with sweat, her tail out straight, ears jerking around frantically. She pawed at her modified rash guard and sweatshirt safety suit. It too was soaked, and it hung from the feline like an extra layer of oversized skin.

"Easy, baby," cooed Jenni, but her voice cracked with emotion.

"Can we peel off some of this stuff?" Ward asked.

Bill said nothing and simply looked at his two partners.

So that was a no.

A cylinder of air and a tank of gasoline were held to the van sidewall via metal straps, and Bill hung the flamethrower gun from a hook to let it cool. There were containers of bug spray with hoses and spray guns, cans of gasoline, and guns. A wooden bench seat ran along the metal wall opposite the flamethrowers supply propellants, and there was a bin with masks and backup clothing, as well as a first aid kit. Bill had thought of everything.

The van's engine roared, and the front tires squealed as they rubbed on the metal plating protecting the wheel wells. Desmond backed the van up Bill's driveway as Ward's nerves scratched and poked his skin. Bill's house had a detached garage, and visions of his own home being overrun sent a tremor of angst through him.

Muffin worked her way to Jenni's side, and she stroked the animal.

Bill tossed Jenni a towel. "Not sure the wife will let that cat in the house. She's not a fan, and with food scarce and all."

Jenni licked her lips but said nothing.

Ward was happy his wife had realized this wasn't the time or place to debate the man who had just pulled their asses out of an acid-filled swimming pool.

"Be right back," Bill said. He collected the flame gun from its hook, lit its end, and opened the roof hatch.

Several stray Crics crawled over the lip of the opening and Bill depressed the flamethrower's trigger and directed its flame through the hatch. Then he was standing on a box, everything from his chest up exposed as he panned the flamethrower around, its dragon breath scorching the land.

Desmond hit a garage door opener held to the dashboard with Velcro, and the rumble of a metal door lifting filtered into the van.

Bill shut down the flame gun, stepped off the box, and slammed the roof hatch closed.

The van jerked to a halt, Desmond hit the door control, and the shriek of a chain rattling signaled that the party was almost safe in the garage.

Ward didn't understand how they were going to get into the house. Then it hit him like a slap in the face. Maybe Jenni and Ward weren't going into the house. Maybe strays were kept in the garage.

Ward rolled his shoulders and got to his feet.

"Wait," said Bill.

A sharp hissing sound, like gas escaping a punctured hose, leaked into the vehicle.

"I used some plastic pipe and made a compressed gas system to fumigate the garage. It only takes a couple of minutes," Bill said.

"How is it powered? Do you have solar?" Ward asked. He didn't recall panels on Bill's roof, but he hadn't memorized every side of every roof on Southwood Street. Not yet, anyway.

Bill chuckled. "Solar? I look like a hippie to you? No, we've got limited power because I'm in top-level fuel conservation mode and the generator is running light."

"Where'd you find the time to do all this?" Jenni said.

"Been going non-stop for two days," Bill said. "We should be good now. Let's go."

Muffin cried and whimpered as Jenni scooped her up and stuffed her back into the leather harness. This time the cat fought the process, but Muffin had no better luck getting through Jenni's protective suit than the Crics had.

Desmond shut down the van and got out as Bill opened the van's rear doors.

"This here is Jody," Bill said as he pointed at his second helper. Jody was his teenage daughter. Bill noticed the cat hanging from Jenni's chest and he shook his head. "The wife…"

"Let me talk to her," Jenni said. "I'll make sure she never sees the cat and I'll give her a portion of my food."

"You've got food?"

Ward said, "We've got a bit in our packs." He grabbed the leaf blower and primed it to start.

Bill said, "Leave that here. You won't be needing it. At least not now."

Ward was reluctant to leave his best weapon behind, but like Jenni, he knew he needed to play the situation carefully. Bill was a good guy, but he was ex-military, very conservative, and he didn't get along with most of the folks on the street.

"Well, OK then." Bill jumped to the garage floor and helped Jenni, Ward, and Jody out.

The garage had a side door, and through its window, Ward saw the deep blue of a tarpaulin. "How are we…"

Bill raised a hand. "You'll see."

Desmond hefted an AR-15 as he peered through the side door's window. "Looks clear," he said.

Bill pulled on a backpack spray tank and primed its pressure bulb. "Open'er up."

Desmond dropped to a knee, pushed open the door, and aimed the AR-15.

With a *woosh* of air, Bill depressed the trigger on his spray gun, and a thin stream of poison coated the area beyond the door.

Bill and Desmond inched out the door and into a tunnel made of plywood and sealed with plastic, tarps, and duct tape.

"How did you manage this?" Ward asked.

"It's like building a dock bulkhead or a dam," Desmond said.

"Or a space station. We built it a foot at a time, clearing Crics, and adding, keeping the sea of mutants at bay as we worked," Bill said.

The run from the garage to the backdoor of the house was fifteen feet or so, and as the party moved through the tunnel, Bill asked, "What happened? What were you thinking going outside that second time?"

"We were overrun and decided to head for the firehouse." Ward asked himself how Bill knew it had been the second time?

Bill and Desmond chuckled, and Ward didn't like the sound of it at all.

"The firehouse was lost yesterday," Desmond said. "We heard it over the emergency band."

"What's happening?" pressed Jenni. "We've heard nothing since the emergency broadcast yesterday."

Bill harrumphed and sprayed poison. "The dipshit in the White House said they're working on more evacuation sites, more boats, and the military is being deployed."

"What about the gassing plan?" Ward said.

"Nothing yet," Desmond said.

"They won't give us much notice on that," Bill said. "Just enough time to protect ourselves."

"And if there's anyone who hasn't done that yet, well…" It was the first time Jody had spoken and she sounded like her dad.

The group arrived at an improvised airlock that led into a tiny vestibule with its windows boarded up. Bill slipped off his poison pack and knocked on the door four times.

When the door swung open a thin woman stood in the opening wearing a house dress and an apron like it was a Sunday afternoon and she was making dinner. A thin smile split her face, but when she saw the cat, she gave her husband a look that could have wilted lettuce.

"I told her…" Bill stammered.

Ward almost laughed. Bill was four times the size of his wife, and twice as loud, but there was no mistaking who wore the pants in the Bugman's house.

"What was I to do, Janet?"

Her hand slashed at the air, and she said, "Come in."

Jenni blurted, "She'll be no bother. I promise."

"We'll see," the woman said.

The group entered a kitchen with boarded-up windows. Ward's neighbors watched with eager eyes as he stripped off his helmet, goggles, and all the rest. He pulled his wetsuit halfway down and tied the arms around his waist. Desmond handed him a glass of water, and Ward sucked it down so fast he almost puked.

Bugman's place was Cric-proofed to the extreme. The guests, more like strays, were only allowed in the living room, the hallway, bathroom, and the kitchen. Bill explained how the house was broken up into several sealed sections that could be retreated to if the need arose, like a spaceship, and the secondary areas were off limits to guests.

"I'm sure you understand," Janet said. "We've got kids."

Ward nodded. In addition to Bill, his wife Janet, and their kids Jody and Timmy, he saw Jazz and her husband, Toby. They lived four houses over from Ward on the same side of the street. He didn't know Desmond, but he did know Lacy, a middle-aged schoolteacher whose life partner Mindy had recently passed away from cancer. She lived next to Ruth. He wanted to ask how these people had all ended up at Bill and Janet's, but there was plenty of time for stories and at the end of the day their tales probably weren't much different than Jenni and Ward's.

"Thank you again," Jenni said.

"How did you... I mean, why did you come for us? I appreciate it, but that was above and beyond," Ward said.

"We were watching you," said Janet. "What you did for Ruth was brave... and good."

"Everything probably would have been easier if she called me, but..." Bill hiked his shoulders. "She don't like me much because I charged her to remove a beehive a few years back. Gave her a discount, but I got bills, am I right?"

"It's hard living alone," Lacy said. Her voice was meek and subdued and Ward couldn't picture the woman in a Cric suit or in the back of Bill's van.

"Janet and Bill are kinder souls than me," Desmond said.

"Oh, shush yourself," Janet said. Then to Ward and Jenni, "Don't mind my brother. He's slow."

Desmond licked his lips, opened his mouth to retort, then thought better of it. Janet wears the pants indeed and apparently always had.

Ward looked at his wife and exchanged what Ward liked to call marital precognition, the ability to read your spouse's mind with virtually no information. Not everyone wanted Bill to risk himself to save himself and Jenni, and now there were two... two-and-a-half... more mouths to feed.

Jenni stroked Muffin's head and moved closer to her husband. The cat's ears were flattened to the top of her head, her teeth bared, and a low hiss like a popped car tire emanated from the beast as she stared at Janet, apparently aware of the woman's disdain.

Outside, Crics hummed and tapped on the house in the eerie rhythm that sounded like rain.

12

Stones Throw, Long Island, New York, 6:57 PM EST, *fourth day of infestation*

The Southwood Crew, as the group of survivors mooching off Bill and Janet Fredrick had come to call themselves, stood in the common room, formally the Fredrick living room. The crew stared at the TV with a heightened reverence even Toby, who was the oldest among them, couldn't fully grasp.

Toby said, "The last time I watched the tube this much was after 9/11."

"The tube?" Jody said. Bill's sixteen-year-old daughter was shy and didn't ask many questions.

"Before televisions were flat, they had a glass tube inside them, and when I was young that's what people called TVs."

Jody smiled, revealing her crooked teeth.

The power generator growled faintly beneath the newscaster, and the picture on the LED screen pixeled due to a weak signal.

Horrific video showed the ongoing crisis on Long Island and things were looking dire. The military and law-enforcement had encircled the island, and the evacuation of citizens along the shorelines was progressing, but the efforts were hampered because the rescue vessels couldn't go near shore or docks, or they'd be overrun with Crics.

The president spoke of the extermination plan and said it was almost ready, but there were concerns about prevailing winds, the type of chemicals, and the necessary protection for the citizenry. All this was still being discussed. In addition, the plan for creating rescue zones was tabled. It was determined that though the military could clear and create such zones on large fields and other key areas, there was no way to control the flow of people to said sites. Therefore, the death toll would be great. Islanders were being instructed to stay indoors and seal up their structure using all possible means. The puppet heads reiterated that oxygen wasn't an issue, and even if there were several people in a given domicile there would still be enough air to last for months.

"They were saying before that the creatures are a mutation of camel crickets. As if that was ever in doubt," Bill said.

"Regular sprickets are harmless," Jenni said. Muffin was in her harness asleep.

Toby coughed, which Ward had learned meant he was about to speak. The old guy's glasses were dirty, his thin gray hair tousled, and his dress shirt was wrinkled and stained. For the tenth time, Ward wondered how he and Jazz had ended up at Bill and Janet's place.

"Spider-crics have been around forever, literally. A picture of Rhaphidophoridae was found engraved on a bison bone in the Cave of the Trois-Frères," Toby said.

Nobody spoke. Ward had no idea what the Cave of the Trois-Frères was.

"The cave is an important historical find named after the French brothers who discovered it," Toby said. "The cave paintings within date to approximately 13,000 BC. So these things are nothing new."

"Minus the claws, stabbers, and teeth," Jazz said. Ward wasn't sure how the middle-aged African American beauty had ended up with a tax accountant, but there it was. Jazz's mocha skin was flawless, her blue eyes striking, her perfect hourglass figure model-like.

"And the poison," Lacy said. She'd been sitting back quietly with the kids, never taking her eyes off the T.V. Her short dark hair was matted to her forehead, her keen gray eyes alert. She reminded Ward of Ellen DeGeneres, except older and with different color hair.

"Poison?" Jenni said.

Ward's skin prickled as he struggled not to look at his wife's legs where he knew there were several Cric bites.

"They don't know anything for sure, but they think the things' bites are poisonous," Bill said.

"Even a scratch might do the job," Janet added. Her gaze was shifting back and forth between Ward and Jenni as if she could see through Jenni's spandex workout pants.

Desmond moved in behind his sister.

Jenni hugged Muffin to her, didn't look in Ward's direction, and said, "Great. Just great."

Ward wanted to change the subject, and fast. He said, "How do you keep the Crics from messing with the wires and the dish?"

"We don't," Bill said. "All the exterior wires have been ripped off the house. The dish's wires come directly through the roof underneath the unit, and we have one of those neat Plexiglass boxes over it. The little ones get in there, but not enough to stop the transmission, though it's only a matter of time before one of the big ones knocks it off the roof."

"You seem to have accomplished a great deal in three days," Jenni said.

"Desmond here is real handy, and so are Janet and the kids," Bill said. "Plus, I've known something big was coming for a while. If not this, it would've been something else. This world is going to shit. You see it, we all see it, you gotta see it, there's no way not to see it. So, I've been preparing for a while. We've got guns and ammo, and a nice…"

"Bill, now these people don't want to hear about your crazy prepper shit," Janet said.

Janet didn't want the world to know what her family's stockpile was. Ward didn't blame her one bit.

"Anyhow, we had a bit of a head start, so we're in decent shape. For now," Bill said.

"What do you think we should do?" asked Jazz, her smoky voice not unlike a jazz singer.

Bill hiked his shoulders, and everyone's gaze shifted to Ward like he knew something.

"Look, I just got here, and I still feel Crics crawling up my ass, so for now, I think we sit tight. If Bill and Janet will have us," Ward said.

"You're welcome to stay, but supplies are already running low," Janet said.

"We'll get to that," Bill said.

"Seems to me, that if we must leave the confines of the house, we should head to the bay. It's only two and a half miles from here," Jenni said.

"It's Cric-infested and might as well be two and a half thousand miles," Desmond said. "Have you forgotten what it's like out there?"

"And on the ham radio bands there are rumors of much bigger Crics than we've seen," Bill said.

"Even if we decide to evacuate to the water…" Jenni sighed. "There's a backup and a long wait for boats. I guess we could light fires and collect gas as we go."

Ward hoped he was the only one who heard the desperation in his wife's voice. In addition to everything else, she was now worried about her bites, and getting out of the Containment Zone had taken on a new sense of urgency.

"How would we get to the water anyway?" Lacy asked. "Can we all fit in the van?"

"It would be tight, but I think we can fit," Bill said. "Plus, I've got a boat."

The living room clock ticked, Timmy coughed, and Jody handed him a tissue as the tapping and fluttering of the Crics outside leaked into the house.

"Are you sure you still have a boat?" Toby asked. "I can't imagine things along the shoreline are orderly."

"Yeah, it's probably long gone, Bill," Lacy said.

"Nope," said Bill. "It's on a trailer behind the garage and it's in perfect shape, ready to roll, and it can fit us all."

"You can hitch it to the van?" Ward asked. An hour ago, he'd never have considered such a crazy plan, but he needed to get his wife medical attention, and that meant getting out of the Containment Zone.

Bill nodded.

The thin rays of sunlight cutting through the boarded-up windows faded as night fell. Bill liked to keep the house dark and conserve fuel, so the generator was shut down for the night as dinner preparations began.

Jenni brought Muffin to the bathroom, and to everyone's surprise, the feline squatted over the toilet for the first time. Keeping the porcelain cleaner than Bill wasn't enough for Janet to spare the cat the stink eye, however, but it was a start.

"He'll sleep in his harness? I can't have him running around," Janet said. "I know cats are… free spirits… which often makes them inconsiderate. I have other guests in here and I don't want that cat walking on them while they're trying to sleep."

"I don't mind," Lacy said.

"Nor me," said Jazz.

Toby was smart enough to keep his opinion to himself.

"She'll stay right where she is. Promise. I'll give her some of my food," Jenni said.

Bill and Desmond had politely but unequivocally outlined their case to go through Ward and Jenni's packs. Their food rations were pooled with the house foodstuffs, which Ward learned after handing the stuff over was kept in a secure section of the house not accessible to guests.

Desmond wanted to take the guns and ammunition, but that's where Ward drew the line, though he did agree to stow his loaded weapons on a gun rack in the kitchen.

"Can I help with dinner?" Ward asked. Jenni was preoccupied with Muffin, who had burrowed into her harness and hadn't made a sound in an hour.

"Yeah," Jazz stood. "I'm bored, and not a great cook, but I can cut up vegetables."

"All right then," Janet said.

Jody and Timmy headed for the closed door that led to their bedrooms.

"Where are you two going?" Janet said. "Thank Mr. Ward and Jazz for doing your chores."

Both kids said thank you with as much enthusiasm as a patient before a colonoscopy, then retreated to their rooms. Ward took note that Jody used a key to unlock the hallway door.

The kitchen was outdated, worn, and very clean. Formica countertops that had been scrubbed so many times the finish had come off in spots lined one wall, and the sink was dented, the cabinetry an homage to classical western. There was a large butcherblock stained with what looked like blood, and atop it was a stack of vegetables. "We're making stew, so we'll need carrots, celery, and onions peeled and cut up. Ward, you want to give her a hand?"

"Sure thing."

Janet nodded curtly. "I'll go get the meat."

Several seconds of uncomfortable silence followed before Janet crossed the kitchen, peered out the back door window into the makeshift airlock, and then deftly pulled a key from her pocket as she approached the basement door. She didn't look back, and as she unlocked the door, she didn't attempt to downplay or conceal what she was doing. The woman of the house closed the door behind her, and the click of the lock engaging echoed through the room.

"I've only lived across the street for over a year. She knows I'm not some criminal," Ward said. He started peeling carrots.

Jazz said nothing as she went to work on the onions.

"It doesn't bother you at all that she doesn't trust you?" Ward said.

"We're in uncharted territory here. End of the world stuff, and it's her house. She has children and limited food. I really want to think I'd let five neighbors into my house under these conditions with those considerations, but I'm not sure I would. If she told Bill not to come get you, where would you be?"

"Next to that bag of bones out in the street."

"Me and Toby would be right next to you," Jazz said. "So I'm thinking we cut slack at levels beyond any slack-cutting ever."

Ward nodded.

Janet returned with a package, unwrapped the white butcher's paper, and dumped the brick of meat in the stewpot.

Ward thought the meat looked awfully dark. Probably venison judging by the two deer heads mounted to the wall in the living room.

The stew smelled fantastic, and with the sweet aroma of caramelized onions and charred meat leaking through the house, Ward was almost able to tune out the click and buzz of the churning Crics.

"I'm afraid the table isn't big enough for us all, so grab a bowl and find a seat," Janet said when she proclaimed the stew ready.

The kids came, glasses of water were poured, and Ward found himself in the living room on the loveseat with Jenni and Muffin.

Jenni tried to feed the cat some stew, but the feline wanted no part of it.

Ward ate his stew in silence, the carrots still crisp the way he liked them. The meat had broken down into tiny pellets, like ground beef, and Janet had spiced it with cumin and paprika and that was all he tasted. Potatoes were needed, but his grumbling stomach was campaigning for more when something crunched between his teeth.

He stopped chewing as he tried to convince himself it was nothing. A shard of bone. Maybe a speck of sand or grit. Ward chewed and felt something stuck between his teeth.

Bill and his family were in the kitchen with Lacy, and Jazz and Toby had their heads buried in their bowls. Jenni had her eyes closed as she stroked Muffin's head, the bowl in her lap empty.

With a trembling hand, Ward fished inside his mouth for the culprit and pulled free an ultra-thin segmented black leg.

13

It was a long night.

Ward kept his discovery to himself, though he'd been unable to finish his bowl of stew... gruel is what it was, and what he had eaten still sat in his stomach like a rock.

The creatures danced on the roof and bounced off the side of the house. Their constant motion and the hum of their legs rubbing together seeped into the house, but all the traditional sounds of the night flora and fauna were gone. He heard no crickets. The trees didn't whisper or sigh. No night owls or birds chirped gently from beneath their tree covers, because there were no tree covers, except for the evergreens, which stood out on the torn-up landscape like reminders of what once was.

He'd been following Jazz's advice when Ward decided not to make a stink over the Cric stew. "We need to cut the most slack in history," she'd said, or something like that. What was he going to do, anyway? Start a fight with Bill? Have a gun fight in the house and rip shit up? That would serve no purpose, and since nobody else seemed to notice the Soylent Green, he'd let it be for now, with the caveat that he didn't like getting lied to. Or eating Crics.

Desmond and Bill's morning rounds, which included a review of the neighborhood via the exterior cameras, as well as clearing windows on each side of the house, revealed two new concerns.

The first was Ruth standing in her front bay window which was clear of Crics. Her place was on the opposite side of the street next to the remains of Ward and Jenni's place, and Desmond spotted her with his binoculars. The old woman stood silhouetted within the window, the word HELP written on the glass with Post-it notes.

Wrinkle number two of the morning was that Desmond and Bill had seen no other signs of life.

There appeared to be fewer Crics, but there were more big ones, almost as if the stronger were feeding on the smaller and weaker and thus becoming bigger and stronger, perhaps even magnifying the effects of their mutations. So it was that the gentle hum and constant titter on the house had diminished, but an occasional shriek or thin cry echoed through the dawn, reminding all within earshot that all wasn't right with the world.

Ward ate the eggs Janet cooked. He'd watched her as she cracked them into the pan. Jenni sat beside him, Muffin puffing steadily as she slept.

Bill threaded through the kitchen and picked up a plate of eggs and a glass of water before planting himself in the seat at the head of the table. He looked around, assuring himself that the entire Southwood Crew was present, before stating, "We need to get Ruth."

Janet paused with a fork of scrambled eggs halfway to her mouth. She said, "You'll do no such thing. It's too risky. Especially now with all these new big ones."

"You approved us saving them," Desmond said as he hiked his thumb toward Ward and the rest of the guests.

Janet ignored her brother and addressed her husband. "How old is she, Bill?"

In the stillness of the Fredrick house, a generator rumbled to life, and the snap and buzz of a compressor coming on filtered up from the basement.

"Nobody's volunteering to go?" Bill asked, but he was only looking at Ward.

Bill's expectation wasn't unfair. The man had saved Ward's ass, and Bill and the others probably felt like Ward had a vested interest in seeing Ruth to safety. He'd already helped her and understood her problem, and Ruth was familiar with Ward and trusted him.

Ward asked himself, "How bad could it be? A little zoom across the street in the apocalypse van, grab her and her tanks, and boogie home. But..." To the group, he said, "Bill, she's got one spare tank in addition to the one I hooked up. I'm no doctor, and I don't know how long those tanks will last, even with a reduced flow and oxygen percentage."

"What else could be the problem?" Jazz asked, and Toby gave her a look that said don't get involved.

Ward hiked his shoulders. "She's alone. Maybe she's seen a few smaller ones in the house. Maybe she doesn't feel well. Who knows."

"You're saying she might not have an actual emergency?" Janet asked.

"I didn't say that," Ward said. "I don't think she would reach out like that if she wasn't in trouble. She pushed me out of her house because she wanted me to be home with Jenni before dark. So, no. I think she's got a real issue, but as Janet pointed out, given we don't have any extra oxygen and her age..." He trailed off because though he knew and understood survival of the fittest was mankind's mantra, he didn't want the words to come from his mouth. They sounded harsh enough in his head.

"I made that same argument with you," Desmond said. His eyes shifted to Jazz, Toby, and Lacy in turn.

"Fair enough," Ward said. "If you send a party, I'm in."

"Ward?" Jenni said, and Muffin screeched. The cat had been behaving perfectly. She'd stayed in her harness, kept quiet, went to the bathroom on command, and ate crumbled crackers without so much as one meow of complaint.

"If we do go," Desmond said, "we might as well make a supply run. Lacy, you said you had a stocked pantry. Canned goods and such?"

Lacy nodded.

Now that the topic of food was being discussed, suddenly everyone was studying their empty plate, including Janet.

"What about you guys?" Desmond pointed at Jazz and Toby.

"Nothing crazy," Toby said. "The freezer is full with rea… meat, and we've got pasta, a few cases of water. A couple of weeks worth for two, I'd say."

Jazz nodded in agreement.

With that, the air left the balloon and the debate fizzled out, at least for the moment.

The morning news, beyond pointing out the obvious that the larger Crics were taking over the landscape, all provided an update on the extermination plan, which was progressing. A more localized approach was being considered that included an advance force of Army and Marine soldiers to clear out the big mutants and douse heavily infested areas. The broadcast created more questions and angst than it did answers and comfort, but the rescue supply run debate had taken on new meaning.

"Do we want to be around when the choppers start spraying?" Desmond said.

"We're sealed up good," Bill said.

"And we've got gas masks, our suits," Timmy said.

The boy hadn't spoken all morning and Bill beamed with pride as he looked at his freckle-faced son.

"They didn't give a timeframe," Jazz said.

"Again," added Toby.

"Like I told Ward," Bill said. "There won't be much warning. It could happen while we're on our run."

"I still think we should hitch up the boat and make a run for it," Desmond said. "What good is living if you've got two heads and your smaller one won't work?"

"Lovely image," Janet said.

"But a valid point," Bill said.

The rattle of Crics jostling on the roof filtered into the house.

Desmond said, "I was in the Army. When they get the order…" He shook his head. "They'll be considering the consequences if these things break containment, and they'll see us as necessary collateral damage."

"The needs of the many outweigh the needs of the few. It's our entire system," Bill said.

"Anybody feel like falling on a sword for the rest of America?" Jenni said.

Thumping on the roof, claws and legs scraping on glass, and the gentle hum of the generator and freezer in the basement filled the silence.

"I assume there's no way of contacting Ruth?" Jazz asked.

Bill hiked his shoulders and looked at Ward, who shook his head no.

"Everything was out at her place. No generator," Ward said. "I had those radios… I should have given her one instead of stuffing them in the storage container."

"Storage container?" Bill said.

Ward swiped at the air. "Lost."

Janet sighed. "I don't like it, but maybe Ruth will have food?"

"Or maybe that's what she needs," Jenni said. "I know she relies fully on deliveries."

"Bill said he's been preparing for a long time and we're already low on chow?" Ward pressed.

"What I should have said was, 'We're getting low on food for our guests,'" Janet said.

A loud thump from above as Janet met the eye of each of her guests. Feeling the heat, she said, "I've got children."

"And you are guests here," Bill added.

"What was in the stew last night?" Ward blurted. He hadn't meant to, but they were discussing matters of life and death and honesty meant something.

It felt like the temperature in the room dropped twenty degrees, but Lacy was the only one who stared at Janet. All the others, including Bill and the kids, were studying their shoes.

Janet smiled curtly. "Was it not to your liking?"

Ward said nothing. He was sorry he'd brought it up. He could feel Desmond and Bill's eyes boring into him as he kept his gaze locked on Janet.

"I don't owe you an explanation," the woman of the house said, and she turned, pulled a key, and disappeared through a door that led into a restricted area of the house.

"What did you go and do that for?" Bill asked.

Desmond's face had gone beet red, and Ward thought that if Bill wasn't between them, Desmond would've punched Ward in the chops. Because he had no answer, Ward said nothing.

"She was the one that wouldn't let you die," Desmond said.

"Understood, but the Crics could be poisonous," Lacy said, suddenly full of fury. "You heard the news."

"That's new information," Bill said. "And she cooked the meat so long I doubt any bacteria could have survived."

"And that's why we need more food," Desmond barked. "We can't use the… mutated fauna as food."

"Not even for guests?" Jenni said, the tone of her voice acid.

"Not even for guests," Bill said.

"So either we get more food, or some folks don't eat," Desmond said. "Any idea who those folks might be?"

Ward understood where Bill and his family were coming from. Thing was, sitting tight was no longer an option for him. With each passing second the worry and desperation he felt grew, and the report from Jenni that her wounds were getting worse and that she felt hot only made him more eager to escape the Containment Zone. He said, "Sounds like a big effort to get nowhere."

"What else can we do?" Toby asked.

"Head for the Great South Bay," Ward said.

"Grab Ruth on the way," Jenni added. She'd deduced her husband's play and drove it forward. "How long can we run around out here? You guys are great shots, the apocalypse van is awesome, but how long before our luck runs out?"

"Pack up and make one run," Ward said.

As the day wore on Ruth was spotted two more times, and the fact that she was standing was considered a good sign, but there was still no agreement about how to move forward. Ward told Jenni he thought it was Janet and Bill's call what happened next. It was their van, their boat, and their house, but as is often the case when a complex decision needs to be made, the universe chose for them.

Jazz and Toby approached Ward and Jenni when Desmond and Bill were tending to chores, and Janet and the kids where in their private section of the house. Lacy was asleep on the couch.

"I think we're going to stay, no matter what you all decide," Jazz said, Toby nodding solemnly behind her. Ward started to protest but she put up a hand. "We've been talking, and aside from the fact that we think going outside unless it's absolutely necessary is crazy, and the fact that we'll hold you back and slow you down, there's no way Ruth can accompany you with her tank, all her ailments, how slow she moves."

"We'll stay behind with whatever food stuffs are left, and keep watch on her until rescue arrives," Toby said.

"That could be…" Ward said, but he didn't have the heart to finish.

"Never," Toby said. "We know."

More talking, considering, and debating, but by nightfall, the consensus was that the Southwood Crew had to try and help Ruth, and with Cric stew no longer an option, more food was needed. At first light, Desmond, Ward, and Bill would go see what was up with Ruth, grab some supplies, and if that went well the trio would probe up Southwood Street to Montauk Highway to see what there was to see.

14

Bill roused the crew before dawn, and as the eastern horizon turned orange beyond the boarded windows, Bill, Desmond, and Ward ate a fast breakfast before suiting up.

Nobody seemed to notice, and Jenni didn't complain, not even to him, but Ward could see that his wife's health had gone downhill overnight. Her eyes were crisscrossed with spidery red blood vessels, her cheeks puffy, eyes glassy. Jenni was quiet, and she and Muffin stayed in the living room on the couch and only got up to go to the bathroom.

Ward didn't feel right leaving her behind, not even for a short time, but what could he do? Like it or not, he was part of this little community now, and he had an obligation to contribute to the ongoing efforts concerning their survival and the support of those around them.

Dawn is a disorienting time of day for many animals. In the gray of the morning, creatures came out to feed and hunt, but Crics became more docile and confused, which made it a good time to move around outside.

Like the prior day, there were fewer Crics, but the ones still around were larger. As they moved around a low rumble rolled through the house, and it got louder as the team slipped into the back porch airlock, Bill spraying poison, though there were no Crics visible.

Ward carried a rubber storage container that contained water, food, and such. He was surprised to find when he looked inside that the supplies he and Jenni had contributed were there. He recognized the peanut butter and jelly sandwiches and the brand of water they'd bought. He felt like shit for a couple of seconds, but then figured the stuff was only there because of what had occurred the prior night. Cric stew still sat in his stomach like a bad memory. He thought of Jenni and hoped she was alright. She had to be alright.

The trio reached the garage, and though there were Crics hopping about, they were small and quickly disposed of. Ward was already sweating his nuts off, despite not having to wear the wetsuit. He wore Timmy's dirt bike outfit, which was a blue leather jumpsuit, with a neck guard and hood. He'd also shed his helmet and ski goggles and donned a loaner gas mask, also Timmy's. The rubber chafed his skin, but as Desmond clicked the garage door opener, the chain rattled, the door lifted, and he felt better than he had upon waking.

If the extermination plan started while Ward and his partners were out and about, at least they were protected. That was more than Ward could have said yesterday.

Carapaces cracked and Crics popped as the van rolled onto the driveway, Bill manning the flamethrower to clear the way. Though the bigger beasts were more daunting, there were fewer of them which made clearing the path easier and faster.

The outside world looked like it had been blasted by a nuclear wind. Clouds obscured a gunmetal sky, the sun hidden on this day, which didn't help. Other than the evergreens there wasn't a single green leaf. The van's exterior cameras were clear—another advantage of bigger Crics, and like the prior day Ward saw no lights on in houses, and no vehicles or people moved about.

As the truck rumbled along Southward Street, Ward wondered what had become of his other neighbors. Had their houses been infiltrated? Or were they hiding and waiting for a miracle?

The remains of the first brave Cric warrior were still in the street, and though the tracks of smushed Crics caused by the miliary vehicle were still there, they were more noticeable with many of the smaller Crics gone.

Gone where? Collective cognition and cannibalism? What an interesting mix.

The van dipped on its springs as Desmond made a slow turn, the tires rubbing on the metal wheel well protectors. He straightened out the van, and backed into Ruth's driveway.

The old woman's front bay window was covered in rat-sized Crics, and the beasts undulated and shifted at the sound of the approaching vehicle.

"I don't see her," Desmond said.

Bill dropped down into the van and closed the roof hatch behind him before stowing the flamethrower. "Beep the horn."

Desmond nodded and licked his lips as he beeped the horn.

No sign of Ruth.

With Bill and Ward looking over his shoulder, Desmond piloted the van over the cobble stones lining Ruth's driveway, across her brick pathway, and brought the van to a stop with the rear bumper pressing against the house's stoop.

The gyrating Crics paused a heartbeat as Desmond beeped the horn three times, the blasts resounding over the neighborhood, each blast a little louder than the one before it.

Nothing.

"OK, we go in," Bill said as he slipped on the backpack sprayer filled with his special brew of bug-dissolving chemicals and grabbed an AR-15 from where it hung by its shoulder strap.

Ward had his Benelli M2 and a pocket full of shells. It was the last of his ammo, though Bill had hinted that he had more. Much more.

"Ward, on three open the left rear door," Bill said as he slung the rifle over a shoulder. He hefted the flame gun, adjusted the pressure and gas flow on the tanks mounted to the van's side, and lit the torch.

"Three," Bill yelled.

Ward chuckled as he threw open the door and Bill sprayed Ruth's front stoop with flames.

Crics burned and popped as they tried to escape, and when the steps were clear Bill killed the flamethrower and leaped from the van.

Ward was right behind him, gun up as he pushed the van door closed.

Bill wore a communication headset under his gas mask that was connected to a radio, and his lips moved as he gave Ward a thumbs up.

Desmond revved the engine as Bill knocked on the door, Ward doing his best to kick and stomp any Cric that came within striking distance.

Ruth's front door was locked, and Bill pounded on it a few more times before deciding more drastic measures were necessary. "Stand down," Bill said.

Ward retreated to the base of the stoop.

Bill blew apart the door's doorknob with a burst of .45 MM rounds from the AR-15 and kicked the door open.

Ward climbed the stoop's steps and surged into the house, Crics chasing him as Bill slammed the door behind him.

Ruth's living room was covered in Crics ranging in size from a mouse to a rabbit. Ward recalled being in the room just two days prior, and nothing had changed much except for the size of the mutants.

Bill swung the AR-15 onto his shoulder, lifted the spray nozzle for the bug poison, and doused the living room.

Crics shrieked and popped as they dissolved under the steady stream, and a group of dog-sized Crics appeared in the entrance to the hallway that ran to the bedrooms and bathroom.

The whoosh and bluster of the flamethrower carried into the house as Desmond kept the entrance clear.

As Bill turned the living room into a sea of gray goo, guts, and segmented legs, Ward called out, "Ruth! Ruth! Are you here?"

"In the bedroom," came a frail voice over the turmoil of the frying Crics.

Ward sloshed through the field of Cric remains, the stench of must so thick he sneezed three times as he crunched his way to the hallway.

The dog-sized mutants didn't move. Their front pincers clicked and snapped, their spiked legs stabbing the wooden floor, translucent teeth glowing faintly in the half-light.

Ward put the stock of the M2 to his shoulder, used the double sight to put two of the large Crics in his line of fire, and squeezed off a shot.

The blast echoed through the house as the Crics were peppered with pellets which tore them apart, along with a large section of the sheetrock wall.

Ruth shrieked, but it wasn't a wail of pain, but of fear.

The remaining large Crics hopped away, their massive legs churning, golfclub-sized antennas swaying.

But the mutants didn't get by Bill, and as the Crics sizzled and popped in their death throes Ward headed down the hall to the bedrooms.

Ruth sat on a chair in a corner, a spray bottle of bug poison in her hand, her facial features painted with terror. Crics sprang about the room, and the old woman aimed her spray with deadly precision. When she saw Ward she screamed, "I knew you would come." She tried to stand up, but her oxygen tube caught on the chair's arm and tugged her back down.

"Easy," Ward said as he went to the woman, stomping and squishing the Crics she'd missed with her bug spray. "Can you walk?"

"Yes."

The plan had been to check on Ruth and help her prepare for the next couple of days. But now, with the house infested, he saw no choice but to bring her back with him. This wouldn't be a popular decision, but since Jazz and Toby had already stated their intention to hunker down and had offered to watch the woman, he didn't see an issue other than he wasn't sure how Janet would respond. No matter. Like Muffin, he'd cross that Cric-infested bridge when he came to it.

Ward helped Ruth into the living room, the M2 on his back, the tall cylinder of oxygen on its wheeled rack trailing behind him.

No communication was necessary and as Ward and Ruth headed for the front vestibule, Bill went to the kitchen to commandeer whatever food stuffs Ruth had.

Three minutes later Bill arrived at the front door holding a trash bag that contained his haul and he informed Desmond he and Ward were coming out with a plus one.

Desmond's upper body protruded from the van's roof hatch as he sprayed fire across the brick stoop. Large Crics were amassing at the edges of the property, watching, claws snapping, legs cycling around as if the beasts were treading water.

Bill took extra time clearing away the Crics, the man howling and hooting as he sprayed the larger beasts with the AR-15.

Ward helped Ruth. Getting the oxygen tank into the van proved more difficult than getting Ruth herself in the vehicle, but after two minutes of struggle the old woman sat in the passenger seat, her oxygen tank in the lineup next to the flamethrower's cylinders.

Bill locked the rear doors and stomped on a stray Cric as Desmond dropped back into the van and closed the roof hatch.

"How are you feeling, Ruth?" Ward asked.

The woman was staring at the windshield which was covered with metal. "How do you see if the cameras fail?"

Nobody answered, but Bill nodded to Desmond, and his brother-in-law sat in the driver's seat. He put the van in reverse, backed off the walkway, and down the driveway to the street.

Bill raised his eyebrows and licked his lips when he got Ward's attention. The unspoken question was unmistakable. "Are we still going for supplies?"

Ward nodded his head yes, and Bill said, "You O.K., Ruth?"

This time the old-timer seemed to hear the question, and her face soured as she looked at Bill, but then softened. "Yes. Thank you. Thank you both."

"Don't thank us yet," Ward said. He told the woman of their plan to do a supply pickup at Lacy's, and then take a ride up to Montauk Highway. "Let us know if at any point you... I don't know... don't feel well."

Ruth smiled, but said nothing.

Ward felt like an ass. The woman was eighty if she was a day, and he was sure it was a difficult chore for her to get out of bed each day.

"Janet, do you copy?" Bill asked over the radio. She did, and Bill told her they had Ruth, that everything was fine, and that he'd be home within the hour.

The rear exterior camera showed a troop of grizzly bear-sized Crics as they bounced up the road, trailing after the van. A river of smaller Crics pursued them like ducklings following their mother, and again, Ward hoped that the mutants didn't possess the collective cognition they appeared to display. There'd been nothing about it in any of the briefing reports, which told Ward information was being withheld. That didn't surprise him, but it did drive home the idea that the U.S. government would nuke Long Island and everyone on it if it meant destroying the Crics and saving the rest of the country... or the world.

Lacy's place had double BILCO doors that led down into the basement where the supplies were, and Lacy had supplied the key.

Getting the van backed up to the doors took several minutes because the vehicle's turn radius was so restricted and he had to plow through a wooden fence, but Desmond managed it.

The team went through the routine of clearing the area, and Ward was happy to discover that when Bill and he closed the metal doors behind them, Lacy's basement appeared free of Crics. The irony of that wasn't lost on Ward. On Long Island, the cave crickets' best habitat was the south shore basement.

A wall was filled with shelves that contained stacks of canned goods, boxes of pasta, jars of sauce, everything that was promised. Ward and Bill went to work stuffing bags, sweat dripping down Ward's face as he cycled beans, corn, and other venerable foodstuffs into his bag.

Bill put his finger to the side of his gas mask as he listened to an incoming message. He doubled his pace, loading cans into his sack as fast as he could. When he was done, he said, "Desmond said we need to get back to the van. We've got company."

15

The company turned out to be six people in full motorcycle garb: boots, leather skin, and helmets with blast shields. And they all had weapons.

Ward had always known that eventually man would turn on man, and survival would be the excuse. Plus, half the population was dying to play a real-life video game, and when you added those two things up, you got a new kind of nutter.

"We've got to get out of here," Desmond said.

"Why not fire up the flamethrower?" Ward said. "Let's settle this before they follow us to the house."

"Love the sentiment, kid, but you saw the outside of this van," Bill said. "We've got shielding on the windows and over key areas, but there are plenty of unprotected areas a shotgun blast would blow right through. No, Desmond is right. We've got to get as far away from these fuckers as possible."

"Just like the Crics," Desmond said.

"They're worse than Crics," Ward said. "These assholes know better, or at least they should."

Desmond put the van in gear and pulled away from the basement doors.

Ruth said nothing as she stared at the screen showing the rear camera's view. She appeared to be in shock, her eyes as distant as Andromeda.

The group of six biker-troopers divided. Three of them disappeared behind the southern side of the house, and the other three strode toward the van.

Something ate at Ward, an uneasy feeling that told him the three biker-troopers that had peeled off were going to the front of the house where they could cut off the driveway exit. If the companions continued the way they were going, they could get trapped in the valley between houses.

"Stop," Ward said. "Stop now."

Desmond looked to Bill for guidance, and the big man nodded in agreement, his eyes bulging behind the glass lenses of his gas mask.

Desmond brought the van to a stop.

"What's on your mind, kid?" Bill said.

Ward explained his theory.

Bill sucked on his lips, then said, "Back it up. He might be right."

Desmond dropped the van in reverse and let the angle of the front wheels guide the vehicle back the way they'd come. The power steering pump whined as he straightened out the van. "Now what? Flamethrower?"

"I'm not sticking my head out there. You?" Bill said.

The two men didn't even look in Ward's direction, and he was simultaneously pissed at the snub and thankful for it.

Large Crics stood between the van and the oncoming thugs, and the three leather-clad figures slowed their advance.

A group of man-sized Crics bounced off Jazz and Toby's roof and landed in the van's tracks. The alpha reared back on tree trunk-sized rear legs, forelegs flying about as claws snapped at the air. Antennas swayed, and even at fifty yards with a weak digital image, Ward could still see the spiked clear teeth that filled the beast's extended jaws.

One of the black-clad criminals put a rifle to his shoulder and fired, the hollow crack of the shots pausing the churning Crics.

Two of the large Crics jerked and spasmed as bullets tore through them, their carapaces cracking and exploding, dark blood-like goo seeping through needle teeth.

The person fired again.

Ward heard the tinkle of buckshot peppering the back of the van, and he knew the vehicle was the target. Though the rear windows in the door were covered with steel, and the bumper had been reinforced to allow for ramming, the doors themselves had no additional shielding, but at fifty yards the door stopped the shots.

"Shit!" Bill raged. "How do we fire back?"

"I'm surprised you don't have an exterior-mounted gun," Ward said.

"That we could fire from within the van?" Bill shook his head. "I'm good, but not that good."

The remaining large Crics scattered, and the three biker-troopers continued their trek across Jazz and Toby's back yard.

"We need cover," Desmond said.

"Yes!" shrieked Bill like it was the most original idea ever conceived. "A place where we can get out of the van and return fire."

A four-foot stockade fence surrounded the backyard, except for the section the van had plowed through, and the detached garage was surrounded by shrubbery that made getting the van close to the structure nearly impossible.

"Just plow into the bushes," Bill suggested.

Desmond shot the idea down. "This thing doesn't have four-wheel-drive, Bill. What do we do when we get hung-up in the stuff and can't get free?"

Bill sighed with the frustration of ten thousand years.

Only two minutes had slipped away since Ward and Bill had returned to the van, but the tension running through the van told everyone time was running short. The thugs who went around the front of the house would be on their forward flank at any moment, then they'd be trapped and caught in a crossfire.

On the northwest corner of the house, there was a tall evergreen that stood out like a daisy growing from a pile of dog crap, and Ward thought the trio might be able to use a combination of the van, the tree, and the house for cover. With no other options, Ward voiced his opinion.

Desmond didn't wait for approval this time. He revved the engine and put the vehicle in gear as he turned the steering wheel and angled the van toward the corner of the house.

The three assailants in the backyard opened up, and the tinkle and pop of pellets and bullets hitting metal filled the van.

A thin ray of light knifed across the interior of the van and Ward traced its source to a small hole in the top of one of the rear doors.

"Get down," Desmond said as he put a hand on Ruth's shoulder.

The old woman hadn't said a word as she watched the screen showing the advancing thugs.

Bill grabbed his AR-15 and Desmond jerked a Glock from his waistband.

Suddenly Ward felt underpowered with his M2. He spared a brief thought for the flamethrower, but their attackers were out of range, and he didn't like the idea of sticking his head out the roof hatch any more than Bill did.

Desmond pushed up from the driver's seat and said, "Cover me." He slid open the van's side door and jumped out, using the corner of the house as cover as Bill fired the AR-15.

There was no cover in the middle of Jazz and Toby's backyard, so all three of the attackers dropped to the ground and lay in the prone position, guns extended before them.

Sensing vulnerability, as soon as the three figures hit the ground a rush of Crics gathered like a tornado and surged toward them.

Bill jumped out the side door next, followed by Ward.

The three goons that had gone around the front of the house appeared on the driveway, but Ward drove them back with two fast shots from the Benelli.

Despite their best efforts, the six biker-troopers had bottled them up, but they appeared to have underestimated the level of Cric involvement.

The three attackers in the backyard were forced to turn their attention from Ward and crew, and that was the opportunity Bill needed.

With Desmond and Ward strategically firing and keeping the three ruffians at the front of the house at bay, Bill went to work with the AR-15. He pulled the trigger slowly, but deliberately, a creepy smile spreading over his face.

Ward recalled how half the population wanted to live in a real-life video game, and though Bill would never admit it, Ward thought the man was enjoying shooting the attackers, and who could blame him? Anyone taking advantage of the Cric situation deserved to be punished, and in the current climate that could mean a death sentence handed down by the judge and jury of a bullet.

Shots thumped into the three men in the backyard, Bill's shooting beyond accurate. Ward felt some semblance of relief and peace when he saw that the three attackers looked to be dead before the tornado of Crics arrived, though he knew they deserved no pity.

The beasts mounded over the corpses, their claws tearing away the biker suits, smaller Crics crawling through the holes created by the .45 MM rounds.

With their rear flank taken care of, Bill moved around the side of the van and used the engine compartment for cover. He joined Desmond and Ward as they fired at the three remaining assailants.

The crews exchanged fire, and groups of Crics gathered to watch, almost as if they knew more free food would soon be in the offing.

Ward fired his last shot and as he fished shells from his pocket and pumped them into the M2, a Cric launched off the roof of the house and landed on Desmond. The creature's legs cycled around his head, claws searching.

Bill sighted his weapon on the beast, but he was in too close, and Desmond would take the brunt of the shot.

Ward, however, was in close and he slammed the butt of the M2 into the creature's gaping maw.

Translucent teeth crunched down on the gun, but Italian metal is stronger than Cric teeth.

With a squeal and crunch, the Cric reared back as it brought its claws in for the kill.

But Desmond had used his time well, and he put two shots into the Cric's midsection and splattered the beast onto the side of the house.

Some of the creature's innards sprayed Ward, whose head rang like the noon bell.

"Back into the van," Bill yelled as the AR-15 barked. When the rifle clicked empty, he slammed home a new magazine, chambered a round, and continued to lay cover fire as Desmond and Ward retreated into the van.

Ward used the break in the action to finish reloading the Benelli.

Crics crawled over the van, the exterior cameras blocked, and Ward and Desmond were momentarily blind, and the only thing that gave them a clue as to what was happening outside was the bark of the AR-15.

A rear door flew open and Bill dove into the van. "Go. Run them down!"

The van door slammed, and Ruth screamed as the van lurched into motion.

"Stay down!" Bill shouted.

The van bumped up onto the driveway, the sound of scratching and tearing leaking into the vehicle as it sideswiped the evergreen tree on the corner of the house.

Desmond pressed the gas pedal to the floor, and the van's engine screamed as the vehicle barreled down the driveway.

Crics were brushed away with the motion and the forward camera lens cleared.

The black-clad figures stood in the driveway, smaller Crics swirling around them as they fired at the van. Bullets tinkled and popped off the metal reinforced grill and peppered the metal covering the windshield.

The losers abandoned their attack when the van was twenty yards away and darted around the corner of the house to the front yard.

Desmond laughed as he turned the wheel, the van hardly bouncing as he drove over the driveway's curb and onto the front walkway.

The three thugs fled across the lawn, but in their heavy suits it was slow going and one of them went down.

With a crunch Ward would never forget, the van rolled over the person, the vehicle swaying on its springs as it crushed the assailant to death along with a smattering of Crics.

The remaining two dirtballs used a thick oak trunk as cover, and when the van ran by them, they disappeared around the southern side of Jazz and Toby's place.

Desmond turned the wheel, intent on pursuing the criminals, but Bill put a hand on his arm. "Let them be."

It was then Ward noticed the blood dripping down Bill's right arm, a hole in his safety suit.

"You're hit!" Ward said.

Bill nodded. "It's just a scratch."

"Looks like a bit more than that," Desmond said as he piloted the van across the expanse of dirt that had once been Jazz and Toby's lawn.

"The bullet passed right through. I don't think—"

The ground trembled, the van vibrated, and Desmond brought the vehicle to a halt. Like a distant earthquake, the ground shuddered again, and the van swayed slightly on its springs. The vibrations took on a rhythm, like distant mortar fire.

"Dear god," Ruth said.

The display showed the rear exterior camera, and a Cric with legs as tall as a three-story building filled the screen.

16

Jenni and the rest of the Southwood Crew stared at the TV in the common room, the split screen showing the two front exterior cameras. Bill had given Janet specific instructions not to waste fuel running the generator to power the cameras, and she'd smiled neatly and reassured her husband.

As soon as the van was out of the garage, Janet sparked up the generator.

Everyone seemed to understand, even the kids, that Bill's main reason for not wanting the cameras on was he didn't want them watching if things went sideways, and he certainly didn't want his family venturing outside to help.

The group watched in silence as the van rolled over Crics, Jenni's heart racing in her chest, the heat of fever leaking through her.

Somewhere the faint call of a dog barking carried into the house and that made Jenni think of Lacy's black lab. "Lacy, where is Fury?" she asked. The canine was a bundle of energy and as coordinated as a newborn calf.

Lacy tore her gaze from the T.V. and stared at the floor, tears welling in her eyes.

Jazz went to her and put an arm around the woman. "That's why we're here," Jazz said.

The camera mounted on the northwest corner of the house showed a zoomed-in view of the van turning in a wide arc and backing down Ruth's driveway.

Jenni had spent so much time worrying about Muffin she hadn't realized Fury wasn't around. She'd become accustomed to the animal's faint barking constantly ringing over the neighborhood, and she was surprised she hadn't noticed the canine was missing until now.

The van made it to Ruth's front stoop, and flames washed the front of the house.

"They made it," Janet said.

"It was my fault," Lacy said. "I should have locked him down as soon as things got dicey, but..." Tears slid down her cheeks.

Jazz hugged her tight and said, "There was no way you could have foreseen what happened."

Janet harrumphed and everyone looked her way, but she pointed at the T.V. as her defense.

Gunshots rose over the sound of Crics scuttling over the house.

Jenni stared at the screen, Muffin purring quietly within her harness.

"One of the big ones was tapping on a window, you know the way they do," Lacy said between bursts of tears. "Fury went after the thing, dove through the window, the screen, and by the time the dope realized he'd made a mistake, he was covered with Crics that bit and tore at him like giant fleas."

"And everything went downhill from there," Toby said. He sat on the couch away from the action.

Timmy and Jody had disappeared into the restricted section of the house and hadn't been seen since Ward and the others left.

"We were watching," Janet said. "Just like with you, Jenni."

Jenni sensed the woman trying to warm up to her. Most likely because she felt guilty about the Cric stew.

"Fury... he didn't last long," Lacy said. "And once the things were in the house... Well, if it wasn't for Jazz and Toby taking me in, I would have been dead the second day of infestation."

The T.V. showed a troop of grizzly bear-sized Crics hopping down the street in the direction of the van.

"I didn't have any guns," Lacy said. "Thankfully Toby did."

"Gun. Singular," Toby said. "The shopvac powered by our little generator was the real savior. Until it ran out of fuel."

"It would've been over for us if it hadn't been for Bill and Desmond. They came and got us when they saw our house was breached," Jazz said.

On the T.V. the van rolled up Lacy's driveway and disappeared around the back of the house. The three bear-sized Crics sauntered up the street as though they didn't have a care in the world.

Muffin meowed and Jenni loosened her harness.

"Will she stay on your lap if you let her out?" Janet asked as she pointed at where Muffin hid.

Jenni nodded emphatically, her neck aching as she did so. The heat that ran through her was intense, yet she was cold. Her vision had grown blurry, her joints ached, and the way she felt reminded her of when she'd contracted COVID-19. She took some aspirin, but other than that there was nothing she could do except hope for the best and tell no one about her bites. The Southwood Crew might understand, but fear of the unknown was running high, and for all Jenni knew, she could be a zombie by nightfall. The thought made her shiver.

"Let Muffin out for a bit, then," Janet said. "Just make sure she's tucked up before Bill gets back. I'd never hear the end of it."

Jenni's head pounded with pain, but she smiled and said, "Oh, thank you. Thank you." She unzipped the harness and lifted Muffin out.

The poor beast looked like she'd been run hard and put away wet. Her orange hair was matted to her thin body, her eyes frantic, her tail between her legs, ears flattened against her head.

Jenni stroked the cat, and the feline sat in Jenni's lap as she took inventory of the rest of the people in the room.

The click of a lock disengaging echoed through the house and Jody entered the living room.

Jenni noticed the door she'd come through didn't fully close behind her.

"Mom, I need…" The teenager looked at her mother, then the others. "Can I talk to you in private, please?"

"Of course," Janet said. She stared a moment longer at the T.V., but the van was still at the rear of Lacy's place and couldn't be seen.

Jody and her mother went to the kitchen.

Jenni wondered what the kid was so embarrassed about that she couldn't talk to her mother in front of her and the others. Her period, maybe? That would be shitty luck. Her head hurt, her vision was getting worse, and the murmur of the Crics seemed to get louder and stronger, their titter and scrapes like an odd language that urged her on, telling Jenni it was a good thing if the kid bled. She shook her head and her vision cleared, her gaze settling on the slightly ajar door.

Muffin was the first to investigate. All eyes followed her as she leaped from Jenni's lap, trotted across the carpet, and sniffed the doorjamb.

"Call her back," Toby said. His eyes darted toward the kitchen. "Now!"

Jenni pushed to her feet, swayed with dizziness, then steadied herself. "You aren't curious what they're hiding?" She knew she wasn't thinking rationally, but suddenly she didn't care.

Jazz stood and put a hand on her arm. "I don't think it's a good idea."

Muffin pawed at the door, and it opened an inch, light spilling through the gap.

Jenni shook off the woman's hand a little harder than she'd intended and said, "Don't come then."

Lacy got to her feet, straightened her blouse, and fell in behind Jenni.

"I wouldn't," Toby said as his eyes strayed to the T.V. "Shit."

On the screen, three black-clad figures in full motorcycle garb bounded around the corner of Lacy's house and ran across the front yard.

The danger didn't even register with Jenni. She was on a mission she didn't understand or want, but she was lost in her fever, and Lacy followed as she pressed into a restricted area of the house.

A hallway ran away into shadow. There were four closed doors, two on each side of the passage. She heard Timmy's muffled voice, and she followed the sound, thirty-plus years of horrific news stories oozing through her head as she envisioned the boy chained to his bed, or worse.

The first door on the right was locked, as was the one on the left, so Jenni and Lacy probed deeper, Muffin leading the way.

Timmy was reading, the steady cadence of his voice filtering through the second door on the left side of the hall.

The door opposite Timmy's was also locked, but the handset was old. Jenni pushed on the door as she jiggled the handle, and a crack echoed down the hallway as the door opened. A thrill of excitement and angst burned through her as she pushed inside.

She had no idea what she'd expected to find beyond the imaginary horrors her overstressed brain had manufactured, but she wasn't surprised.

A tousled bed was the centerpiece of the space, and supplies were stacked against the walls and covered the dresser top. Canned food, cartons of ammunition, and four large plastic containers of water. The ham radio sat silently atop a card table, and there were piles of clothes, paper goods, and secondary weapons like machetes, knives, hunting bows and arrows, and what looked to be a crossbow.

Plastic covered the walls, duct tape sealing every crack. The windows were double-boarded—inside and out—and rifles stood at the ready.

The faint rumble of gunshots from outside tore Jenni from her inspection.

"Can't say I blame them," Lacy said.

Jenni did, but she didn't know why. Anger surged in her as she said, "And we didn't see the other two rooms."

More gunshots outside.

Muffin hissed.

"Don't move." Janet stood in the doorway holding a pistol bigger than her forearm, Timmy and Jody peeking around their mother.

"Easy, Janet, we're jus—" Lacy started.

"Shut your piehole," Janet barked as she thumbed back the hammer on the massive revolver. "Is this how you repay our generosity? By proving me right? I knew you 'all couldn't be trusted."

"Trust!" Jenni shouted as she motioned around her.

Janet thrust out the gun as she took a step back, the furiousness of Jenni's tone giving the woman pause.

"We just sent Ward and the others on a mission to get food, and you've got days... maybe weeks worth here. Enough for everyone," Jenni said.

Janet bit her lower lip as the tip of the gun's barrel dipped. "I've got children, and I don't owe you shit!"

That truth cleared Jenni's head, the chatter of the Crics fading. "No. No, you don't," she said.

"We're sorry," Lacy said. "We didn't touch anything."

"And it won't happen again," Jenni added.

"It sure won't." Janet waved an arm, indicating the exit.

Lacy said, "Jazz and Toby said not to come in here."

Janet nodded. "I know. They told me. Though they should have done so as soon as you came in here. And Bill is going to be pissed about the lock so you 'all can explain it to him."

That burned Jenni a bit, but what choice did Jazz and Toby have? Janet had the gun, and Jenni and Lacy would've been discovered without their help, so why piss the woman off?

"Get in here!" yelled Toby from the living room.

Janet un-cocked the gun's hammer and let the pistol fall to her side.

Jenni scooped up Muffin as she left the bedroom with Lacy in tow.

The floor shook, and everyone paused for a heartbeat.

Timmy's face was red, and he looked upset. The boy eased back into his bedroom and closed the door as Jenni, Muffin, and Lacy jerked into motion.

Janet and Jody followed, and when Janet entered the living room, the woman of the house made a show of locking the door and putting the key in her pocket. She stuck the revolver in her waistband, focused on the T.V., and gasped.

The floor trembled.

Bill and company were still up the street, the van stopped in the center of the road. The biggest Cric Jenni had ever seen vaulted down the street, the ground vibrating beneath the behemoth's weight.

Teeth the size of broadswords filled its open maw, the beast's humpbacked carapace arcing back to its rear legs, the tops of which looked like bridge supports. Five-foot pincers snapped and searched, the second row of legs stabbing the ground, the creature's huge antennae swaying wildly.

The ground trembled as the massive Cric advanced.

"Why aren't they moving?" Jenni asked.

Janet stared at the T.V. and didn't even look Jenni's way when she said, "My husband will handle it. Like he always does."

To Jenni, it didn't appear Janet was buying what she was selling.

"Do you know I called him crazy when he started stockpiling a few years ago?" Janet asked as she stared at the huge Cric hopping along the street, the house shaking.

All eyes turned toward the woman of the house.

"I never would have thought..." Janet shook her head and stared at the floor.

Jody's eyes were wide as quarters and she said, "Dear God."

"Don't think he can help," Lacy said.

"And if he can, where the hell is he?" Toby asked.

"Don't talk like that," Janet admonished, and she licked her lips, her eyes straying back to the horror unfolding outside on the street.

Jenni's head hurt as her consciousness was raped and a million voices screamed and ranted. The sounds weren't words, and she didn't understand the message. Confusion paralyzed her, the heat of fever pressing on every muscle, her heart racing so fast it felt like it might explode. In her mind, the great Cric shrieked, and Jenni fell to her knees as Muffin hissed.

17

The road vibrated and the van listed.

"You wouldn't happen to have a stinger missile in your arsenal, would you?" Ward said.

Bill chuckled. "You joke. I tried. Way too expensive and if the feds find out you have one, they call you a terrorist and put you in a hole so deep nobody ever hears from you again."

The huge Cric filled the screen showing the front camera view, its huge legs churning as it bounded up the street.

Desmond and Ward looked to Bill for guidance, but the big man was tending to his wound. The hole in his arm still bled profusely and he was wrapping it with a rag. When Bill was done, he looked up and found Desmond, Ward, and Ruth string at him.

The massive Cric was a hundred yards away.

"Ram it," Bill said, his voice as cool as an autumn morning.

"Say what, now?" Ward said.

"We've got a reinforced front bumper and a steel windshield," Bill argued.

"Still, I don't see how—"

"You just don't see," Bill said. "The flamethrower has a limited range. Meaning we would have to get close, and even then, I wouldn't have enough time. And you've seen it takes direct shots to take these things out with slugs and bullets. It takes many. Are you gonna hang your ass out there and shoot for five minutes?"

Desmond pressed the gas pedal to the floor and the van lurched forward, the power steering pump wailing as he straightened the vehicle out. Crics crunched beneath the van's tires as the beasts struggled to get out of the way, their bodies smashing against the front camera enclosure.

The colossal Cric didn't slow. It raised its spikes, forelegs cycling, pincers forward as if the beast was beginning a breaststroke, rear legs churning so fast they were a blur. Translucent teeth glinted in the gloom and bulbous tennis ball-sized eyes focused on the van.

Crics gathered around the huge beast like rats on rotten meat. They surged around houses, from under cars, and launched off tree branches stripped clean of leaves. Sucked in by the great mutant, the mountain of roiling teeth, legs, and pincers gathered like a storm, encircling the massive Cric which was only sixty yards away.

Desmond and the big boy played a game of chicken, the van steady, the front camera intermittently obscured by angry Crics. A house cat-sized Cric leaped onto the box protecting the forward camera, and for ten tense seconds, Desmond drove blind, gripping the wheel as churning legs and the pale underside of a black carapace filled the viewscreen.

The Cric bounced away, and the view of the street reappeared with a flash of gray.

"Ruth, tighten your seatbelt!" Desmond yelled.

When Ruth gave no sign she'd heard the command, Ward tightened the woman's chest strap as she stared at the approaching Cric.

Bill pressed his back to the van wall, the AR-15 in his hands, a thin smile cutting across his face.

"You almost look happy," Ward said.

Bill shrugged. "If you've got to go, what better way?"

"How about no way?" Ward said.

"Hold on!" Desmond yelled.

"Ramming speed!" Bill shrieked, doing his best D-Day impression from the classic Animal House.

Ward closed his eyes and gripped one of the straps holding the flamethrower's fuel supply.

"It's been a pleasure, boys," Bill said.

The Cric pulled up short as it raised its claws to take a chunk out of the van. But the beast didn't understand that its pincers couldn't cut metal like butter and a chunk of steel moving at thirty miles per hour was tougher than its carapace and bone-like legs.

With the thump and screech of breaking bones and tearing metal, the van plowed headlong into the Cric's open maw. The vehicle listed hard to the right as the reinforced bumper broke off crystalline teeth like a snow shovel clearing icicles off rain gutters. The beast's jaws snapped closed, and metal stretched and bent, but the van stayed upright.

The engine raced, the van's rear drive wheel fighting for traction, its tire shrieking on the pavement, clouds of white smoke obscuring the camera lens.

Thumping, shrieks, and rending metal thundered through the van as the vehicle settled on its springs.

A spike the size of a fencepost pierced the roof of the van, missing Ward by inches before retracting.

"Come get it, you bitch!" Bill screamed as he pressed the tip of the AR's barrel into the hole the beast had made and squeezed the trigger. The roar of the shots hammered through the vehicle and Bill fell back as the massive Cric screamed and collapsed onto the van.

A front tire popped, the roof crunched, and the van almost flipped over.

Desmond smashed the gear shifter into reverse, and the van drove back, Crics popping, the big boy jerking itself upright. Separated from the tangle, Desmond put the van in forward and sideswiped the flailing Cric as he piloted the van around the floundering titan.

Bill laughed as the view of the rear camera cleared and he saw that a portion of the massive Cric's head was missing.

But still the mutant came on.

Half the Cric's body didn't appear to be following commands, and only the legs on the creature's right side were moving. The unbroken legs and pincer on the left side hung like so much overcooked spaghetti, and as the Cric moved, it lurched to the left.

"Screw this," Bill said. He shed the AR, gripped the flamethrower gun, adjusted the nobs on the tanks, and lit the torch, a gentle blue flame appearing at the gun's tip.

"Bill, I don't think that's a good idea," Desmond said.

"Then don't think," Bill said. "When I say so, jump on the brakes." He mounted the box beneath the roof hatch, took a deep breath as he gathered his courage, and threw open the hatch. "Now!"

Tires shrieked as the van skidded to a stop, and the huge mutant stumbled into the back of the van.

Flames tore through the roof hatch, Bill clearing his path as he popped out. The flamethrower roared, and the scent of charred musty Cric and burning gasoline filled Ward's mask.

Bill let loose with a battle cry as he sprayed the massive Cric with fire, the beast squealing as its insides boiled beneath its red-hot carapace. Spiked legs lashed out at the van, and the beast's antennas caught fire, then the fine hair covering its face, and for an instant, the Cric's head was wreathed in flames.

Then its carapace cracked, its torso sagged, and the beast exploded in a hail of skin, viscous fluid, legs, and broken teeth. The arced rear legs fell in on each other like a collapsing building, and when Bill finally let the flamethrower's fire die away the big mutant was nothing but a heap of smoldering goo and blackened tree-like legs. Skin and pieces of leg fell like rain, pattering on the van's roof.

The mass of Crics following their dead leader broke over the van like a cresting wave.

Bill stuffed the flamethrower into the van, dropped back inside, and gripped the handle on the roof hatch.

Two Crics, each the size of a small dog, bounced through the opening into the van.

Ruth screamed.

Desmond pulled his Glock.

Ward swung the Benelli off his back.

Bill reached for his rifle.

They were all too slow.

One of the newcomers landed on Bill's head, the other on his shoulder. Both went to work with their pincers, grabbing and pulling at Bill's protective suit. The creatures were mostly mouth, and their sharp needle-like teeth tore and pulled at Bill's gas mask and leather jacket.

Desmond waved his Glock around, but the beasts were on his brother-in-law, and any shot the Crics took would be shared by Bill.

Ward thrust the butt of the M2 at the Cric alighting on Bill's head, and a satisfying crack reverberated through the van.

The beast wailed, a thin cry that sounded like paper tearing. It hopped forward, pincers out, but then froze and fell to the floor, all six legs searching for the ground.

Ward put a hail of buckshot into it, a cloud of tiny pellets going through the beast and peppering the metal floor.

The Cric on Bill's shoulder twisted and impaled the black nail at the end of its second foreleg through the side of Bill's head via his ear. A *smack* echoed through the van, and a splatter of blood sprayed the inside of the eye lenses on Bill's gas mask as the Cric retracted its spike with a *pop* of rubber.

Bill's eyes crossed, and the stench of human waste seeped into Ward's gas mask as the big man's bowels let go and he fell to the floor. The Cric stabbed Bill's head again, but there was no third.

Ruth screamed and tried to press up from her seat, but she was jerked back by her seatbelt. Her old boney hand released the belt's clasp, and she lunged at the Cric poking Bill's corpse. Her spidery hands found the pincers, but the dog-sized Cric was stronger, and with a crack and crunch that turned Ward's stomach the old lady's right hand was severed.

That just enraged the woman. She threw herself forward in her fury, her eyes red as cinders. Blood spurted from her stump, her shirt ripped, her oxygen tube flying.

Ward saw festering Cric bites on the woman's arm.

As it had with Bill, the Cric used its pincers to hold Ruth as it impaled her in the face with one of its spikes. Blood speckled the van's wall, and Ruth's corpse fell atop Bill's, her body nothing but a bag of skin filled with bones.

With a wail of anger, Desmond fired the Glock, and the crack was deafening within the confined space.

The remaining Cric was splattered on the flamethrower canisters, dark entrails leaking down the stainless steel cylinders.

Ward and Desmond both stared at the bullet hole between the oxygen tank and the flamethrower propellant.

"Shit," Ward said, the stench of blood driving out the musty smell of roasting Crics.

Smaller Crics cycled into the van via the roof hatch, and Ward pulled the hatch closed as Desmond stomped the life out of four newcomers.

"Oh, God. No. No. Noooooooooo!" shrieked Desmond as he turned the last Cric into a stain on the metal floor. He pressed the tip of the Glock's barrel to his forehead and screamed.

Ward dove across the van and bounded into Desmond, knocking the gun away. The weapon discharged and the bullet went through the van's roof, a thin ray of light cutting across Bill and Ruth's corpses.

Desmond struggled with Ward, but the guy's heart wasn't really in it. He gave up and Ward snatched away the Glock.

Desmond began to cry. "What am I going to tell Janet? What are she and the kids going to do?" Tears slipped down the tough guy's face, and it nearly broke Ward's heart.

"The first thing you need to do is pull it together," Ward said. "If we're lucky there will be time to mourn them. I think, if Bill were here, he would want you to take care of Janet and the kids right now."

Desmond nodded and wiped his face as he pressed to his feet.

For the next five minutes, with Crics tapping and scraping on the van, Ward and Desmond did their best to clean the van and preserve their companions' bodies. Bill wasn't in horrible shape, but Ruth's head was a mess, and they used towels to cover the faces of the lost. The Cric remains were put in plastic trash bags to be disposed of later, and as Desmond drove the van back to the garage, Ward did his best to clean up the blood that covered the van's floor.

Ward didn't want to think about what they'd do with the bodies. Maybe hide them in the garage for burial at a later date? But without refrigeration... And they couldn't be left anywhere unattended, or... He pushed away the thought, the idea of Bill and Ruth being consumed by Crics too much to stomach.

A sense of utter hopelessness spread through Ward as Desmond spun the steering wheel, the flat tire thumping and shaking the van. As he backed up the driveway Ward saw Jenni and the others watching them through the front window of the house, Toby holding a blow-dryer.

Everything he'd done on this day had failed, and now the man who had saved his life was dead. Janet would have to raise two teenagers alone... if she was lucky. He had to remind himself that Bill's death wasn't his fault, and if things continued the way they were going, he and the rest of the Southwood Crew would be joining him soon.

18

When Ward and Desmond were safe in the garage, the rollup door closed, Bill's automated insecticide system spraying, Desmond killed the engine and let his gas mask-covered head fall to the steering wheel.

Then it hit Ward between the eyes. The Southwood Crew had lost their field general, and no army won a war without one. Jenni needed help, and he couldn't get it for her alone. The thought of failing her burned his stomach and made his chest ache.

Aside from the heat and smell, the garage was a good place to store the bodies until permanent plans could be made. Desmond and Ward stowed the corpses in silence, Ward's skin crawling. He was numb, and the Ward of a week ago would have tossed his cookies at the sight of two dead neighbors. As it was, seeing Ruth's stunned face through the clear plastic as he wrapped her up hardly elicited any emotion.

"You've got a spare for that, I assume?" Ward said as he pointed at the flat tire.

Desmond nodded, his eyes glassy behind the lenses of his gas mask. "Bill has... had snow tires. Still does. I don't know." He lifted the spray backpack from where Bill had left it.

"How do you want to handle... you know?" Ward said. He knew the answer and just wanted to hear Desmond say it, so he knew where he fit in.

"She's my sister," Desmond said. "My niece and nephew. I'll break it to them."

Ward nodded.

"Just keep in mind I might gild the lily a little. I want his kids to think... to know... their dad died a hero."

"He did," Ward said. "I wouldn't be here if not for him. And you..."

Desmond nodded, opened the side garage door, and stepped out into the tunnel of plywood and tarpaulins. He said nothing as he walked, and his pace slowed as the duo approached the backdoor porch airlock. The astringent scent of the bug spray leaked into his gas mask, and suddenly Ward's body itched all over.

Crics tapped on the tunnel, the low hum of their churning legs sending bolts of nervous energy down his spine. Ward saw Janet staring through the backdoor window, her face creased with worry lines.

Ward and Desmond knew the airlock routine almost as well as astronauts trying to get back into the International Space Station, and it only took a couple of minutes to ensure they were Cric free. The duo retreated into the house where they were met by the flock, and they looked angrier than a horde of Crics.

In the kitchen, with the remaining members of the Southwood Crew looking on, Desmond and Ward pulled off their gas masks and stripped off their safety suits.

Janet screeched, "Where is he?"

Desmond licked his lips and looked at the floor.

Janet grabbed her brother's shirt. "Where?"

Jody started to cry, and Timmy inched up beside his mother and stroked her back.

"He didn't make it, Janet." Tears leaked down Desmond's cheeks.

The crack of Janet slapping Desmond across the face echoed through the room.

Lacy gasped.

The dam broke then. Janet dove forward and threw her arms around her brother, weeping uncontrollably.

Ward went to Jenni and was startled to see how red her eyes were.

Muffin stuck her head out and meowed softly.

With the entire group listening, Desmond filled in the gaps of what they had seen on the house cameras, and when he got to Bill sacrificing himself to save Ward, Desmond, and Ruth, the woman of the house growled.

In the heat of the retelling Ruth was almost forgotten, but Ward added a description of the old woman's final act, her attempt to save Bill.

"Did you bring him back to me?" Janet asked between halting bursts of tears. It bothered Ward to see a woman as tough as Janet reduced to a dysfunctional mess, but he knew it was best to get it all out. When the dark clouds in her head cleared, she would focus on the children, and life would go on.

The group broke up, and Janet and the kids went to their private quarters.

Ward pulled Jenni aside. "You look like… not so good," he said.

The fear in his wife's eyes stirred his stomach and a wave of nausea ran through him like a roadside burrito, and he gagged.

"It's getting worse," she said. "Like I have COVID, but…"

He put an arm around his wife.

"I can't think straight, and I'm having weird dreams and strange ideas, like… I don't know how to explain it."

Ward put a hand on his wife's forehead. "You're not burning up, but you do have a fever, and that does sometimes lead to confusion and difficulty understanding the surrounding environment. Unstable emotions can cause delirium."

"Do you think that's what it is?"

Ward said nothing.

"I'm worried I might…" she said.

"What?"

Jenni told Ward how she'd snuck into Janet's room, what she'd seen, and how she'd almost fainted.

Ward didn't know whether to be angry at Janet and the others for hiding the size of their stash, or at Jenni and Lacy for risking their situation. If Janet decided she wanted Jenni and him out, none of the others would oppose her.

"I apologized, but there was only so much I could share," Jenni said.

"So she's unaware of… your condition?"

Jenni harrumphed. "That woman is aware of everything. If you're asking did I tell her how I felt, about my wounds, the answer is no."

Ward nodded. "Let's keep it that way."

The Southwood Crew gathered around the T.V. to watch the evening update, and the news was grim. Nobody was in the mood to do anything, and the entire group was just as lethargic as Jenni.

Mutant Crics had been found in Connecticut and Jersey, but the creatures had been dealt with, the areas cleaned, and no more mutants had been found outside the Containment Zone.

Inside the zone was a different matter. Scientists, politicians, generals, local authorities—they all agreed something needed to be done, immediately, but what was to be done was still a question for debate.

Images of huge Godzilla-sized Crics had made it to the airwaves, and the sight of the giant creatures pushed the establishment over the edge. MEMEs, videos, and cartoons already could be found in every corner of the internet showing the mutilation and destruction caused by the Crics. This stoked fear, and when the president announced that the military would be taking care of the big ones and supplying citizens in need with necessary protection before the entire island was gassed, there wasn't much resistance.

The science behind the mutations of the camel crickets was still fuzzy, but lab tests on the creatures revealed what Ward and the others had seen with their own eyes; bug poison killed the things, so as long as people wore protective clothing, masks, and stayed indoors, the citizenry should be unaffected when the island was doused with airborne insecticide.

Research relating to the Crics' poison, which was injected via its teeth upon piercing flesh, was ongoing, but biological experiments are time-consuming. In the interim, the CDC was recommending basic cold remedies and topical creams, and if severe symptoms emerged, antibiotics—specifically amoxicillin and doxycycline had shown positive results in driving back the infection. When Ward asked Janet if she had any of the listed medications, she responded, "We use old-fashioned aspirin, hon."

Ward didn't ask for any of Janet's stash because it would raise too many questions, but with his wife's condition worsening that bridge might have to be crossed soon.

With the main report over, the puppet head droned on about how there are more than 500 species of camel crickets, and many of them called the basements of Long Island their home. That made locking down the exact biology difficult because it appeared that the mutations affected the 500 species in slightly different ways. The bigheads believed that was the reason some of the creatures grew at different rates and to abnormal sizes, while others had only the mutations of mouths of teeth and pincers.

The crew's debate about how to proceed was tabled because Janet and the kids were still shaken up, and Desmond was focusing all his attention on his sister, niece, and nephew. Jazz and Lacy were asleep on the couch, Toby staring at the dark T.V. The generator had been shut down, and as the sun dipped below the horizon the gray streaks of dusk leaking through the boarded windows faded to black.

Outside the Crics stirred with newfound energy.

Jenni and Ward were in the kitchen, Ward eating a can of soup, when Jenni said, "I'm going to let Muffin out so she can eat and stretch."

Ward glanced at the closed kitchen door.

"It's O.K. When you were gone, she said I could let Muffin loose for a bit," Jenni said.

"And that led to good things?" It had been the cat that nudged open the door to the private section of the house.

She made fish lips. "She's been such a good girl. She needs it, Scott."

"Fine."

Jenni unzipped the leather jacket harness and Muffin jumped to the floor, shook herself, and sauntered over to a bowl of water. As water sloshed onto the floor, relief flooded through him. At least the water was still running.

Muffin hissed and darted across the kitchen.

Ward looked at Jenni, who shrugged. He pressed to his feet, grabbed the Benelli M2 from the collection of guns next to the refrigerator, and went to investigate what had gotten the feline's hackles up.

Jenni flicked the light switch, but with the generator off no blossom of illumination pushed away the grayness.

Muffin mewed and pawed at the wall molding next to the refrigerator.

An LED flashlight sat on the countertop and Ward grabbed it and turned it on. Under its unwavering eye, he saw nothing unusual except the cat pulling dust bunnies from behind the refrigerator.

"What do you have there, Muffin?" Ward bent low to get a good look and a Cric hopped into the air and landed on Muffin's head.

The feline shrieked as she bucked and heaved, tossing her tiny head in an attempt to dislodge the creature, but the Cric held on tight.

Ward's hand shot out, then retracted just as fast. The cat's head was moving too fast, and he didn't want to get bitten.

"What's going on in here?" asked Janet as she entered the kitchen, and when she saw Ward with the flashlight, she pulled her revolver and pointed it at the cat.

"Wait. Janet, you don't—"

"Shut it! I was nice. That was my fault. But I should have never let that cat in here. He just might…" Her voice trailed away like she'd run out of gas as her eyes found the Cric.

The Cric hopped off Muffin's head, and the cat bolted to Jenni.

All eyes watched the mutant as it hopped around the kitchen. It came near, then moved away just as fast, testing its boundaries as if uncertain whether the humans were friend or foe.

Ward leaped at the creature twice, trying to make it acquainted with the bottom of his boot, but the mutant was agile and motivated, and like a spider, it sensed approaching danger.

A gunshot thundered through the room, and a bullet punched the kitchen floor.

The Cric was gone.

All eyes swung to Janet, who held the pistol in a double-handed grip.

A smell like burnt hair wafted through the room and Ward pointed the LED flashlight at the hole in the floor, and pieces of leg, skin, and a splash of dark fluid were all that remained of the Cric.

Jazz, Toby, and Lacy pressed into the kitchen.

"What's happening?" Jazz asked.

"I'm sorry… not sorry, but I…" Janet said. The pistol fell to her side. "That was reckless and unnecessary. I apologize."

Lacy said, "What? Stop. You were protecting us. If that—"

"That bullet could have ricocheted and killed someone!" Janet railed before deflating like a balloon.

The Southwood Crew stood silent, staring at the hole in the kitchen floor.

Outside the Crics were oddly subdued.

The door to the basement opened and Desmond appeared. "Who the hell is shooting?"

Janet put up a hand. "It was me. Everybody is fine."

Ward looked around at the rest of the gang, pausing briefly to stare at his wife. Jenni was bathed in shadow, the flashlight's cloud of light shrinking as darkness engulfed Long Island.

The companions stood there for several minutes, and the kids joined the group. That one little mutant inside the house meant so much. Was it a stray that snuck into the house on Ward or Desmond's boots? Had it come through a crack? Had it always been in the house undetected? Did it matter? Because if the Cric spread eggs around...

Like a final bell or a game-ending whistle, the Cric inside the walls said only one thing to Ward, and Jenni's condition only drove it home. But before he could start campaigning, he gained an unlikely ally.

"Desmond, in the morning you fix the flat on the van and hitch up the boat," Janet said. "We're getting the hell out of here. This house is no longer safe."

19

The Southwood Crew took turns keeping watch overnight. In a reversal of policy, Janet announced that since they were leaving the next day the generator could run all night and she commanded that every light in the house be turned on. So it was that while others slept, or tried to sleep, a member of the group stalked the house, searching for any sign of Crics inside the castle walls.

There were no more private areas in the house. Janet dropped all barriers, and supplies were being shifted and moved. The team had to travel light, which meant they weren't taking much. As Timmy had so eloquently put it, "If we're still running around at nightfall, we're in big trouble."

Through all this, Jazz and Toby kept their desire to stay behind to themselves, and neither of them even looked in Ward and Jenni's direction when matters of longevity concerning the house were discussed. With the captain of the team gone, decision-making took a little longer. Make no mistake, Janet was in charge, but without her husband by her side, she listened to the group, considered what they had to say, and sometimes shifted her position. Still, Ward was worried about not having Bill with them out on the road.

The crew did have one thing going for them. There was an incoming rainstorm expected to hit the island. But on Long Island in the warm months, thunderstorms had a mind of their own, and they appeared as if from nowhere and disappeared just as quickly. There was a brief discussion about waiting for the storm, but because of the sporadic nature of the thundershowers, the idea was rejected.

Three more Crics were discovered. Two of them were so small Muffin was the one that found them. Not unsurprisingly, Janet had softened her position on the beast after it became clear the cat was the best Cric hunter in the house.

"I may have misjudged you, Muffin," Janet said with a smile as she stroked the feline's tail.

The group was in the living room, taking a break and eating fresh hamburgers.

"Such a treat," Lacy said as she devoured her burger with cheese and fries.

"No sense saving the stuff anymore, right?" Janet took a bite.

Toby coughed.

Ward licked his lips and exchanged a glance with Jenni that said, "Here it comes."

"About that," Toby said. "Janet, is it O.K. if we stay behind in your house?"

Janet stopped chewing and looked at Ward. "Did you know about this?" she asked.

Ward shrugged. "I knew they were thinking about it."

The woman of the house shook her head in frustration.

"Look, it's O.K.," Jazz said. "We just… we'll just hold you back and we think, given our age and athletic abilities, that our best bet is to stay here."

"We've already nabbed four Crics in the house. You know what that means," Lacy said.

"We do," Toby said. "With Janet's permission, we plan to hide in her ultra-Cric-proofed bedroom and see if we can hold out until they gas the island, which can't be more than a couple of days off, tops. Right?"

"That's how it's looking, but a lot can happen between now and then," Jenni said. "There's a storm coming, and the military is bound to break some eggs."

"They won't take long," said Timmy. The kids were standing guard behind their mother. "Dad said our troops are the best."

"Desmond is in the garage fixing the flat on the van. I need to make sure he doesn't need either of you," Janet said. "But if he's O.K. with it, I guess I am."

"Can Muffin stay with us, Jenni?" Toby asked.

Hearing her name, Muffin froze where she patrolled by the front door, ears twitching as her head swiveled.

Jenni opened her mouth to protest, but then her face twisted, and she looked to Ward for answers.

Ward pulled a Toby and coughed, all eyes on him. "Do we want to leave Muffin behind? Not a chance." Jazz started to protest, and Ward put up a hand. "But what we want isn't the question, is it? It's what's best for Muffin."

Outside the Crics scuttled over the house, their constant shuffling like background static.

Ward pointed at the boarded-up front window. "Out there we might have to literally run for our lives. Muffin is small and fragile—ferocious in her own way, yes, but she won't stand a chance against any Cric bigger than she is and there's nowhere to hide out there."

"And Toby and Jazz need her here. Like an alarm system," Lacy said.

"Are you alright with that, Jenni?" Jazz asked.

The backdoor slammed and the sounds of Desmond stripping out of his protective suit carried into the living room.

Jenni nodded as she stared at Muffin.

The feline appeared to know she'd been traded, and she turned, raised her tail in the air so the assembled got a good view of her poop chute, and disappeared behind the couch.

"That's decided then if Desmond approves," Janet said.

"Approves what?" Desmond strolled into the living room holding a beer.

Janet's eyes narrowed as she studied the Blue Point Summer Ale in her brother's hand. She explained the plan, and when she was done, Desmond nodded his approval and took a long pull of beer.

"I was considering how to broach leaving the cat behind," Desmond said. "It'll be easier with fewer people to keep track of, so what Jazz and Toby do is their call as long as they don't burn the house down."

Jenni sniffled.

"Sorry," Desmond said.

There had been little time for Ward to consider what he and Jenni would do if they managed to escape the Containment Zone. The newlyweds' house had burned to the ground, and he had no idea how long it would take to get it rebuilt, and he wasn't sure that was what he wanted. The island was going to be a wasteland for a long time, and he wasn't sure he wanted to be around for the rebuild.

"With all that settled, can we talk about the elephant in the room?" Janet asked.

That question sent a shiver of angst traipsing down Ward's spine, and it bounced and banged on each vertebra on its way down.

Nobody spoke, the hum of the house and the prattle of the Crics outside the only sounds.

Janet and Desmond stared at Jenni, and she wilted under the gaze.

"Do you have a question you'd like to ask?" Ward said.

"Yeah," Desmond said. "Jenni, do you have any Cric bites?"

Jenni put a hand on Ward's arm and said nothing, but the large tears that rolled down her cheeks left no doubts about the answer to Desmond's question.

Jenni looked like hell, and a stranger would be able to see she was sick. Ward said, "We don't *know* anything. She hasn't been—"

"Do you have bites?" Janet asked, her tone motherly, yet stern.

Jenni nodded.

"I kind of figured it out when Ward started asking if I had those drugs the CDC recommended," Janet said.

"That's why I've been staying away from everyone," Jenni said. "I don't know if I'm contagious."

"Nonsense," Toby said. "There's been no news of that at all."

"That they've told us about, you mean," Timmy said. The apple didn't fall far from the tree.

Toby shrugged and pressed his lips together. The kid had a point. A good one.

"Do you think Daune's Drug might have amoxicillin or doxycycline?" Lacy asked. The old family drug store was on Montauk Highway and was nearly on the route the Southwood Crew planned to take to the shoreline.

"Before the names of the drugs were mentioned on the tube? Definitely. Now?" Desmond shrugged. "Might be worth checking out, though, if we're going right by it."

"There's no longer a reason to consider commandeering a second vehicle, right?" Ward asked. There had been talk of a car running interference for the van, but the modifications would take time and Bill had been the welder.

"I never liked the idea of splitting up," Jenni said. "Strength in numbers and all that rot."

"And we're down to seven people," Desmond added. "So there's plenty of room in the van."

With the major decisions made, the group set about preparing.

Bill and Desmond had recently used his eighteen-foot V-hull center console, so it had fuel and Desmond knew the engine was in turnkey condition, so there wasn't much to do there.

"I'm thinking we get everyone into the van, then trailer up the boat," Desmond said.

"One trip out there. One suit up. Sounds good to me," Ward said.

The crew cleaned and loaded guns, secured extra ammo, and fine-tuned their makeshift safety suits. Then everyone helped Jazz and Toby go over Janet and Bill's bedroom, and the plan was for the entire group to spend the night in that one room together. Supplies were loaded up, waters packed, and when the sun started its descent to the horizon, preparations were substantially complete.

Even with Jazz and Toby staying behind, there was still enough food for Janet and Jazz to prepare a feast. Desmond repeated what he'd learned from his drill sergeant in boot camp; eat and sleep when you can because you never know when you'll get the opportunity to do so again.

Wine was opened and Janet tapped her glass. "Would anyone like to say grace?"

For a heartbeat Ward had no idea what the woman was talking about. Ward had given up on the church years ago—that wasn't true. He'd never believed, not really, though his parents had forced him to follow the path to communion and confirmation.

Nobody spoke up and Janet said, "Jody?"

The teenager steepled her hands, and in a voice that sounded like someone was forcing bamboo shoots under her fingernails, she broke into the standard "Lord thank you for the food you have provided…" It all burned Ward a little, but he stayed silent. If there was a God, where the hell was he and why had he allowed Long Island to become infested? Ah, the grand plan, and yet again he was a tool.

Jody finished, accepted compliments with a smile, and roasted chicken, fresh vegetables, and dirty rice were eaten. If it wasn't for the patter of the Crics an observer might have thought a close group of friends was having a peaceful dinner.

Ward raised his wine glass and said, "To Bill."

"And Ruth," Jazz said.

The companions clinked glasses and ate in silence. Like a sports team before a big game, the Southwood Crew was beyond chitchat, and everyone had their heads down as they focused on eating and thinking about what was to come.

It was an uneventful night, and no Crics penetrated the bedroom where everyone slept. Ward didn't sleep well, and Jenni tossed and turned all night, muttering in her fever-induced dreams. Janet had given her all the aspirin she had, but it wasn't doing much except easing the pounding in Jenni's head.

With the sun creeping over the eastern horizon, the Southwood Crew put on their protective suits. Jazz and Toby helped the others with gas masks, putting on gloves, and pulling on hoods and helmets.

Muffin stared at Jenni with eager eyes, and when she didn't drape the leather jacket harness over her neck the cat meowed and brushed against her legs.

Ward might have been the only one to notice, but the pain cutting his wife's face to ribbons turned his stomach. He said, "We'll come back and get her when this is all over."

Jenni nodded and licked her lips.

When everyone was suited up, gas masks in place, the breaking of the Southwood Crew commenced as those departing said goodbye to Jazz, Toby, and Muffin.

"You better hold her as I go," Jenni said.

Jazz lifted the cat gently.

Muffin didn't struggle, but she looked anything but comfortable as she watched Jenni with eyes that seemed to understand betrayal was on the horizon.

"Let's do it," Desmond said as he opened the backdoor and passed into the back porch airlock.

Muffin hissed and scratched at Jazz's arm as she jumped to the floor. The feline darted to Jenni and sat at her feet, crying.

If there weren't mutant Crics attacking the house, Ward would have felt sadness at seeing the display, his wife in so much pain. He did feel sad, but also angry. His wife was sick, and he didn't have time to soothe the feline's feelings.

Ward picked the cat up, stroked her back, kissed her on the head, dumped her on the basement stairs, and quickly closed the door, locking her within. The wails of pain and the mewing cries made Jenni weep.

"I'll let her up as soon as you're gone," Jazz said.

"You take good care of her," Jenni said.

"And yourselves," Janet added as she followed her brother out the back door, her kids in tow.

With nothing left to do, Ward followed his wife as he hefted the Benelli, Muffin's strangled cries echoing through the house.

20

Desmond had done his best to hide Bill and Ruth's bodies, but Janet was no fool. Upon entering the garage, the woman set out on a search to find her husband, the children trailing behind her. The stench of freshly decaying flesh pervaded the air, but with the gas mask on the smell was minimal. Desmond stepped in front of his sister. "There will be time for that later."

"That time is now," Janet said.

Desmond nodded and led his sister and her children to a corner of the garage where various crates filled with sporting equipment, tools, and other minutia were stacked in a neat pile, creating a makeshift mausoleum that held the bodies of Bill and Ruth.

The rest of the group crowded in behind Janet and her children as Desmond and Ward opened the newly created tomb. Even the Crics seemed to respect the moment and the static of their constant movement decreased.

Ward's head pounded as he watched Janet and her kids. His endless supply of guilt poked at him, eating at his rationality, and making him feel somewhat responsible for the two people who lay dead within their rubber shrine.

Janet was the first to pay her respects, and she dropped to a knee before her husband and caressed his face through the plastic. "Goddamn you Bill, you son of a bitch," she screamed, and slapped the dead man across the face. She cried in earnest then as she pushed to her feet and turned her back on the man who had saved Ward and Jenni.

The children clung to their mother, staring at the bodies sheepishly. One by one the rest of the Southwood Crew came forward to pay their respects.

When he felt the right amount of time had passed, Ward said, "Thank you, Bill. We'll be back to take care of you right and proper."

Desmond put a hand on Ward's shoulder. "We promise, bro," he said, and turned to his sister. "I promise."

The team piled into the van. Desmond drove and Ward was in the shotgun seat. Lacy, Jenni, Janet, and the kids were in the back. The cargo van only had two front bucket seats, and the back was packed with equipment, gear, guns, and the flamethrower and related tanks, including Ruth's forlorn oxygen cylinder. They didn't need oxygen anymore, but Demond didn't see the purpose in getting rid of it. There was space in the van, and who knew what they might need between the house and the Great South Bay? The van's cameras had been repaired, all the holes fixed, and when Desmond turned the key, the engine rumbled to life

"Hold onto something," Desmond said. "I'm gonna go as fast as I can, and it might get bumpy."

Ward had been assigned the passenger seat because it would be his job to hitch the boat after Desmond threaded the needle.

The outside world was a Boschian nightmare. The larger Crics had taken over, and the smallest beasts Ward saw were the rat-sized things that looked twice their size because of their gigantic legs and huge pincers.

Ward's mind wandered as he stared at the Crics. Would all the surviving Crics be huge? Would the entire landscape eventually become the domain of the big boys? Huge monsters hopping around like Kuju endlessly hunting for food, having eaten every living thing, even their kind? Would the large mutants eventually turn on each other?

Rubber squealed as the tires scraped on the protective wheel well covers and the power steering pump whined as Desmond arced the wheel and backed the van through the backyard to where the boat waited.

"Get ready with that flamethrower, Lacy," Ward said.

Lacy stood and grabbed the flamethrower gun from where it hung on the van's wall. Desmond and Ward had suggested sending Timmy up with the flamethrower. The boy, being much more agile, his senses and reflexes tuned from live-action video games, was more qualified to work the device. But when Janet objected, Ward realized she was right. Whatever the situation, Timmy was a teenager. He had his whole life in front of him and there was no way Ward, Desmond, or anyone else was going to play a role in cutting that short.

Desmond adjusted the angle of the rear camera so he could see the hitch as he backed up the van, and when he was an inch away from the boat trailer's receiver tongue, he said, "Get ready."

Ward was far from ready, but he nodded, gas mask slipping on his face. He pulled on the mask's straps and tightened its seal.

"Do it!" yelled Desmond.

Lacy ignited the flame gun as she stepped up onto the box, which had been fortified to give it extra height. She opened the roof hatch, and sprayed the opening with flames, clearing a path and burning up any Cric brave enough to perch on the van. Crics popped and sizzled as they charred, the flames blinding the forward camera.

When Lacy had cleared the larger Crics away from the van, Ward slid out the passenger door and ran to the boat.

Desmond backed up the last inch, and when the ball hitch was under the receiver tongue, the van clunked into park.

Ward cranked the jack handle, and the tongue of the trailer slowly dropped until it settled on the hitch ball. Heat burned through him, sweat running down his back, as Ward pounded the hitch lock into position, put on the safety chains, and quickly removed the blocks holding the wheels in place. Then he double-timed it back to the front of the van, kicking and stomping Crics as he went. The bigger beasts were hanging back, watching, waiting.

Fire scorched the area, and Ward felt the heat of the door handle as he got back into the van.

The entire task had taken less than thirty seconds.

Through the barren trees and gaps between the houses, the forward camera showed the approaching storm on the horizon, a dark line of smudged clouds marching west. It looked a long way off.

Crics hopped and skittered all around the van, the sound of cracking carapaces carrying over the hum of the mutants as they gyrated. Janet and the kids were getting their first closeup view of the new world, and judging by the sour milk expression on Janet's face, it was a bit more than she'd anticipated.

Southwood Street ran north to south and turned into Atlantic Avenue when it crossed over Montauk Highway. Atlantic was a major road, and it was straight as an arrow until it got to the bay. That was the most direct path to the shoreline. If all went well an attempt would be made to enter the drug store and retrieve Jenni's much-needed medicine, but Desmond had reserved the right to call off the attempt if he felt leaving the van was too risky.

A large Cric the size of an elephant stepped out onto the road, blocking the van's way.

Janet gasped.

Desmond chuckled and pressed the van's gas pedal to the floor.

"What are you doing?" screeched Janet.

"Watch," said her brother. "We'll be fine."

Ward looked up at the patch of steel Desmond had bolted over the hole the big boy had made with one of its forward spikes, and skepticism campaigned for control of his mental dashboard, but he said nothing.

Jenni was slumped against the van's wall, her eyes half closed.

Janet hugged her children, and Lacy grabbed the flamethrower gun.

The charge didn't last long, and the van struck the Cric head-on.

Teeth snapped, legs broke, and the beast's torso beneath its shell deflated as the van ran down the Cric, dark goo covering the forward camera enclosure as the van bounced and jostled over the monster's remains.

Ward listened for the devasting sound of a tire being punctured, but no such sound came, and the van rolled on. The rearview camera showed the boat, and it swayed and listed severely as it passed over the pile of goo, legs, and cracked shell that had been the giant mutant.

The first non-Cric obstacle was an abandoned car slanted awkwardly across the street. Ward recognized the blue Honda Accord. He'd seen the vehicle around town but didn't know its owner. Two corpses picked clean by Crics occupied the front seats, and Janet told her children to cover their eyes as Desmond worked the wheel and brought the van and trailer around the abandoned car.

Ahead the road looked clear of impediments other than Crics. Desmond zoomed in the forward camera, but the lens was partly obscured by the Cric goo covering the camera's protective housing.

Montauk Highway was a quarter mile to the north, and Ward marveled at his neighborhood as Desmond slowly piloted the van over Crics.

The view from the cameras back at the house hadn't done the devastation justice. Ward and Jenni's place wasn't the only one that had burned to the ground. Three other houses on the street were in smoking ruin, and many houses showed no signs of life and there were many broken windows.

When they were halfway up the street, Montauk Highway visible through a halo of barren tree limbs, Janet chirp-screamed.

All heads turned toward the mother of two.

"You don't see that?" Janet said.

"See what? Where?" Desmond said as he slowed the van and studied the view of the front and rear cameras.

Janet inched between the bucket seats and pointed at the view of the rear camera. "Zoom that in."

Desmond touched the screen and widened his fingers as the image zoomed.

At first, all Ward saw was the brown dirt of a destroyed lawn, tiny pinpricks of green marking the grass where it had been eaten to the ground.

Desmond moved his fingers around, shifting the image.

"Oh, let me," Janet said as she brushed away her brother's hand. She worked fast, her fingers flying as she focused the image.

A block of ice formed in Ward's chest.

The screen showed the front window of a blue house, and within its frame, a young woman had a baby in a sling across her chest, a candle in one hand, and a sign in the other. It read simply, "I have an eight-month-old. Please help."

Desmond brought the van to a stop with an exaggerated sigh.

"Why have we stopped?" Janet asked. "Do you know her?"

Desmond shook his head no.

"You?" She was looking at Ward, Jenni, and Lacy.

Ward shook his head no.

"I know her," Lacy said. "She's in my Pilates class. Her name is Trinty."

"And?" Janet said.

"You're saying we should just leave her?" Desmond said.

Before Janet could knock back her brother, Ward did it for her. "This is horrible. I get it. But do you know how many people we're going to come across on this little journey?"

Desmond looked at the steering wheel and said nothing.

"She doesn't look in that bad a shape to me," Timmy said.

"But the baby," Jenni forced out.

"We can't take on a stray every time we see someone in need," Janet said. "We won't get to the end of the block."

"What the hell did you show us for, then?" Desmond said.

Janet shrugged. "I... I'm not sure, but better to have this talk now than in the heat of the moment, no?"

Desmond licked his lips, dropped the van into gear, and continued up the street.

Ward stared at his boots, then looked over his shoulder at Jenni. Her eyes were closed, but her chest slowly rose and fell. It was moments like these that Ward wished he didn't think about every decision like it might be his last. He'd overthought things his entire life, and now that meticulous plans were needed, his mind was a mishmash of half-truths, fears, and fantasies of escape and survival.

Jenni mumbled in her delirium and Ward felt Janet's eyes on him. Regardless of the situation up on Montauk Highway, he was getting Jenni her meds, or he'd die trying.

21

Ward's heart sank when the team reached Montauk Highway. Stones Throw's main thoroughfare ran west to east, and the road was blocked in both directions with crashed cars covered in Crics. Light poles were down, and a tangle of electrical wires stretched from the forlorn commercial buildings along the south shore's oldest highway. Energy drained from Ward's overheated muscles, and in that moment he wanted to give it all up.

The front camera went dark as a large Cric crawled over its protective housing.

Desmond stabbed the brake hard, and the van rocked forward. The Cric obscuring the camera was tossed from its perch, the devastation coming back into focus. Desmond inched the van and its trailer across dirt lawns and around stalled cars to the edge of the Montauk Highway.

To the party's left on the north side of the highway, there was a strip center that housed three stores: Nilly's Nails, Joe's Deli, and Shaolin Dojo. Across the street was an open building lot that until recently had contained a dilapidated commercial building that had been one of the oldest structures in town. To the west on the northern side of the highway was the vast parking lot before Don Quijano Mexican Grill. The lot, which was normally full of cars, was a sea of mutants.

Dwayne's Drug was a historical landmark. Originally a trading post that serviced the harbors of Long Island and related transport companies that brought the incoming cargo into New York City, it had been in existence since 1730 when the first bill of lading bearing the name "Sag Harbor" was recorded. The business transformed over the centuries, growing from a mom-and-pop to a mom-and-pop with a big franchise shine. Dwayne's was on the southern side of the highway past the mechanic shop that was across the street from Don Quijano's. Its parking lot was meager because one didn't shop in Dwayne's, one merely collected that which was not sold elsewhere.

The van was silent, and nobody spoke because the problem was obvious. The crew could see the drugstore, but it might as well have been a thousand miles away due to the maze of cars and devastation on the highway and in the surrounding lots. The van expertly driven by Desmond might make it through the chaos, but with the boat on the hitch, there was no way the rig would make it through.

"We could unhitch, leave the boat, do what we've got to do, then hitch back up," said Ward, doing his best to sound like that was a wise course of action. It sounded beyond stupid, especially after his recent speech about taking in strays.

"Or we can wait here while you give it a shot. It's not that far and I don't see any big boys in the immediate area," Desmond said.

"But the longer we sit, you know that will change, so…" Janet said, and looked at the floor.

"I'll go," Ward said. "And you'll wait here as long as you can?"

Desmond nodded. "I can't go with you." He didn't have to say why. Janet and the kids were his responsibility now because Bill was dead.

Jenni pushed to her feet, rolled her shoulders, shook her head, and flexed her jaws. "I'll watch your back. You have to do all the hard work, but I can still shoot straight."

But for how long? Ward wanted to ask, but he said nothing. He had little chance of success alone, and she was fighting for her life, but… Ward just didn't want her out there with him, didn't matter if she was sick or healthy as an ox.

"Let me go," Timmy said. The kid's eyes were alight with excitement.

Before Janet had to be the bad guy Ward shot the idea down citing all the same reasons why the boy wasn't allowed to use the flamethrower.

Jody made no offer to help, and the teenager hadn't spoken since the crew had piled into the van.

"I can clear a path for you," said Lacy.

Ward nodded his thanks.

"And here," Desmond said as he handed Ward one of the team's AR-15s. "It's ready to fire." Bill's armory had included two ARs, along with pistols and shotguns, so when Ward offered up the Benelli in trade, Desmond shook his head. "Naw. Let Jenni use that."

Ward and Jenni inspected their safety suits, tightened their gas masks, and checked their weapons. Jenni had the M2 loaded with one in the chamber, and two pockets full of shells. Ward had his Colt .45 in a holster slung from his hip like a gunslinger, the AR-15 fully loaded, and a second loaded magazine.

"We'll be watching," Desmond said as he pointed to the camera. "If you get in a bind, head south and meet us along the road. There's a copse of trees behind Dwayne's, and then you'll hit houses."

Ward nodded.

Jenni was on her feet, marching in place as she got the blood flowing, cheeks red, eyes burning embers.

Desmond held out a hand. "Good luck."

"Let's do it!" Ward screeched as he shook the man's hand.

Lacy lit the candle and went through the motions of clearing Crics away from the roof hatch and the area around the van. Ninety seconds later the roar of the flamethrower ceased, and Lacy yelled, "You're good!"

Jenni pulled open the side door and Ward jumped to the street, the pop and crack of fried Crics beneath his boots rising above the chatter of the wind and the ever-churning mutants.

Ward slammed the van door, and then the pair was moving in and out of smashed cars, crunching and kicking Crics as they ran, the smaller beasts hesitant to attack on their own.

Several large Crics appeared between a turned-over box truck and a sedan filled with blood-covered skeletons picked clean.

The AR-15 barked, a staccato of bursts that blew the creatures to shards of legs and goo, and cleared their path like Ward was Moses, and the Cric-infested highway was the Red Sea.

Ward was sucking for air, the lenses of his gas mask fogging. The Mexican restaurant's front plate glass window was shattered, and the joint's interior was infested. The gas station was clogged with abandoned cars, and Ward pictured the frenzy to get gas in those early hours. His vision went red with the thought of it.

Beep. Beep. Beeeeeeeeeeeep. The van's horn shrieked, and Ward and Jenni both turned back the way they'd come.

Two horse-sized Crics had bounced from under a turned-over pickup. Huge legs splayed out as the creatures jumped, pincers biting, teeth glinting in the half-light beneath the thickening cloud cover.

"Let's get a move on," Ward said as he cut across a thin shoulder of grass before reaching the sidewalk, which was littered with forlorn cars that had tried to drive around the chaos.

"Head to the entrance," Jenni said. "I'll cover you."

Ward shook his head. "I've got better fire power for long-range shooting. You head to Dwayne's, and *I'll* cover *you.*"

Jenni nodded, put the stock of the Benelli to her shoulder, flexed her fingers around the pistol grip, and threaded through the Cric-littered destruction to Dwayne's Drug.

Ward waited until his wife had her back pressed to the front of Dwayne's before he turned his attention toward the two huge mutants. The beasts were forty yards off now and had picked up a Cric flock like Pied Pipers. He cleared a white Hyundai's hood of Crics and braced himself as he raised the rifle.

He squeezed the trigger twice and two bursts tore into the creatures.

The huge mutants staggered, mouths hanging open, their insides splattered on their brethren. As if controlled by one mind, the smaller Crics paused as the giant beasts folded in on themselves and fell from view between the abandoned cars.

With time moving ten times faster than normal, Ward double-timed it to his wife, firing at the largest beasts.

The M2 barked as Jenni helped clear a path for her husband. With the death of the big boys, the smaller Crics lost some of their vigor, and many fled before Ward as he crossed the last forty yards to Dwayne's.

Ward wished for his portable flame stick, but in its absence, the pair used their guns and boots to clear the entrance. As Ward pushed open Dwayne's front door, any Cric smaller than a cat scurried back into the dark places.

The interior of the drugstore had been fully ransacked. The shelves were empty, broken boxes and containers littered the floor, and the locked closet that normally contained the controlled substances was busted open and empty.

Ward's heart sank, and he felt his wife's eyes boring into him. He wasn't surprised the place had been looted, but still… The hope of getting Jenni the medication she desperately needed had evaporated, and he didn't know what to do next.

Six minutes had slipped away since the partners left the van, and he couldn't expect Desmond to wait much longer. Ward's heart hammered, sweat poured down his back, and his muscles ached, but those same muscles also trembled in their eagerness to be in motion. Dwayne's was lost, and any help he'd find for his wife wasn't there.

The faint moan of the van's horn snapped Ward from his reverie. He said, "How you doing, babe?"

Jenni tore her gaze away from a group of cat-sized Crics gathering at the end of the aisle she stood in. There were tears in her red eyes, the absence of all hope turning her laugh lines into bulging blood vessels. "What are we going to do now?"

Ward stared at his wife, but he couldn't find any words.

"I see two of you, Ward!" she screamed.

The beeping of the van's horn became more incessant.

"Let's retreat to the van and figure something out," Ward said.

"What?"

"Come on." Ward grabbed his wife's arm as he made his way to the front of Dwayne's.

In the rear of the store, a swarm of Crics gathered around the group of larger beasts, the sound of thousands of legs cycling over one another scratching Ward's last nerve.

When the duo reached the exit, Ward saw why Desmond was beeping.

A person wearing a black leather motorcycle suit, tall black leather boots, gloves, a hood, and a modern gas mask strode across the parking lot. He held a pistol in one hand, but it was pointed skyward. "Don't shoot!" the newcomer pleaded.

Ward and Jenni took up positions on both sides of the front door, but there was little cover with the windows blown out.

"What do you want?" Ward said.

"I have what you need." The voice was muffled behind the gas mask, but the tone was unmistakably male.

Ward said nothing, hope and fear coursing through him in equal measure.

"What are you talking about?" The desperation in Jenni's voice was obvious.

"Yes… you do need help, don't you?" the guy said.

Anger surged through Ward. He didn't like the sound of the guy's voice. Not at all.

"Do you ha—" the man started.

"Put the gun down and we can talk," Ward interrupted.

Laughter. "You're joking, right? Let me come in. It's getting… crowded out here."

Ward told Jenni to cover him, and he army crawled below the frame of the broken front window to a side window with an eastern view.

A horde of Crics of various sizes had surrounded the van and the boat on its trailer. The rig was inching forward and was almost across Montauk Highway. Desmond's words came rushing back; "If you get in a bind, head south and meet us along the road. There's a copse of trees behind Dwayne's, and then you'll hit houses."

Ward pressed to his feet and sprayed the front of the store with bullets, making sure to hit the floor and the wall below the window. The diversion worked, and by the time the echo of the shots had died away, he was standing next to Jenni. He pointed toward the rear of the store and Jenni nodded. Dwayne's had an employee entrance at the back.

"Wait!"

Ward and Jenni turned to locate the source of the command.

The black-clad man stood ten feet from the entrance, his gun at his side.

"I've got drugs. All kinds," he said.

Ward sighted the AR on the man's head.

The nosecone of the guy's gas mask lifted as he threw back his head, extended his arms, and strode forward. "Go ahead. Do it! You'd be doing me a favor."

"What've you got?" Ward asked.

"I was here when that happened," the guy said as he pointed across the ravaged store at the broken-open drug closet. "Got a bit of everything, I think."

"Do you have amoxicillin or doxycycline?" Jenni blurted.

The guy nodded. "Popular selections. I've got both."

"Where?" Ward pressed.

"In a safe spot only I know about."

Ward's focus strayed from the AR's sight to Jenni. His wife's eyes were so red he couldn't see his wife in there anymore. The cold creep of worry made Ward's decision for him, and the tip of the AR dipped as he said, "What do you want from us?"

"This is just for show," the guy said as he lifted the revolver. "No ammo left. No food other than some candy, but I got drugs. I'll give you what you need if you take me out of here with you. I'll give you everything I've got."

"What makes you think we're going to get out?" Ward asked. As he heard himself ask the question he wondered at the answer. Their effort was already waylaid, and they'd only made it to the end of the street.

"I saw your van," the man said. "I'm sure you can fit one more."

"Show us the drugs!" wailed Jenni.

Ward couldn't see the man's face, but his eyes narrowed behind the gas mask's eye lenses and Ward was certain the dude was smiling.

22

"Name's Dan. Dan Ricker." The man didn't offer a hand.

Ward introduced himself and Jenni. "It's not my van, so we'll have to clear things with our group. How close is your stash?"

"Close."

The sharp crack of something falling in the rear of the store made the trio turn in the direction of the sound. The larger Crics and their horde were advancing up the ravaged aisles.

Ward and Jenni swung their weapons toward the disturbance and Dan took cover behind a fallen display case.

Tittering, scraping legs, as more Crics inched from the shadows.

"Take us to your stash. Now!" Ward spun and aimed the AK at the man's chest, but even as he did so he knew he wouldn't be able to pull the trigger. The man's gun was at his side, and so far, he'd shown no signs of aggression. But there was no trust in the air, and there wouldn't be any until this ordeal was over, and probably a good way beyond that.

"Cover me," Dan said.

"Where are you going?" Ward asked.

Dan didn't respond as he threaded down an aisle toward the remains of the makeup case, clearing away smaller Crics as he went, and ignoring the advancing swarm. The glass front of the cabinet behind the makeup counter was smashed, as was the glass counter. Lipsticks, compacts, powders, eyeliners, and a myriad of other beauty items were strewn about having been tossed aside in the frenzy to acquire items that would aid in survival. Ultra rose lipstick and classic rouge didn't qualify.

The thump of Crics throwing themselves at the front entrance echoed through the store.

"What are you doing?" hissed Jenni, her voice cracking.

Dan dropped to a knee and pulled keys from a pocket. There was a cabinet beneath the glass countertop, and he unlocked it.

Ward held his breath. If the guy was going to try something, now was the time.

Dan pulled a box from the cabinet and hurried back to where Jenni and Ward stood wide-eyed behind the glass lenses of their gas masks. The open container was filled with pill bottles, boxes, and clear bags holding syringes.

Letting out a breath he hadn't known he was holding, Ward felt the pressure leave the room, despite the frenzied Crics leaking through the store.

Jenni dropped her pack and dumped the drugs into it. Then she zipped it up, slung it onto her shoulder, and said, "Let's get back to the van so I can take some of these."

Ward headed for the front entrance, but a crowd of man-sized Crics loitered out-front Dwayne's Drug, and smaller creatures cycled into the store through the broken windows. A gathering swarm swirled around the larger mutants, the thick scent of must filling the air.

The entrance door buckled and banged as the larger Crics worked on the closed door. Dog-sized mutants leaped through the broken windows, their pincers snapping, the low hiss of their movement like swaying water reeds in the wind.

Jenni fired the Benelli twice, and two rat-sized Crics were sprayed across the empty shelves. This gave the smaller beasts pause, but the shots seemed to anger the big boys pounding on the door. With a shriek of tearing metal and splintering wood, Dwayne's front door gave way and a wave of Crics poured into the store.

The larger Crics had a much harder time. Though their carapace-covered torsos were small enough to fit through the gap, their arced legs weren't.

Ward and his partners opened fire and cleared a path as they fled to the rear of the store.

The beasts pushing through the front entrance got tangled up and began fighting amongst themselves, stabbing with their spiked legs, and tearing at each other with their pincers.

Crics hopped and sprang in every direction like rubber balls on crack. Ward shifted his aim and fired like he was playing a video game, and when he was done the store was coated in dark viscus fluid, broken legs and carapaces, and shredded skin.

There was a closed door that led into the storage room, but it was locked. Ward cursed as he kicked the door, but it didn't give. He rolled his shoulders, blasted the doorknob with the AR, and kicked the door open.

The storage room beyond was shrouded in darkness. Like the front of the store, anything of value was gone, and rubbish and useless items littered the floor. A cone of light cut through the room from the backdoor that was swinging in the breeze.

Jenni and Dan pushed into the room behind Ward, and they closed the door and secured it.

Eyes glowed in the darkness, and the shuffle of legs and the titter of gnashing teeth filled the room.

"Stay close," Ward said. He pressed the stock of the AR-15 to his shoulder as he got low and inched into the grayness.

A Cric launched from the darkness and Ward brought up his arm to block the attack. The beast's left forward pincer latched onto his jacket, but the cat-sized mutant wasn't strong enough. Ward shook the creature loose and it hit the ground up-side-down and struggled to right itself.

Ward's boot came down with a satisfying crunch, dark goo jetting from the corpse like jelly from a smashed donut. He lunged forward, the column of light growing as the door got closer.

The shotgun discharged, and Ward felt hot air brush his face as a Cric to his right lost the entire right side of its body. Jenni fired again, and the pop of a beast exploding carried through the room like thunder.

More creatures crawled from the shadows, antennas swaying, bulbous eyes glowing.

Ward's ears were ringing like a fire alarm when he reached the rear door and slipped through it. When his two companions were free, he slammed the door and put his back to it, panting.

The door heaved and rattled but held.

As promised, there was a grove of trees behind the drug store, and with every leaf stripped clean, Ward could see the houses and devastation to the south. His view of Atlantic Avenue and Montauk Highway was blocked by the building.

The alleyway behind the drugstore was relatively free of Crics.

"Heads on swivels," Ward said as he surged into motion, working his way along the back of the building, using the structure as cover. When he paused at the corner of the building Jenni bumped into him.

Jenni's eyes had no white left, and she looked possessed, the gas mask's eye lenses magnifying and brightening the crimson.

Dan dutifully trailed after and appeared content to be led.

The Cric chaos at the front of the building had yet to spill around to its sides, but Ward heard the creatures hissing. Jaws crunched and leg bones snapped, and in the reflection of a broken car window, Ward saw two man-sized beasts circling each other, stabbing with their spikes, and grinding their translucent teeth.

"Do you hear that?" Jenni asked.

Ward filtered out the Crics, the whispering wind, and he heard the faint *womp womp* of helicopter airfoils pounding the air. He pointed toward the woods, peeled away from the building, and ran for the tree line, Jenni and Dan on his heels.

As they entered the thin woods, Atlantic Avenue could be seen through the defoliated trees, but Ward didn't see the van. "I don't want to go back up to the highway. Too many Crics. With any luck, Desmond won't wait much longer." He would have traded the .45 in that moment for his old-school walkie-talkies.

With no leaves on the trees and the ground cleared of underbrush except the whips of pricker vines and hardened weed trunks, the trio was exposed. As they entered the grove of oaks, their brown trunks like giant toothpicks sticking from the dirt, Ward and his companions used the tree trunks for cover.

The thumping of the chopper was getting louder.

Crics scuttled out of the trio's path, but larger beasts appeared on the fence that separated the commercial properties from the residential section. Houses loomed to the south and east, and going over the fence was the only way to get to Atlantic Avenue.

The ground trembled and the Crics paused.

When the companions reached the fence, Ward said, "Make us a door, babe."

Jenni leveled the Benelli and pulled the trigger twice.

Booms pierced the day, and Ward hoped Desmond had heard the shots. He could use the sounds to pinpoint their position, not that he could do anything to help until Ward and his partners reached the road.

Ward went through the hole first, gun at the ready. A vast backyard with a pool stretched to an old house with peeling white paint. Smaller Crics hid in the shade, but larger beasts hopped and scampered about the hardpan, the grass gone, the white concrete apron around the pool like a magic demarcation line separating the water and the Crics.

The heat was getting to Ward, and his knees ached as he ran across the backyard, firing strategically and making a path for Jenni and Dan. His stomach screamed for food and water, and it felt like days had passed since he'd eaten with the Southwood Crew, but it had only been a couple of hours.

Ward and company slipped through a gate and stopped at the front corner of the house. Atlantic Avenue was quiet except for Crics, and a pulse of energy sparked Ward's nerves.

The van was stopped on Atlantic just south of Montauk Highway, a fallen tree lying across the road and impeding its forward progress.

"Shit!" Ward screamed. "Can we get one break? Just one!" His frustration boiled over, but he had little time to feel sorry for himself.

Two horse-sized Crics leaped from their hiding place behind an abandoned vehicle, and Jenni only got one before the survivor hopped, twisted in the air, and landed right next to Ward, its legs arcing above him.

Pincers clicked, spike-tipped legs stabbing the road, and an image of Samwise Gamgee piercing Shelob danced through Ward's subconscious as he drew down the .45 and put two bullets into the underside of the Cric's yawning mouth.

Half the Cric's body dissipated in bloody black and blue mist, legs dropping, antennas flopping and falling still.

The thump of the helicopter rotors was loud now, the tips of the surrounding trees swaying.

A swarm of Crics gathered on the road, blocking Ward's view of the van. He and his companions needed cover, and fast.

The open building lot that until recently had contained one of the oldest buildings in Stones Throw, was now nothing more than a forlorn foundation and a real estate sign, the tall grass and weeds that had sprung up on the site long gone. Ward thought he, Jenni, and Dan could take cover in the old foundation until they could get to the van. He'd heard teenagers hung out there, so how bad could it be?

Ward broke into a jog and crossed the street.

Jenni and Dan needed no instructions, and though both their gas mask cones turned toward where the van sat hidden by a building Cric horde, they both followed.

The old foundation was caved in on two sides, and there were several smaller cave-ins that Ward thought were caused by the Crics tearing weeds and grass from every crack and mortar joint.

Within the crumbling foundation walls, piles of brick and wood littered what had been the building's basement, but none of that was what drew Ward's eye.

At the center of the exposed cellar, there was a giant black hole with a diameter of forty feet. Crics of all sizes spilled from the pit, and a steady stream of larger creatures carrying bits of food marched back in. Two black antennas rose from the hole like fast-growing palm trees with no leaves.

An enormous Cric rose from the pit, manhole-sized glistening eyes rotating and searching. A bulbous white egg sack pushed around the edges of the behemoth's carapace like gelatinous white meat gushing from a boiled lobster tail.

Ward staggered as he stared at the hole, a jumble of news reports about Crics and collective conscious stinging his extremities. Terror froze him in place. Had he found the entrance to a hive?

As the Apache AH-64 came in low over the defoliated trees, Ward's brain started following orders again, and he ran.

23

The ground vibrated, and the Crics scattered like a flock of cave bats when a flashlight came on.

Ward's vision grew blurry, the intense heat inside his protective suit suffocating. All the same, he didn't need twenty-twenty vision to know that the massive Cric was crawling from its lair behind him.

The Apache thundered overhead, the crew of two staring down at Ward and the others from the chopper's cockpit. Crics swirled in the air like trash as the twin-turboshaft attack helicopter glided past just above the emaciated tree canopy. Ward had to smile as he eyed the war machine and saw the Boeing AH-64's nose-mounted sensor suite, which was used for target acquisition, and the 30 MM M230 chain gun beneath the aircraft's forward fuselage between the main landing gear. The hunter-killer also had an array of AGM-114 Hellfire missiles and Hydra 70 rocket pods mounted on its stub-wing pylons.

As the chopper hovered, the boom of the pilot issuing a warning was barely audible above the pounding of the bird's rotors. "Clear the area! Clear the area!"

The trio picked up their pace, sprinting toward Atlantic Avenue where Ward hoped the van waited. Though the tall grass and weeds had been razed, the ground was still littered with bricks, discarded wood, pieces of metal, and chunks of roofing material left behind by the demolition crew.

Ward's toe caught on a cracked cinderblock and his arms cartwheeled, the AR-15 falling from his hands, the rifle dangling before him as it swung on its shoulder strap. The world spun, brown dirt, dark clouds, and a giant mouth of clear teeth. He crashed to the ground, his head bounced off a length of rotted lumber, and the right lens of his gas mask spidered, but didn't break.

His heart leaped into his throat, but then Ward remembered the masks were for protection only, and as far as he knew, there were no issues with the ambient air.

Dust clouds obscured ground level, but the tips of the gigantic Cric's antennas and legs could be seen above the haze of grit and dust. The wind gusted, and Ward's breath caught.

The queen Cric was four stories tall, and its arced rear legs and twenty-foot antennas rose even higher. Huge bulbous eyes locked on Ward, its jaws falling open, dark sludge-like saliva leaking onto the hardpan. Pincers that could squeeze the life out of a full-sized car cracked and snapped, railroad tie-sized spikes at the ends of its second set of forelegs stabbing the dirt.

A dark shadow fell over Ward, and he looked around frantically, searching for his wife.

Jenni and Dan were still running for the road, and the Apache was settling and preparing to fire.

Ward dropped to the ground and rolled onto his stomach, the AR beneath him as he covered his head with his arms.

In his mind's eye, Ward pictured the Apache's pilot dipping the bird's nose, waiting on a missile lock, the red square slowly shrinking and becoming green.

A single hollow fart carried on the breeze, and it turned into a whistling shriek that cut through the chatter of the Crics and the helicopter's pounding airfoils.

With a cacophonous roar and a thud that shook the ground, the Hellfire missile streaked through the air and hit the giant Cric. An explosion rocked the day, the shrill death call of the Cric rising above the chaos.

A gust of hot air and debris pushed over the clearing and Ward crawled behind an abandoned car, the AR-15 swinging around his neck. Crics swirled in the air, clouds of dust spinning like tiny cyclones, debris, and Cric parts and innards raining down on Ward as he tried to get his bearings, a hand searching for and finding the .45.

He couldn't see anything, so he bolted in the direction he believed Jenni and Dan had gone.

The Apache rose, the field and destroyed foundation beneath it an inferno of fire, smoke, and cooking Crics. The bird's pilot leveled out the craft, the killer's engines cycling up, its airfoils spinning faster.

Ward had a brief thought about the Apache landing and picking him up along with his companions, but he didn't even finish composing the fantasy before the rational side of his brain, which had taken control, burned the idea to the ground. There was nowhere for the chopper to land, and it was a two-person craft.

The Apache eased away, fried Cric parts swirling, the leafless trees swaying, the thinning dust clouds eddying and twisting.

Ward didn't see his attacker until she was on him.

A woman wearing a hunting outfit, and a green JETS football helmet with ski goggles was wedged beneath the car Ward hid behind. Arms wrapped around his legs as he struggled to aim the AR-15.

The woman squeezed Ward's legs together and pulled.

Ward toppled backward like a rotten statue as he stitched a line on the hood of the car with the AR. The rifle clicked empty as he hit the ground, and Ward shifted his attention to his grandfather's Colt Government.

The woman was a human octopus, and she surged from underneath the car and pounced on Ward, her thin arms and legs surprisingly strong. As the pair wrestled and rolled on the hardpan, Ward fired wildly, the crack and pop of the .45 deafening.

Ward saw the woman's blue eyes through her ski goggles, the tuft of blonde hair leaking out from under the JETS helmet, and he thought of Jenni. With any luck, she and Dan were already in the van and his wife was sucking down meds.

With a scream of rage, the woman worked the fingers of her gloved hands beneath the straps of Ward's gas mask, his right eye blinded by the kaleidoscope of color swirling in the cracked lens. Grunts of exertion, then the strangled call of a Cric echoed over the devastation.

The woman's grip eased as her head swung toward the wail.

Ward followed her gaze, and as the smoke and dust cleared, he saw a swarm of large Crics amassing around the pile of legs, cracked shells, and dark goo that had been the queen Cric.

With renewed vigor, the woman turned her attention back to Ward, and for a brief instant, their gazes met.

The woman's eyes were bloodshot, and not just 'stuck in the Containment Zone running from Crics' bloodshot. Hers were worse than Jenni's, and he opened his mouth to tell the woman he had drugs that might help her when she tore off his gas mask.

She backed off as they both stared at the gas mask. The breeze stirred Ward's hair, the musty scent of burning Crics tickling his nostrils.

The woman was the first to recover, and she delivered a bone-rattling punch to Ward's jaw that bounced his head off the ground. Stars danced before his eyes, the world going dark, the storm clouds reaching down to suck him in. The woman's hand darted out and snatched the .45.

With the .45 in his face, Ward lying on his back, the woman sat atop him like he was a bronco, and she was going to ride him until he dropped.

Ward raised his hands above his head and waited for the shot, a deep sorrow of having failed Jenni engulfing him. If this was it, he'd failed at life, despite the extenuating circumstances.

The woman licked her lips and stood, the pistol aimed at Ward's head. Ward was certain he was going to die, and suddenly he didn't care. He'd been fighting and scraping, but for what? He was tired. So very tired, and he didn't think he had any fight left in him. He was overheating, and it was only a matter of time before his body gave up the ghost.

Then Ward's attacker did something he never would have expected. She ran.

Ward's heart pounded, pain knifing down his back. What game was she playing? What trick? He looked around expecting to find a huge Cric standing behind him, but there was nothing but the dying flames and the gathering Cric swarm.

The woman didn't look back as she ran, her legs pumping, the .45 in her hand but pointed at the ground.

Why hadn't she killed him?

Ward rolled, snatched up the AR, and pressed to his knees. The gun was empty, so he clicked in the spare magazine, chambered a round, and sighted the weapon on the back of his fleeing assailant.

He stared through the sight, his finger wrapped around the trigger, sweat dripping into his eyes.

The wind gusted, the Crics tittered, and underneath it all he heard the fading *womp womp* of the retreating Apache.

Ward lowered the rifle. Desperate times called for desperate measures, but he was still human, and he couldn't shoot a woman in the back in cold blood. Not yet anyway. Yes, she'd attacked him and taken the .45, but she could have killed him, and she hadn't. She was just desperate, like everyone else in the Containment Zone, and in Ward's book that didn't add up to a death sentence.

Jenni's voice came to him then. "Ward! Ward!"

He lurched from his knees to his feet, his joints bitching, back screaming. As his vision cleared, he saw the van on Atlantic Avenue. Ward rubbed his eyes to make sure what he was seeing was real, the rough leather gloves irritating his skin. He'd worn the gas mask for so long his face tingled with every new sensation.

The van was there, and Ward didn't have time to consider how Desmond had gotten past the fallen tree. It didn't matter, and he didn't care. He broke into a run and beelined for the van across a section of lawn that had been eaten to the hardpan.

Lacy's upper body protruded from the van's roof hatch, the flamethrower spitting fire.

Ward spared a glance over his shoulder and saw a wave of writhing Crics tumbling toward him. Crics of all sizes climbed and hopped over one another in a roiling knot of legs, pincers, and teeth. A deep grinding noise drove out all other sounds, and Ward realized it was the Cric horde churning up the stripped ground. The creatures were fifty yards out and closing at an astonishing speed.

Lacy aimed the flamethrower in his direction to clear away any stray Crics.

It was going to be a delicate thing getting into the van and he had to be fast. With the vehicle's nose pointed south, the rear sliding door was on the opposite side of the van. Ward angled around the boat trailer, legs churning as fast as they'd move.

Crics climbed and jumped on the covered boat. The rattle and hum of the churning mound behind him got louder, but Ward didn't look back. He focused on the van's sliding side door and ran at it like he was going to run through it for the win.

When Ward was five feet away from the van's side, his muscles tensing as they tightened and prepared to come to a stop, the door slid open. Ward dove into the van and the sliding door slammed closed behind him.

Everyone searched for Crics that might have joined Ward on his jump into the van, but when none were found, Jenni threw her arms around her husband. Heat radiated from her like she was a mini sun.

Ward pulled his glove off and put his hand on her forehead as his nerves danced just beneath his skin. "Did you take the meds?" he asked, sparing a glance for Dan who stood in the rear of the van alone.

Jenni nodded. "A double dose."

"And?"

She hiked her shoulders. "It's only been five minutes."

Ward laughed. "It feels a little longer than that. I thought w—"

The wave of Crics broke on Lacy's sword of fire and the van rocked on its springs. The stench of burning Crics assailed him, and Ward covered his nose with the back of his hand.

Lacy dropped back into the van and slammed the roof hatch shut.

Outside the Crics covered the van and the cameras were obscured, but the sound of tapping legs and the grinding of teeth told the group everything they needed to know.

Desmond slammed the van into drive and the vehicle lurched forward, the sound of crunching carapaces music to Ward's ears.

"What... what happened?" Jenni asked as she caressed the smooth skin of Ward's bare face.

Ward filled everyone in, and when he started recounting how he'd met Dan, Jenni stopped him because that part of the story had already been told.

Desmond said, "That's amazing. I mean, what isn't these days, but still."

"You didn't recognize the woman?" Janet asked, her eyes constantly shifting from Ward to Dan. The mother of two and her children sat against the van's wall out of the way, Janet's arms wrapped protectively around her kids.

Ward shook his head no. "I think I might have recognized her from around town, but I can't be sure. How did you get around that fallen tree?"

"Slowly and carefully," Desmond said. "Slowly and carefully."

And with that the gas ran out of the conversation and Desmond drove on in silence.

Ward and his friends had traveled an eighth of a mile, but now they had the drugs Jenni needed. He felt relief funnel through him as Desmond piloted the van south on Atlantic Avenue.

24

It's always calm before a storm, and as the dark clouds marched across the western horizon, Ward wished for rain. Black cotton candy fingers reached east, a thick haze of rain bearing down on Atlantic Avenue. Summer thunderstorms on Long Island are unpredictable, and since it was suspected that the weird island weather patterns had enflamed and helped create the current crisis, the hope was this time around the island's maritime climate might help the situation.

Ahead the street was a sea of rabbit-sized creeks, and bigger beasts hid behind abandoned cars, houses, and tree trunks. Desmond had the van humming at a cool twenty mph, the Crics bouncing off the grill popping and cracking as they busted open.

Desmond loaned Ward his gas mask and he worked the flamethrower. As Ward sprayed flames his thoughts drifted into the van where his wife's condition had gotten worse.

Janet explained that antibiotics take time to work, but that there should have been immediate improvement. Doxycycline wasn't a dangerous drug, except in cases of extreme overdose, so Janet said to take two more pills in hopes of sending extra troops into the battle. Ward's stomach squirmed and told him that a pill wasn't going to solve this problem.

Hill Street slid by to the east and beyond it Tuthills Creek ran from the bay, under Montauk Highway, and all the way to South Lake. The estuary became a trickle and went below ground as it passed under the railroad tracks and there was a sandspit just beyond the tracks with a small pond, but it was extremely shallow and was unpassable by anything bigger than a kayak on its deepest day.

The cloud cover thickened, and the beasts slipped into night mode. They no longer fidgeted in the shadows or the cool insides of abandoned buildings, but instead frolicked openly, frenzied in their search for prey, of which there wasn't much left. Except for each other.

Ward recalled the fight between the bigger Crics at the front of the drugstore. How they fought, but he didn't recall seeing the victors eating the vanquished. Did cannibalism fade when the beasts reached a certain size? Were certain camel crickets spared that particular genome mutation?

Desmond brought the van to a stop at the T intersection of Atlantic and Broadway. Ahead the train tracks loomed, a bump in the road as the tracks ran through the heart of Stones Throw.

Ward eased off the flamethrower's trigger and dropped back into the van. "Why did you stop?" he asked.

"I don't know," Desmond said. "I've got a bad feeling. Something."

Ward saw the concern on Desmond's face, and it was contagious.

"We have to go slow over the tracks because of the boat trailer, and it would be a perfect time for somebody to hit us," Desmond said.

Cric legs inched over the edge of the open roof hatch and Ward burned them to cinders before pulling the hatch closed.

"Wait for the rain?" Lacy suggested.

"You heard him," Janet said. "It's not the Crics he's worried about."

"And it looks bad out there, but..." Dan trailed off when all eyes fell on him. As a stray, he had no role in the Southwood Crew's decision making process, but Ward still felt bad. The man had provided the drugs that might save Jenni's life and he owed the guy. Before he could help him out, Desmond did.

"But who knows?" Desmond said. "When I was a kid my friend Tom lived across the street, and one summer day he was sitting on his curb, me across the street from him on my curb. Rain fell on my side, but not on his."

"That can happen anywhere," Lacy said.

"True," Desmond said. "But on Long Island, you can literally have a dark cloud over only your house."

To that, nobody had anything to say.

"And I hate to dump more bad news on everyone, but see those taillights up the road there?" Desmond asked. "That's not far and it looks like things are backed up down at the shore just like we thought."

"What are you saying?" Janet asked. Jody was asleep, her head on her mother's shoulder, and Timmy watched the proceedings, his eyes glassy and distant.

"I stopped at Broadway because this is our last chance this side of the tracks to head west," Desmond said. "If we go straight, we're kind of locked in because getting through the neighborhoods south of the tracks will be..."

What more was there to say? The longer it took to get to the bay, the smaller their chance for survival.

"Stones Throw Avenue will be more packed, no?" Dan said.

"I'd think so," Desmond said.

The railroad tracks ran east to west, and there were only two crossings in Stones Throw: the underpass at Stones Throw Avenue and the crossing at Atlantic Avenue. There was no way over the tracks in-between, not in a vehicle, and not towing a trailer with a boat on it.

Lacy stated the obvious. "We shouldn't sit here."

"What do you think, Ward?" Desmond said.

"If it looks like a trap and smells like a trap, it's probably a trap," said Ward. "But if you see another way, enlighten me. Because I agree with Dan; Stones Throw Avenue will be worse."

"Janet?" Desmond said.

"I didn't come all this way, lose my husband and my home, only to be killed by highwaymen," Janet said.

"Highwaymen?" Ward said.

"I just watched a stream of Outlander," Janet said as she pursed her lips.

The red warning lights on the crossing gate poles came to life, bells chiming as the gate arms came down, the yellow lights atop the white, red-stripped barriers flashing as the road was blocked.

A stunned silence fell over the van, and even the Crics stopped hopping and creeping around to watch the display.

Red and yellow lights flashed, and the warning bells rang. This went on for sixty seconds, and then the chiming stopped, the lights went dark, and the barrier arms lifted like soldiers moving their guns to right shoulder arms during a parade.

"What the hell was that?" Ward said.

"Exactly what I was talking about," Desmond said.

"It's probably nothing," Dan said.

Silence filled the van, the hum of churning Crics outside background static.

Ward saw the suspicion in his companion's eyes. They didn't know this man and they hadn't even seen his face. Ward said, "Why do you say that?"

"There are relay switches that an incoming train triggers, which control the crossing lights and gates," Dan said calmly. "A Cric was probably messing with one and tripped the relay."

That made a lot of sense, but Ward said nothing.

"O.K., then," Desmond said. "Full steam ahead?"

When nobody protested, he put the van in gear.

Ward took up his position with the flamethrower, but only smaller Crics barred the way. A massive X and RR were painted on the road in white, and a thick hedgerow of evergreens created a barrier on the eastern side of the street, a house with a lawn picked clean to the west.

It was odd seeing the lush green trees after the constant devastation, and though the scent of gasoline and burning Crics filled the air, Ward caught the fragrant undertone of bitter evergreen.

"Those bushes are a good place to hide," yelled Desmond from below.

Ward considered spraying the greenery with fire but decided to hold off. It wasn't that he cared about preserving the island's vegetation, but a wall of flames would provide cover smoke for an ambush as well as limit their options.

A Seussian oak tree twisted by time and hurricanes and missing several large appendages reached over the road, and upon its thickest branch sat a wolf-sized black Cric. The mutant's legs cycled around the tree limb as the beast struggled to stay perched atop the branch, wet eyes aglow, pincers searching for prey. Smaller creatures climbed the old trunk and scuttled about on the emaciated limbs, the click and patter of their legs grating on Ward's last nerve.

The immediate area around the van was burned clean of Crics, so Ward put the flamethrower gun down, swung the AR off his back, and sighted the beast, but didn't fire. He caught a flash of light in the trees to his left, and as his eyes tracked the light, he shifted his aim.

With the line of evergreens running along the eastern side of the road, and a hedgerow lining the opposite side of the street, a tunnel of green led to the tracks. Ward saw nothing within the vegetation, the thick smell of evergreen leaking into the gas mask. He shifted his aim back to the large Cric sitting on the tree branch.

The Cric was gone.

Ward swung the rifle around as he searched for targets. He saw the Cric in question as it climbed over a fence and disappeared into a backyard. A nervous itch developed in his stomach, the river of sweat flowing down his forehead and back doubling in volume. Had something scared the Cric off?

Mutants crawled over the road, and a swarm gathered beyond the tracks. He switched back to the flamethrower.

Desmond proceeded with caution, the van rolling forward slowly.

The van was twenty feet from the railroad tracks when the signal lights came to life and the white and red-striped barriers came down and blocked the road. The chiming of the crossing echoed down the road, the thick evergreens on both sides of the road boxing in the sound.

Desmond didn't slow, and the van's engine growled as the vehicle surged toward the barriers.

Gunshots rang out, and bullets tinkled and popped as they hit the van, sparks flying as a bullet ricocheted over the van's roof and missed Ward by inches. Multiple assailants were attacking the van from within the cover of the evergreens on both sides of the road.

Ward dropped back into the van, pulled the hatch closed, and killed the flamethrower, its blue flame dying away with a gentle *whoosh*.

"Get flat!" Desmond yelled as he spun the steering wheel, and the van angled left and brushed against the hedgerow.

Bullets peppered the van, some finding their way through the sections of thin metal that hadn't been reinforced.

A sickening *plunk* followed by a *splat* echoed inside the van, and the side of Dan's head blew out and Janet and the kids were sprayed with blood, brains, and bone.

Lacy screamed as a puddle of blood formed around Dan's head, the crimson pool spreading toward her.

The van crashed through the railroad crossing gates, and wood snapped as the warning bells fell silent. With a shriek of metal, the van listed hard and bounced on its springs as it crossed the tracks, the trailer riding on one wheel, the safety chains shrieking.

With cameras on the front and back of the van, the side views were limited. So it was that nobody saw the makeshift railcar as it streaked down the tracks and smashed into the van.

Metal crunched, and had everyone not been lying flat, the crew would have been tossed like Crics in a gale. The rear camera showed a small flatbed railcar with two men atop it, an old school pump handle between them. The steampunkian railcar was wedged between the van and the boat trailer. As the van powered forward, tires shrieking, black smoke pouring over the road, the trailer jackknifed. The safety chains screamed under the strain as they twisted, and Desmond slammed on the brakes before the trailer broke free.

"We've got to take the fight to them, or we're done," Desmond said as he slammed the van into park and grabbed the AR-15 wedged between the bucket seat and the transmission tunnel.

He slipped between the seats into the rear of the van and headed for the back doors.

"What are you doing?" Janet asked.

"Saving our asses. Stay down," Desmond said.

The ratatat of gunshots had slowed, and yelling could be heard outside the van.

Ward's eyes strayed to Dan's fallen body, rivulets of blood running in the channels that ran the length of the ridged floor.

Jenni got to her feet, and with an obvious effort, lifted the Benelli and prepared it to fire.

Desmond screamed, a full-throated battle cry, and as he kicked open the van's rear door, mist from the coming rain pushed into the van.

Two men sat on the railcar, and both looked a bit dazed from their assault. They wore improvised biohazard suits: their cuffs and wrists silver with duct tape, and football helmets and safety goggles completed their ensemble.

Desmond fired, the AR barking as he riddled both men with bullets.

Lacy screamed as people poured from the evergreens, some holding clubs, others knives, and shovels, anything that could kill.

25

Ward froze, his world spinning as he stared at the two bullet-ridden corpses on the railcar. Blood and bone covered the machine's deck, both men's open eyes staring into the next world.

With the echo of Desmond's gunshots still hanging in the air, and misty clouds of blood floating over their two dead mates, the approaching mob slowed and came to a halt. Pledging to die during a planning session doesn't always equal kamikazes, and bringing a knife to a gunfight was never a good move.

Ward thought of Bill, how just a week ago he would've called the man a nutter for having such a large arsenal. How many guns do you need? That was the common refrain from those who saw guns as evil. Until recently, Ward would have said no more than five firearms per person, and in his opinion—past opinion—an AR-15 was a bit much for standard home defense, let alone two. Ward silently thanked Bill for being so paranoid.

Desmond and Ward retreated into the van but didn't close the open rear door. Gunshots dinged and popped, but they were sporadic and off the mark.

"They're coming around the front!" Janet yelled.

A shotgun blast in close made Ward duck.

Janet screamed, "They blew out the forward camera!"

"Cover me," Desmond said.

Ward stared at him, confusion tearing at his emotions and fogging his muddled mind.

"I'll handle the hitch while you cover me," Desmond explained.

Then Ward saw it. With the makeshift railcar wedged between the jackknifed trailer and the van, there was no way for the vehicle to move without unhitching the trailer. That meant giving up on the idea of the boat ever touching water, but at least they'd have a chance.

As Desmond unhitched the trailer, Ward eased around the van door, peppering the evergreens, and putting rounds at the feet of anyone brave enough to still be in the open.

Opportunistic Crics encroached on the scene.

To the north, arched legs cut through the evergreens on both sides of the road, and tall antennas stuck above the greenery. Ward's mind stuttered as it searched for a question the answer to which was evergreens. Was there an evergreen glade nearby? There was one along Tuthills Creek just beyond the tracks.

The rattle of the safety chains hitting the road pulled Ward back to the here and now.

Desmond scrambled into the van, and Ward closed the door behind him.

"Did you see if there was anything ahead on the road?" Ward yelled as Desmond threaded through the openmouthed crew to the front of the van.

"We're good for about fifty yards and then there's a stalled car.. a bunch of them. It's gonna be hard to get around, but we could turn back."

Ward said nothing, the pessimistic portion of his brain reminding him driving the van through a Cric-infested disaster zone was going to be a difficult task and doing it in reverse would make it even harder.

Gunshots pinged the van and the rear camera view showed Crics amassing on Atlantic Avenue north of the railroad tracks beyond the abandoned boat on its trailer. Bigger creatures were working their way around the evergreens, avoiding them as if they were toxic.

"What are we going to do?" Lacy shrieked. "The trailer is blocking the way behind us."

"We'll see. We'll see," Desmond said. He dropped into the driver's seat, put the van in gear, and pressed the gas pedal to the floor. As the tires hissed and carapaces cracked and popped, the van surged forward, rocking on its springs, the engine racing. Desmond drove the van blind, the front camera obliterated.

Ward's stomach grew hot as he watched the covered boat separate from the van and recede into the distance.

When the van was forty yards away from the boat Desmond slammed on the brakes, jacked the gearshift handle into reverse, and spun the steering wheel as far as it would go.

The van bucked and heaved, the power steering pump squealing as the van turned in a tight arc until the rear camera showed a southern view of Atlantic Avenue.

As the van inched up the road, Ward said, "Desmond, the things don't like eating evergreens. Nothing new there. But did you notice them avoiding the hedgerow back there? Like the bushes were on fire?"

He nodded. "Your point? I'm a bit busy." Desmond had the van going at five miles per hour as he traversed an abandoned car.

"You know that small forest of evergreens that leads down to the creek?" Ward said.

Desmond nodded slowly, understanding spreading over his grief-lined face, Ward still wearing the man's gas mask.

The camera showed Crics of all sizes spilling around houses and cars and launching from tree branches and fence tops.

Ward's skin crawled with the idea of not having a rear view, and as that worry weed sprang up in his mental garden the ground shuddered.

"Janet, get yourself buttoned up. We might have to move," Desmond yelled.

"Move? Move where?"

"Do it!" Desmond yelled.

"I'll get the flamethrower going," Lacy said.

"I can handle—" Ward started, but Desmond cut him off.

"I want you focused on your wife, Janet, and the kids. Don't let them out of your sight, no matter what happens."

Ward nodded.

The ground shook harder and a massive Cric three stories tall appeared on the road ahead. It reared back on its hindlegs and jumped, its huge form leaving the camera's eye for an instant before landing ten feet from the van.

Lacy lit the flamethrower, and as she opened the roof hatch, she depressed the trigger and fire charred the Crics loitering on the lip of the hatch.

"Shit!" screamed Desmond. With the Cric blocking the road, he spun the wheel and the van bumped up over a curb onto a lawn of dirt.

Lacy screamed as fire spat from the flamethrower, the giant Cric's pincers, forelegs, and the bristly hairs on its face catching fire.

The beast squeaked and thrashed, but that only helped spread the flames.

"Desmond, we've got company!" Lacy screamed.

"More!" Desmond bellowed, and his voice cracked.

Janet told Timmy to pass around water.

"Six people approaching through the evergreens to the south," Lacy yelled, the whoosh of the flamethrower dulling her voice. "Three stopped at the boat, but…"

Sparks flew as bullets tore into the metal roof around Lacy, and she fell back into the van, the flamethrower still ablaze. Fire scorched the propellant tanks strapped to the van's wall, and several sections of the rubber tubing connecting the canisters burned away.

Janet shielded her children, and Ward dove in front of Jenni, fully expecting the canister of gasoline to explode.

Instead, the tip of the flamethrower gun faded to a thin blue flame like the dying of the day's sun and went out with an inrush of air.

Gasoline spilled onto the van's floor, and a thin line of fire ran down the center of the van, burning away the trickle of gas and racing toward the leaking canister. When the flames reached the supply tank the fire grew.

A cat-sized Cric bounced through the roof hatch.

Jenni fired the Benelli and splattered the beast on the van's wall, but more Crics poured into the van.

The metal canister holding the gasoline was getting pinkish-white at its bottom and the blue paint was peeling away.

"Get out of here!" Ward yelled, his ears ringing as he stomped at the fire heating the canister, but with gas still trickling out there was no stopping it.

Desmond abandoned the driver's seat, bolted to the back of the van, kicked open the rear doors, and sprayed the area outside with bullets.

There were Crics everywhere, though some of the beasts were staying away from the clouds of black smoke pouring from the van.

"Let's go!" Ward yelled as he jumped to the road.

Next came Jenni, gun up, and she took up position behind the other van door. Next came Janet and the kids. Jenni and Ward provided cover as the group ran for an abandoned pickup truck.

Lacy emerged from the van next, Desmond behind her, his AR spitting bullets.

Flames leaked from the van's roof hatch, and as the van caught fire, tires bursting, windows shattering behind their protective metal shields, a paralyzing sense of all-consuming despair froze Ward in place as he watched the van burn.

Waves of heat and dark smoke rolled over the street, hot ash speckling the lenses of Ward's gas mask as the Crics backed off.

The six assailants coming up Atlantic Avenue from the north didn't back off.

"Get down!" Desmond yelled, and everyone dropped like a stock after Ward bought it.

Everyone except Lacy. She was a heartbeat too slow.

Gunshots rang out, three fast shots.

The first shot pinged into the van, the second hit nothing, but the third ricocheted off the van's door and caught Lacy in the face. With a strangled cry and gurgle that rose above the chaos, the back of Lacy's head was blown out, blood, brain, and bone hissing in the air as they sprayed the flames and were charred to ash. She fell in slow motion, Desmond reaching out to stop her fall, crimson splatter covering his bare face.

Ward, Jenni, Janet, and the kids reached the abandoned white pickup and Ward helped Jenni and the others into its bed before jumping in himself. "Lay flat!" he screamed as he searched for targets, but though he saw a few large Crics, none of them were in the immediate vicinity so he didn't waste ammunition. He didn't know how many shots he had left, and he had no time to reload the magazine with the bullets that stuffed his pockets.

Storm clouds exploded overhead, tall streams of mist reaching the ground, clouds of fog mixing with the smoke.

The canister in the van took off like a rocket, the gasoline finally igniting and completing the combustion process which released devastating energy in the form of heat and expanding gases. As the fuel, oxygen, and gasoline erupted, a bang echoed over the scene, flames shooting into the air. The canister came down and hit the road with a clang as the van burned.

A shockwave of heat and debris knocked Desmond from his feet, but that probably saved his life.

Two figures in improvised safety suits and wearing motorcycle helmets with dark face shields inched around the van, firing as they moved, but with Desmond on his back, the shots sailed over him and smacked into the open door.

Jenni was the first to react. She'd reloaded, and now she used the side of the pickup's bed to brace the Benelli. Two clean shots and both the thugs went down.

Ward was staring at his wife in amazement when he said, "What?"

Desmond broke into a run as a wave of Crics broke around the burning van, giving it a wide berth.

Gunshots pierced the gloom, but the shots weren't aimed at Ward and his team. The enemy of your enemy is your friend, and as the Crics began their assault in earnest, the remaining four attackers ceased firing at Desmond and the crew and turned their aggression toward the Crics.

The van was nothing but a blackened burning husk when Desmond reached Ward and the others, and he joined them in the pickup's bed.

A loud *crack* reverberated over the devastation and all eyes turned to see Lacy's corpse get crunched between the jaws of a man-sized Cric missing both forward pincers. The beast tore at the dead woman, ripping her safety suit, its translucent stiletto teeth tearing the corpse apart as its head jerked back and forth.

Ward sighted his AR and put two bullets between the Cric's two bulbous eyes. The freak deflated like a balloon, but that didn't stop the inevitable. Crics cycled around the burning van, taking turns darting toward the heat and fire to pull the corpse away from the flames. Ward didn't dare waste ammunition on the smaller beasts, and soon Lacy's body was far enough away from the dying flames and red-hot metal for the beasts to begin working on her. As the creatures swarmed over the dead woman Ward looked away.

"We can't stay here!" Desmond yelled. "Let's head to that evergreen glade you mentioned. We might be able to regroup there."

The party was ensconced in the pickup bed, but with the fire dying, Crics were coming from all around to investigate the disturbance.

Ward's gaze shifted to the east, where a row of houses blocked the view. Fences separated front yards from back, and Ward knew there was another row of homes directly behind those. He didn't know that part of the neighborhood well. He briefly considered backtracking and walking along the railroad tracks but quickly discarded the idea when he recalled that was where most of the mob had come from. Could they be hiding in the evergreen forest?

He had no time to consider.

Desmond said, "Let's do this." He leaped from the pickup, helped the others to the road, and set off toward the row of houses to the east, kicking and driving away curious Crics as he ran.

The heat of failure stung the tips of Ward's fingers and toes. Regardless of the spin he put on it, Lacy was dead, the van and boat were lost, and now they'd have to get to the shoreline on foot with no supplies and dwindling ammunition.

26

The trouble started when it began to rain.

Jazz sighed as the van disappeared from the camera's eye. The house was eerily silent with the crew gone, and the tapping and scraping of the Crics seemed louder.

Toby was in Janet and Bill's bedroom, which the couple had dubbed "the Lockbox," searching for cracks and shoring up the room's defenses.

Muffin was on patrol, and the feline had found two small Crics since the crew departed.

Jazz didn't want to get up from the couch, so she sat staring at the camera feeds for over an hour, watching the Crics as they scoured the neighborhood. Though she had done little more than spectate, the events of the last few days had drained her batteries to the point of shutdown. She'd never felt this tired in her life, not even when she'd had chemotherapy for breast cancer.

There was plenty of fuel left, but it was in the garage and neither Jazz nor Toby wanted to venture out there, so the couple had agreed to conserve gas when they could. Jazz pushed up from the couch and went to shut down the generator.

She paused in the kitchen and drank some water, ate the rest of her sandwich, and checked the back airlock for Crics. Nothing moved on the porch or in the tunnel of wood and tarps beyond. It was like the calm before a storm, and her palms itched with nervous energy.

Jazz was assaulted by the musty scent of stale air, gasoline, and laundry detergent as she opened the basement door. She took a gas mask from a hook and slipped it on as she pulled the door closed behind her. The generator ran on gasoline and wasn't supposed to be run indoors because of the harmful carbon monoxide produced during the combustion process. Bill had rigged an exhaust system that dumped the fumes into the cesspool, but the gas mask was a necessary precaution.

As soon as she shut down the generator and its gentle rumble died, she heard the pitter-patter of raindrops.

"Jazz, you better get up here," Toby said.

She listened hard. The Crics had gone strangely still, and only the slap of water against roof shingles and the tinkle of drops trickling down the gutter leaders broke the stillness.

A crack of thunder like the Earth itself had been cleaved by Thor's mighty hammer shook the egress windows and vibrated the basement floor. For a brief instant Jazz thought a huge Cric had hopped onto the driveway next door.

Jazz restarted the generator, and the basement light flickered back to life.

More booms of nature flexing its muscles—yet, they sounded more hollow and the floor didn't shake. Jazz headed for the stairs, her mind conjuring a series of problems and incidents that all ended with her husband being torn apart by a swarm of Crics.

When she reached the top of the stairs, she replaced the gas mask on its hook and eased into the kitchen. She wished she was carrying one of the shotguns Desmond had left behind. Neither she nor Toby had experience with guns, but Desmond had given them some basic instruction, and she was confident she could fire the weapons at need. Both guns were loaded and at the ready in the Lockbox.

The kitchen was quiet save for the gentle hum of the house and the mewing of Muffin as she stalked the outer walls of the room.

"See anything, sweetie?" Jazz said to the cat.

Muffin paused in her search long enough to give Jazz the stink-eye before moving around to the back of the refrigerator.

When Jazz returned to the living room, she found Toby staring at the exterior camera feeds.

Like a sheet hanging on a drying line and rippling in a gentle wind, the Crics rolled and undulated as the beasts staggered on their tall legs, antennas drooping as the rain soaked them.

"Finally, a little luck," Jazz said.

Toby said nothing. His eyes were locked on the lower quarter of the television that showed the view of the northeast camera.

In the distance, something massive moved through the rain and fog, its image blurred. Fog billowed before the creature, two dark eyes materializing out of the rain, a formless shadow coming together like a deadly puzzle.

The house shook, but there was no crack of thunder. No lightning to turn the T.V. white.

Like the heavens had busted open, the rain came in buckets, a heavy downpour that drove against the house and pushed the Crics to the ground. It was a pleasure to watch, and Jazz found herself hugging Toby, a smile spreading across her face.

Muffin's screech tore Jazz from her moment of bliss and hope. She shared a worried glance with her husband.

"Wait here and I'll grab the guns," Toby said as he bolted down the hallway toward the Lockbox.

The camera lenses blurred with water and Jazz struggled to see the massive creature. The rest of the Crics were beaten down by the rain, and fog limited visibility. Every few seconds the floor vibrated, the windows rattling in their panes as the mountainous dark shape separated from the gloom as if the rain and fog were coalescing to form the creature.

Toby returned with a Mossberg pump-action and Remington auto-loader, both loaded and ready to fire. He handed the Remington off to Jazz and eased through the swinging door into the kitchen.

At first, Jazz didn't see Muffin, but she heard the feline's hissing and screeching.

A Cric the size of a mouse jumped from behind the refrigerator, then another, then a third.

Muffin launched from behind the fridge, the cat in pursuit, and her front paws came down on one of the beasts. Her sharp claws didn't penetrate the Cric's carapace that covered its soft innards and the beast hopped away.

Toby took four long strides and crushed the creature beneath his boot, pivoted, and crunched another one.

Muffin jumped straight up as only cats can, and when she came down her jaws locked down on the last Cric, its head disappearing in her mouth, pincers and antennas flailing. The feline shook her head until the Cric's legs stopped moving. Then she let the dead mutant drop to the floor and looked up at Toby.

"Good girl," Toby said. "Good girl."

The rain eased, and the pounding on the roof fell to a dull roar.

Toby stared down at the remains of the Crics, went to his wife, and put his arm around her. There was nothing to say or do. They both knew the house would be breached eventually, but Jazz had hoped to have a little more time.

The house shook harder than before, and window glass rattled behind protective shielding.

With guns in hand, the couple went back to the living room.

Outside, drizzle dulled the scene, but the Crics stirred with renewed vigor as they shook themselves off and began searching for shelter. The creatures took the break in the storm to crawl under cars, perch beneath the eaves of houses, and to Jazz's dismay, many of the larger Crics had gathered around several of the windows and were attempting to peel away the sheets of wood covering the glass. The creatures had tried this before, to no avail, but with bigger Crics in play, a bolt of worry-pain marched down Jazz's spine and drove a nail into her lower back.

Muffin hissed and screeched from the kitchen, and Toby said, "I've got it."

Despite the offer, Jazz followed her husband and she gasped when she entered the kitchen and saw mouse-sized Crics marching from behind the refrigerator again.

Muffin gave up and bolted toward Toby and Jazz, but one of the Crics hopped in her way, legs cycling, pincers grasping for feline flesh.

Jazz had once seen a cat thrown from the roof of a burning house by a fireman desperate to save the beast's life. The tiny gray beast had arced through the air, twisting end-over-end like a badly thrown football, only to wiggle and adjust just in time to land on its feet and scurry away from danger.

Muffin deployed her feline guile in a similar manner. Without stopping her forward progress, the cat changed course and used her rear legs to launch off the kitchen floor. She lunged at the Cric with her nails out, tail straight, her rear legs forward like an attacking eagle.

The clash was an epic knot of legs, claws, and teeth.

Muffin raked out the Cric's eyes and the mutant squealed and thrashed, jaws and pincers snapping, but that only made things easier for Muffin. The feline shifted position and clamped its jaws down on the Cric's torso, its shell cracking with a *pop* as dark goo sprayed the cat's face and leaked onto the floor.

"O.K., I've seen enough," Jazz shrieked. "Let's go." She kicked open the kitchen door and held it open for Toby and Muffin. Then she slipped into the living room and secured the door behind her.

As soon as the doorlatch slammed home, Toby was on his hands and knees stuffing towels under the door. When he was done, he fell back onto his butt and let his head fall into his hands.

Outside, the camera's eye caught a Godzilla-Cric shuffling through the drizzle and fog, arced legs rising above the house's roofline. Based on the creature's current course, it would pass between Bill and Janet's place and the house to the north. A bit too close for reasonable comfort.

"Turn off the lights," Toby said.

Jazz stared at the flatscreen and said nothing.

"Kill the lights Kill the lights!" he yelled as he set about shutting down the lights in the living room. The last thing to go dark was the display screen.

"Good call, babe. Good call," said Jazz. They had no idea what might attract larger Crics, and rays of bright light leaking through the boarded-up windows might catch the massive mutant's attention.

The crack of breaking wood made Jazz jump, and she almost pulled the shotgun's trigger. She gripped the weapon so tightly her fingers had turned pink, and her knuckles hurt.

Muffin paused in her patrol, her eyes shifting to the front of the room.

The tip of a pincer worked its way behind the thick plywood covering the front window like a nail claw on a hammer. Wood creaked as it bent, the five-inch nails holding the wood to the window frame slowly easing out.

Jazz and Toby watched, mouths hanging open, terror rooting their feet to the floor.

Muffin hissed, the hair on her back standing on end as she backed away.

The pincer worked its way in further, and a two-inch gap opened between the plywood and the window frame.

Rat-sized Crics squeezed through the gap, filling the space between the wood and the window. Soon the glass was covered, and as the huge pincer continued to flex open and closed, slowly working its way under the wood, Jazz found her voice.

"We need to—"

Wood cracked and nails shrieked as they pulled free, and a three-foot pincer pulled the corner of the plywood back.

The wood held and snapped back, but it drove the pincer into the window glass, and it shattered.

Crics poured in through the gap and Toby grabbed a can of bug spray from a nearby table and doused the beasts as they hopped into the house.

Red hot anger boiled over in Jazz. She'd lost so much, and she didn't have any more to give. She strode forward, Crics jumping all around her, and shouldered the gun, placed the tip of the Remington against the huge pincer. She pulled the trigger, pumped another shell into the firing chamber, and pulled the trigger again.

Cacophonous booms echoed through the room as the recoils knocked her back, her ears ringing as the pincer was pelted with #4 turkey shot. The claw broke open, translucent meat streaked with black veins leaking out. With a squeal that sounded like a pig getting a rectal exam, the pincer fell back.

But it was too late.

The window was broken, the plywood bent and cracked, and mutants cycled into the house through the gaps.

Jazz scooped up Muffin and she and Toby ran for the hallway that led to the bedrooms.

The plywood was torn off the front window, and a huge Cric with a shattered claw stared into the living room, its dark eyes searching, antennas swaying.

Toby put the stock of his shotgun to his shoulder, aimed between the beast's eyes, and fired. He pumped the forestock and chambered a round, then fired again.

Once in the hallway, Jazz dropped Muffin, who bolted for the Lockbox.

Toby secured the door, stuffed towels in the gap along the floor, and the couple retreated.

The lights were on in the bedroom, and as Jazz secured the door and Toby stuffed towels, her heart sank. The generator was still running, and it would be a major task to shut it down. So it would run dry, and if they still needed power tomorrow they would have to venture out to the garage for gasoline.

Jazz and Toby climbed onto Bill and Janet's bed and huddled together, the sounds of Crics trying to get out of the rain echoing through the house.

Muffin sat at attention, ears flicking wildly, her eyes shifting about the room. Much of the day remained and Jazz's thoughts strayed to Janet and the others. They were beyond her help now, and she beyond theirs.

But if she and Toby could make it through the night… If they could just make it through the night.

27

Ward had never believed in God. Not really. He'd gone through the motions, made his parents happy, taken his tax deduction, and when he saw the social and economic benefits of being a believer, he'd decided the "there is no God" mountain wasn't one he wanted to die on. As the Crics descended on the crew it began to rain, and a ray of sunlight pierced the cloud cover, and Ward thought maybe he needed to reconsider his position.

A Cric pounced on him from behind a tree trunk and drove the thought from his mind.

Ward stumbled as he fought to get the creature off him, but the beast's pincers had taken hold of his jacket. The Cric rocked back and forth, jaws flexing as it tried to take a bite out of him.

With a squeal of terror and anger, Timmy smacked the beast with a baseball-sized stone.

A satisfying crunch rose above the din, and as Ward regained his balance and ran on, he high-fived the kid.

Thunder exploded and lightning crackled as the driving rain subdued the Crics. Some of the beasts pressed themselves to the ground, trying to make themselves small, and others scurried for cover.

Desmond was on point, followed by Jenni. The children, who still played night tag in the summers, were guiding their mother around trees, and helping her avoid roots reaching out to trip her up. Ward was rearguard, and he turned as he ran, trying to watch everything and everyone at once.

A narrow tunnel-like alley ran between two houses boxed in by tall six-foot stockade fences, and Desmond made for it. Crics scurried out of their way as the rain fell, antennas drooping, their thin legs sluggish.

Desmond leveled the AR and popped off a few shots to scare away the larger beasts as he ran.

The party reached the back of the house where a six-foot stockade fence blocked their path.

There was a gate, and Desmond and Jenni took up positions on each side of it, and Janet and the kids took cover behind Desmond.

Ward kicked the gate open and eased into the backyard beyond, AR-15 up and ready to fire. The crew rushed through behind him, and Ward slammed the gate closed and secured the latch.

Desmond huddled up the team as they took cover against the house, gusting wind blowing the rain sideways and pushing the Crics around like dead leaves. But still, a horde of smaller beasts were already gathering in a corner of the yard and several larger beasts were perched atop the stockade fence.

"We need to conserve ammunition," Desmond yelled.

Jenni stuffed shells into the Benelli, doing her best to keep them dry. Her eyes were solid red, and now that she'd stopped running, her shoulders slouched, and she swayed on her feet.

Reloading the AR-15 magazines without clips was a bit more complicated and would have to wait. Ward had lost count of how many shots he had left. The rifle's magazine held thirty rounds, and he'd used at least twenty, and his spare magazine was empty.

"Do what I do," Desmond yelled. "Keep your back to houses, cars—though keep in mind the Crics seem to like hiding underneath vehicles. Tree trunks, use whatever you can to protect your back. Fire only when necessary. Janet, you and the kids stay between Ward and I."

Desmond worked his way along the back of the house, then stopped short.

Jenni bumped into him, but Janet and the kids managed to pull up.

A picture window revealed a woman and a young child. The woman's hair was disheveled, but otherwise, she looked alright. She held a young boy in her arms, the kid's blue eyes glistening with curiosity and fear. The kid waved at the party as the group surged back into motion.

Ward hadn't had time to consider the other residents of Stones Throw. There were many broken windows along Atlantic Avenue, but other than that it looked like people were following the government's advice and had holed up. During the COVID pandemic, and after, there had been insane accusations that wearing masks had been more about making people comply than it was about safety. So Ward was a bit surprised most people had accepted the government's advice. Surely the arrival of the military helicopter and the subsequent explosion would be building hopes of rescue.

There was no gate on the back portion of the fence and with the fence crossbeams turned outward it would be a difficult climb for a sick Jenni, two teenagers, and a woman who probably hadn't climbed a fence since she was a teenager back when Jimmy Carter was president.

Booms of thunder, cracks of lightning, and the rain came in buckets.

In a way it was refreshing. Ward had been in his safety suit for hours, and though it was harder to run with the heavy gear wet, the cool water running down his neck charged his batteries. Plus, it was nice not having to deal with the Crics every step of the way. Though some of the creatures made halfhearted attempts to snag them with their pincers, for the most part, the crew crossed the house's backyard unscathed.

When they reached the fence that separated the backyard from the one beyond it, Desmond stopped to regroup. "We're six houses from the railroad tracks, but Mark Drive runs north to south beyond this double row of houses and intersects with Richlee Street. We can use the houses for cover, and when we hit the creek, we can work our way to the evergreen glade. If my memory serves, it's in the sandspit that used to be Week's Pond long ago."

Ward recalled the map he'd studied just yesterday, and what Desmond said sounded right. He'd hiked up that way when he and Jenni moved to Stones Throw, but it was months ago, and he didn't remember the finer details.

Lightning backlit the dirty cloud cover, and for a heartbeat, the world flashed white, as if some god somewhere had just taken a picture using a celestial flashbulb. The rain eased, but it was still coming down hard.

Desmond and Ward tore down a section of rotted fence and the party spilled into another backyard. Huge oak trees and vast gardens surrounded a gazebo infested with Crics. The beasts piled and climbed over one another in an attempt to get out of the rain, and Ward noticed the creatures were more frenzied than when the heavy rain was coming down.

It hit Ward then. These creatures had never experienced rain, so it made sense that the first time they got wet they'd be disorientated. But now the mutants knew they didn't like rain, and as soon as it let up a little, they sought shelter.

The party reached Mark Drive. There was a large house on the corner of Richlee Street, and most of its windows were broken. Crics fought to get inside like a horde of rats fighting for a single piece of cheese, and the team gave the area a wide berth.

When Desmond made the right onto Richlee, Jenni went down.

Ward saw it happen in his mind's eye before it actually occurred. Jenni slowed, and staggered, but before Ward could get to her side to support her, she faceplanted onto the blacktop, the M2 clattering to the road beside her.

Janet was the first at her side, and as Ward skidded to a stop, he saw that his wife's eyes were closed.

The rain had become a thick drizzle, and Crics were shaking themselves off and venturing from their shelters.

Janet lifted Jenni's head off the road and Ward knelt beside her.

"She's breathing," Janet said. "But she's burning up."

Ward gently tapped his wife's cheek. Nothing. Then he slapped her a bit harder, and her eyes popped open. "Sorry, honey, but you need to stay awake."

Jenni's eyes darted about, and to Ward, it appeared as though her tears were tainted with blood.

"We can't stay here!" Desmond screeched.

"Can you walk?" Ward asked.

Jenni's eyes rolled in her head, her breathing erratic.

"O.K., then," Ward said. He snatched the Benelli, handed it to Janet, and scooped up his wife.

"She needs…" Janet trailed off. Whatever Jenni needed, no one present could provide it for her.

"Hold onto my neck," Ward said. He hung the AR over a shoulder by its strap, and hoisted his wife onto his back, gripping her legs at the knees as he wrapped her arms around his neck.

There were only six houses on each side of Richlee, but with Ward carrying Jenni piggyback, it was slow going. The Crics were stirring, and many sets of black eyes watched the party as they ran down the center of the street.

"See that house," Desmond said. "The white one with the rusted black wrought iron railings?"

Ward nodded as he ran, Jenni's head resting on his shoulder as he clung to his neck.

"The old lady that lived there… I can't remember her name… a dictator's name, but I can't recall it. Me and my friends egged her house every Halloween."

"Why?" Ward forced out, though he didn't care.

"She didn't answer the door."

On Halloween, that would do it.

The crew reached the end of the road and Desmond bolted down a long driveway that ran behind a large house set on the creek. The railroad tracks were to the north, but houses packed the road in that direction.

A tall stand of trees, a mix of oaks stripped bare and pitch pines filled with pinecones, marked the rear property line. There was no fence, and the scent of wet evergreens wafted on the breeze as Desmond plunged into the trees without pausing.

Jenni mumbled something in Ward's ear, but he couldn't make out the words. His heart pumped wildly, the AR smacking his leg as he ran.

The rain stopped and mist hung five feet above the ground, the scent of moist earth and must creeping up Ward's nostrils.

As the woods thinned the ground became soft, and the hardpan gave way to marsh. Water reeds ran along the edge of Tuthills Creek, but the thin stream was only a couple of feet deep.

Desmond laughed as he crashed through the water reeds, sinking knee-deep in mud as he waded out into the water.

"Look!" exclaimed Jody as she pointed downstream. The teenager hadn't said a word since she saw Lacy's head blown apart, and she clung to her mother like she was a life raft, and the kid was tumbling on a raucous sea.

Janet ventured hesitantly into the marsh, her head twisting so she could see what Jody was pointing at.

A burst of Crics sprayed from the forest downstream and pulled up short at the edge of the creek.

Ward and the rest of the party struggled through the mud toward Desmond, who was sloshing through the river as he headed toward the pine forest.

A group of elephant-sized Crics appeared on the eastern shoreline, and the crew was boxed in on both sides of the creek.

The water reeds thinned as the party struggled on, and pitch pines appeared on the western shore.

Crics struggled in the mud, but the beasts found their footing as the bog slowly transformed into a sandy hardpan. The evergreens grew thicker, as did their underbrush of scrub pine, the Crics screeching like the trees were dripping acid and not sap-infused droplets of rainwater.

A man-sized Cric launched across the creek and landed on the opposite shore, crushing several of its smaller brethren beneath its girth. Its jaws dropped open as it came at the party, but pulled up short at the edge of the water.

Tree by tree the evergreen forest formed along the shore, the mutants wailing and bitching as they backed off.

The western shore turned sandy, and Desmond trudged from the river and entered the trees, the shrieking of the Crics fading as they stopped at the edge of the evergreen forest. Fog snaked between the trees, the scent of pitch pines like perfume.

Like giant bonsai trees, the pitch pines were irregularly shaped, their branches twisted. The evergreens ranged in size from ten to sixty feet, and their bundled needles were strong, narrow, and sharp. Sap ran down many of the trunks, and with the trees wet, the pinecones glistened.

Ward's back ached from carrying his wife, and when the party was well within the evergreens he stopped and laid his wife on the pine needle-covered ground.

As the party caught their breath, Janet went to work on Jenni, waking her up and pulling off her gas mask so she could wipe her forehead with a wet cloth.

It hit everyone then, losing Lacy, Dan, and the helicopter taking out the momma Cric. Ward was exhausted. Done. Spent, and as he bent and put his hands on his knees, he didn't think he had anything left to give on this day.

"We should hunker down here a bit. Reload and regroup," Desmond said. "It seems you were right, Ward. The creatures want nothing to do with the pitch pines."

"At least in daylight," Timmy said.

"The boy has a point," Janet said.

"What we need to do is take care of Jenni and get her help," Ward said.

"I saw flashing red lights downstream at Weeks Bridge. Beyond the bridge the creek becomes a passable canal," Janet said. "I'm sure soldiers will be coming this way soon."

Ward knew it was chaos at the shoreline. He'd seen the pileup of cars at the end of Atlantic Avenue with his own eyes. The authorities had their hands full and who knew how long it would take for them to reach their position? Ward had to bet that Jenni didn't have that much time.

"We're sitting ducks here," Ward said, but his heart wasn't in it and the tone of his voice let everyone know it.

Jenni moaned in her delirium as Janet wiped her forehead.

Ward wandered through the evergreens, and when he reached the edge of the forest, he found a horde of huge Crics stacked ten rows deep.

28

"We're surrounded," said Ward. "They're at the edge of the forest riling each other up. When it gets dark…" Ward looked at the ground. He didn't know what would happen when it got dark, all he knew was Jenni might be dead by then.

The group stood at the center of the small evergreen forest, tension and the remnants of the storm crackling in the air like static electricity.

"Maybe it will rain again," Jody said.

As if the child had spoken some ancient wisdom, all heads except Jenni's swiveled to the west. The sky was already clearing, and patches of blue could be seen through the black cotton candy clouds. When Long Island's weather forecasters said isolated thunderstorms, they meant isolated.

"We've got hours of daylight left," Janet said. Though she tried, Janet couldn't stop her gaze from drifting to Jenni. Janet reached up to itch her neck, and when her fingers found rubber, she pulled her gas mask off.

Everyone stared at her like she was an astronaut on the Moon who had just pulled her oxygen tube out. But then one by one the group removed their masks and protective gear, their helmets, ski goggles, and heavy jackets. The party was soaked through, and Ward rolled his shoulders. It felt good to get the heavy wet clothing off.

Noticing Janet's concern for Jenni, Ward said, "Is there anything we can do for her?"

Janet shrugged. "Give her more antibiotics? I'd rather have an overdose issue than see her die of whatever she's got."

Ward took a moment to consider the risks. His wife was lying half-dead before him, and they had medicine that might help. But how much was too much? In the end, he figured Janet was right. If they did nothing she would surely die. "Do it. Please," he said.

Janet nodded and she and Jody tended to Jenni.

Desmond said, "If we're going to get her anywhere, we need some type of stretcher. You can't carry her on your back like that the whole way to the bridge."

Ward inventoried his surroundings for the first time. Most of the pitch pines were lush and clean, but there were plenty of pinecones and dead undergrowth on the trees themselves, as well as twigs and other dried brush littering the needle-covered sand.

"We could start a fire," Ward said. "We can make torches, set the evergreens on fire if need be."

"Let's take fifteen minutes," Desmond said. "Drink some water, get something to eat, reload, and let's see if we can get that fire going. I don't see a downside."

Janet and Jody stayed with Jenni, and Desmond collected all the ammo and reloaded the magazines. Ward and Timmy went in search of firewood, pinecones for kindling, and vines and long branches or evergreen trunks for the side rails of Jenni's litter. Pinecones and branches were plentiful, and soon the duo had a nice pile of firewood, but no vines and no stretcher poles.

As the pair worked their way deeper into the pitch pines, Ward felt the need to say something to the boy. They'd never been alone together, and Ward wanted the boy to know his dad was a hero. "I'm sorry about your dad, Timmy. He was a brave man."

Timmy shrugged. "And now he's gone."

"Oh, don't be like that. He didn't choose us over you," Ward said. "There are people that run and hide when trouble comes calling. Then there are those who run toward the fight with a total disregard for their own safety. Your dad was one of those."

"But why?" said the boy as he disappeared between two lush scrub pines.

"Because he cared so much and didn't want to see anyone hurt," Ward said.

"And he thought he could save them?" Timmy asked as Ward's heart cracked a little.

"That's right." Ward pushed through the trees to find the boy standing by a bronze evergreen that looked like a dead Christmas tree. "Perfect. That's one rail." The tree had been dead for some time, and it broke away from its base easily.

As Ward stripped the branches off the tree trunk with a stone, Timmy went in search of a second side rail.

"I've got another one over here," Timmy called out.

The crew had no rope, but there was a vine coiled around the dead tree Timmy had found. The vine twisted down the trunk and crawled across the ground before disappearing into the sand.

It had been stripped of its leaves.

Ward and Timmy exchanged a glance, but it was Timmy who broke free of his paralysis first.

"Desmond! Desmond!" the boy yelled as he ran back through the trees toward base camp.

Ward was going to yell and tell the boy to slow up, but then he decided he should probably be running himself.

Desmond met Timmy in the forest, and when Ward arrived Desmond had his hands on the boy's shoulders and was trying to calm the kid down. When Desmond saw Ward he said, "What the hell happened out there?"

"Come see for yourself."

So it was that the three companions stood gaping at the vines creeping over the dead evergreen, the implication clear; the leaves had been consumed by Crics—there were scratch marks all over the vines' thin brown bark—which meant now there were no doubts as to what would happen when darkness fell.

With everybody gathered at the center of the small forest, Jenni moaning gently, Desmond told the rest of the group what Ward and Timmy had discovered and what it meant.

Wind gusted through the evergreens, and the distant rattle of the Crics amassing on the borders gnawed on Ward's last nerve.

"So what we need is a diversion," Janet said.

"Exactly," Desmond said.

Jody had managed to hold onto her backpack, so the companions shared three bottles of water and four packages of peanut butter and cheese crackers. The guns were made ready, the stretcher constructed, and spears were made for the kids.

Desmond got a fire started with the lighter used to start the flamethrower.

"Good thing you grabbed that," Janet said. The lighter gave them the ability to light torches and set fires on the go, though the yellow BIC only had a trickle of fluid left in it.

An hour after entering the evergreen forest, Jenni was on her stretcher and strapped in place with Desmond and Timmy's belts. The party was exhausted, but everyone had agreed that the longest day of their lives needed to be a little longer because making a run for Weeks Bridge gave them the best chance of survival.

Back in their safety suits, the crew prepared to leave as Timmy took up one end of Jenni's stretcher and Ward hoisted the other. That would allow Desmond and Janet to run point, so Janet traded the Benelli M2 for Ward's AR-15.

In summer pitch pines release sap that is highly flammable, and the fine pointy leaves are also rich in combustible oils. Desmond had smothered several pinecones in sap, and when the time came, they could be easily ignited and thrown.

"The wind is out of the south now," Desmond said. "So, I'll light the fire on the northern edge of the woods. If there are—"

The ground trembled.

Jenni's eyes opened and she mumbled something unintelligible.

"We're making for the creek," Desmond said. "Is everyone ready?"

Ward looked around at his companions and they appeared anything but ready. He knew he wasn't. He was tired, hungry, and with his wet makeshift safety suit back on each step was an effort, but all it took was a glance in his wife's direction to find his motivation.

"Let's do it then," Desmond said. "I'll meet you guys along the eastern edge in two minutes."

With all the planning done, and everything at the ready, there was nothing else to say, yet Desmond lingered, his eyes locked on Janet.

"Be careful," Janet said. Then she gathered Jody and headed east.

The Benelli was slung over Ward's back, and he and Timmy followed Janet as they hauled the stretcher.

Jenni moaned, her eyes closed, her head slowly moving back and forth as she shook her head "no" in slow motion.

The stretcher wasn't that heavy, and as Ward pushed into the trees he didn't look back. He and Timmy wove through the evergreens, branches whipping their faces, tree roots and pricker vines reaching up from the sandy hardpan searching for feet to trip.

A cone of sunlight cut through the clouds and illuminated their path, and the ground vibrated as the Crics squealed.

Ward and Timmy reached the eastern edge of the forest and found Janet and Jody staring at the army of Crics waiting just beyond the woods border.

The Crics climbed and harassed each other, the larger mutants moving forward, crunching and brushing aside smaller beasts in the process.

A faint *womp*, like all the air had been sucked from the world, carried over the scene. Ward sniffed, and beneath the intense scent of wet evergreen the astringent smell of smoke filtered through the air.

Desmond arrived and said, "It only took two pinecones. Even with everything damp, the dead underbrush caught like balsa wood."

Clouds of smoke poured through the forest, and the Crics backed away, many of the smaller beasts scurrying north to see what all the excitement was about.

The crackle and pop of flames echoed through the forest, and only the largest Crics remained, watching the party as they formed up.

Ward and Timmy put down the stretcher, and Ward swung the M2 off his back into his hands.

"On three," Desmond said.

"Three!" Janet screamed as she pulled the AR's trigger as fast as she could, spraying the Crics with lead.

Ward and Desmond did the same, and with piles of legs, mounds of goo, cracked carapaces, and torn skin littering the sandy hardpan, the party bolted for the creek.

To the south emergency lights spun atop Weeks Bridge.

Desmond led, the stock of the AR pressed to his shoulder as he trudged through the mud to the creek. Jody trailed after Desmond, but Janet waited for her son, and when he arrived, she kissed him on the cheek.

"Mom!" the kid exclaimed, like she'd bitten him.

Janet put her hand atop the boy's helmet and said, "You did good. I'm proud of you."

With help from Janet, Ward, and Timmy managed to get through the mud while hauling Jenni on her stretcher. She hadn't made a sound in some time, nor had she opened her eyes, but Ward saw her chest slowly rising and falling.

When Ward stood in two feet of water, the finish line in sight, he took a moment to gather his courage and catch his breath.

Gunshots rang out, and the water rippled.

To the north just beyond the evergreen forest, the naked trees swayed, branches cracked and snapped, and a Godzilla-Cric trundled into view, the thinning fog and thickening smoke eddying around the creature like a cloak.

Ward's breath caught. The thing was all black, its wet eyes glowing. Its turkey leg rear limbs were five feet thick at their widest point, and the beast's pincers were the size of a full-grown human. Claws flexed open, searching for prey as steel cable-like antennas swayed and broke tree branches as the Cric inched forward, avoiding the water. Six-foot clear teeth gleamed, the beast's jaws flexing open and closing as if chewing.

No words or commands were needed. Ward and Timmy hefted the stretcher and started downstream, water splashing around their legs, their feet sinking into the sandy bottom.

Jody stayed close to Ward as Desmond went on point and Janet took the rearguard.

The crack of the huge Cric's pincers and the gnashing of its teeth echoed on the wind. Waves of heat and thick plumes of smoke rolled off the evergreens as tall flames licked the sky. The fire had spread, and the forest was being consumed along with everything in it.

Ward struggled to keep the stretcher from being jostled, but when the huge beast screamed, he almost dropped his wife.

"Are you O.K.?" Timmy asked. The kid had been a trooper and had done a great job carrying the litter with Ward.

In the cold chaos of that moment, Ward's chest grew warm, and he said, "I don't know, Timmy. I just don't know."

29

Guilt cascaded over Ward in the form of invisible spiders clawing at the underside of his skin. He was an adult, the role model, and dumping his insecurities on a teenager was the pinnacle of weakness. Timmy's question was like a jab to the jaw.

When was the last time he'd been O.K.? Ward didn't even know what being O.K. meant anymore. Shame flooded his muscles and weakened his knees. It had taken the mutants for Ward to understand he was coasting when he should be living. Now that he was forced to fight for his life, he realized he wanted to live, but that brought on an even deeper sense of gloom because he didn't understand what that might mean.

The huge Cric pursuing the crew along the stream's edge disappeared into the smoke and fog, and Ward experienced a brief moment of relief.

It didn't last long.

The creek bent west and narrowed to ten feet across. Water reeds packed the shoreline, and sandspits reached into the water. Adventurous Crics ventured out onto the spits, and in spots, only feet separated the mutants' pincers from the crew as Ward and company threaded downriver.

The creek water rippled, and the ground vibrated as all the Crics along both sides of the stream froze as if they'd been hit with a blast of subzero air. Two thunderous thumps and the Crics were moving again, gyrating, and hopping in a frenzy.

As the party worked their way south, houses appeared in the trees beyond the reeds to the west, and to the east, a barren field dotted with tall, deformed pitch pines stretched to a condo complex on River Avenue. Ward recalled having dinner at a place called the Tiki on Patchogue River, which was just beyond River Avenue.

A blur of motion as a shadow fell over the party.

Godzilla-Cric was back. It bounced over the creek and landed with its legs splayed on either side of the water, the beast straddling the stream. Its black-striped brown carapace rose fifty feet in the air, its arched legs rising another twenty. Garbage can lid-sized eyes stared down at the party, the smaller Crics rallying around their master, a swarm forming.

Janet opened up with the AR-15 and peppered the Godzilla-Cric with .45 MM NATOs.

"Hold your fire!" screeched Desmond.

Janet spun on her brother-in-law, swinging the AR around like Desmond was going to be the next one to get some lead. "What?"

Desmond said nothing as he watched the massive Cric rear back and scream, enormous pincers snapping. The mutant jumped and landed directly in the team's path, straddling the creek, the spikes on the beast's second set of forelegs stabbing the ground on the banks of the stream for support. The creature rocked forward, its pincers searching for prey, jaws snapping closed on air.

"Follow me!" screamed Desmond. "We can't take this thing down." He turned east as he fired his AR, clearing a path on the shore of the creek.

The huge beast reached out for Ward and Timmy as they fumbled with the stretcher, but Janet stepped in and fired her AR at point-blank range into the meat of the claw. The *crack* of the shots and the *pop* of the giant pincher exploding reverberated over the creek, and the massive Cric drew back.

Fight or flight had never been clearer, and with no options left, Desmond had made the only decision possible. Leaving the water was a tough blow, but there was no way the party could have made it through the gathering swarm and past Godzilla-Cric, especially with Ward and Timmy hauling Jenni.

Ward's stomach tightened, but he smiled as the sound of helicopter airfoils beating the air rose above the commotion. He and Timmy struggled on, Jenni moaning faintly, her eyes moving around wildly beneath their closed lids.

Desmond flattened water reeds and splattered the marshland with Cric guts as he drove forward, the party trailing after, Janet serving as rearguard.

The party broke free of the water reeds, mud clinging to their legs, the ground pillow-like and wet, the dry bog stinking of rot.

A barren field infested with Crics stretched out before the crew. Ward got lunch sometimes at The River Deli and he drove by the open area often. In summer, tall grass dominated the field, the spattering of oaks, pitch pines, and maple trees like flowers painted on a green canvas. What he saw now rivaled Mordor.

Of all the memories and knowledge, all his experiences, all the suffering, celebrations, the life and death, it was a smidgen of bible verse that forced its way through years of adult callus. "Then I will make up to you for the years. That the swarming locust has eaten, the creeping locust, the stripping locust, and the gnawing locust. My great army which I sent among you." Though he never really believed in God, being forsaken by him could still have its downsides.

Every blade of grass on the field had been gnawed to the hardpacked brown earth. Every leaf had been stripped from every tree and vine. There were no weeds, no dead grass, or wild berries. Stones, piles of rubble, and holes marred the hardpan like a battlefield, and the thick trunks of the bare trees looked dead. They weren't, and many would survive once the Crics were gone, and the grass would grow anew as if rejuvenated by fire.

As he stumbled on, his feet finally leaving the soggy bog and finding sand-encrusted dirt, he thought perhaps things weren't that bad. The island would recover and do better without as many people infesting its ecosystem like civilized Crics. He thought of that Ray Bradbury story... he couldn't recall its name, but the last line of a poem by Sarah Teasdale therein had stuck in his head like a fishhook his entire life: "And Spring herself, when she woke at dawn, would scarcely know that we were gone."

Ahead, a thick copse of naked oak trees separated the field from the Creekside Landing condo complex. Normally the gray wood facades of the community's buildings wouldn't be visible from Ward's position, but with the world stripped of life, the party could see their goal; a red brick wall to put their backs to.

All they had to do was cross the two hundred yards of open country infested with hangry Crics.

An Apache thundered over the trees and tread air above the barren field. The bird was too far away to issue orders, but Ward didn't need to be told what to do. "When they fire hit the deck!" he screamed, his legs buckling as he dropped to a knee, the stretcher tipping sharply to port. Had it not been for the belts holding Jenni in place, she would have hit the hardpan.

As it was, Ward staggered but managed to stay on his feet as he held onto the stretcher and brought it level.

The party ran, Crics scattered, and the smaller beasts twisted in the air as the Apache churned the landscape with its downwash. Ward could almost feel the pilot's tension reach out and grab him. The bird's pilot was waiting for him and his companions to get clear before he put a missile up Godzilla-Cric's gullet.

Ward stumbled as the land became uneven, shallow pits and valleys normally hidden by the leveling agent of field grass now pronounced and visible. Old foundations, piles of ancient wood framing, and other remnants of the distant past pocked the landscape like traps, and Ward struggled to focus on his next step and ignore the hunter-killer floating in the sky.

Godzilla-Cric screeched, the ground shaking as it hopped forward, tree trunks snapping, the *womp womp* of the bird's airfoils beating the air exploding over the clearing. Dog-sized Crics swarmed around Godzilla, and the smaller mutants were churned under the advance like pebbles being sucked back into the bay with the tide.

Ward spared a glance over his shoulder and as the wind pushed away the thinning fog the gargantuan Cric jumped from the mist. It was fifty yards back, its pincers searching, antennas cracking like bullwhips, its mouth hanging open in a rictus grin.

If the beast jumped toward the party again it would have them.

A klaxon pierced the day, a steady electronic alarm that emanated from the Apache.

Ward opened his mouth to yell, but Desmond beat him to the punch.

"Hit the deck!" Desmond yelled.

Realizing Jody and Timmy might not know what that meant—the lesson of the tube as slang for the television a recently learned lesson—Ward screamed, "Get down! Get down!"

The shriek of the whirly bird's klaxon ceased, and a sharp hiss cut through the confusion.

Ward and Timmy put down the stretcher and Ward shielded his wife as the rest of the party dove to the ground.

A Hellfire missile streaked through the air, thumped into the huge mutant, and detonated with an explosion that rocked the clearing. A shockwave of hot air, Cric innards, legs, and shattered carapace blasted Ward as he buried his head in Jenni's jacket. Heat scorched the back of his neck, then eased, and acrid smoke poured over the barren field as it rained Cric.

Ward sat up.

The Apache's engine cycled up, and the pilot waved as he dipped the bird's nose, spun the chopper around, and darted east toward the river.

A dog-sized Cric bounced from the smoke, its front forelegs missing, the tips of the appendages charred black. A ragged hole showed the inside of the beast's head where its right eye had been, and its left tennis ball-sized eye rolled in its head.

Ward pressed to his knees, swung the Benelli off his back, and put a cloud of #4 turkey shot into the beast's flexing jaws. The gun's pistol grip felt good in his hand, and the roar and the tight recoil pressing his shoulder, and the chiming midnight bell tolling in his head, all sent a zap of energy through him and jumpstarted his muscles. He got to his feet, hung the shotgun over his shoulder, lifted the end of Jenni's stretcher, and said, "Let's go, kid. It's not that much farther."

30

When the party reached the wall that marked the northern border of Creekside Landing, Desmond laid cover fire as the rest of the team put their backs to the red brick. Ward and Timmy put the stretcher down and flexed their fingers, arms, and legs as the last of the water was passed around.

Janet sucked both of her children to her, kissing the tops of their heads, and this time Timmy didn't pull away.

Out on the battlefield, the Crics were inching forward and probing the remains of Godzilla-Cric. Huge chunks of cracked carapace littered the hardpan like the Apache had destroyed a giant's Easter egg hunt. Gray goo tinged with blue and pink covered the ground, and all the mutants that were in tight and close when Hellfire was unleashed were covered in their master's lifeblood.

Ward's heart raced so fast he was dizzy, and a static-filled his head that made his ears hurt. The gunshots and the missile explosion had rung his bell, and if his eardrums weren't blown it would be a miracle.

To the south, the condo complex rose above the red brick wall. A thin line of tree trunks marked the backyards of houses that ran along River Avenue and beyond that lay salvation.

"I'd love to be on the other side of this wall. Does anybody know if there's a gate?" Desmond asked.

Ward had no clue, and apparently, neither did anybody else because nobody spoke.

The wind whispered and sighed, Crics tittered, and the pounding of helicopter airfoils beating the air filled the silence.

"There is one, but it's always locked," Jody said.

The group all turned to look at the girl. She'd done such a good job blending into the background and staying close to the group and keeping herself safe, that Ward had hardly noticed her. She was like a ghost, and to Ward she'd been invisible, just another person he was trying to protect.

"How do you know that?" Janet asked. Armageddon, the apocalypse, the end of all things, but moms gonna be moms.

"Kristal lives... lived here with her mom, remember?" the teenager said.

Janet said nothing, her eyebrows knitting.

"We go to the candy store that way, her mom said—"

"That's fine, sweetie, where is it?" urged Desmond.

To Ward's amazement, and her mother's, judging by the expression on her face, Jody didn't answer, but instead took the lead.

"Hold up, now," said Janet, but she didn't stop her daughter. Instead, she hefted the AR and followed her daughter as she threaded east along the wall.

"Do you need a break from that?" Desmond said to Timmy as he pointed at the stretcher.

The kid shook his head no.

Desmond smiled and nodded at the kid, pride brightening his face despite the dark bags beneath his eyes and the dirt smudged on his face.

As the party eased along the wall, Crics amassed on the barren field. But the beasts were still concerned with the remains of the monster Cric, and they were munching and eating, gnawing on any bit of flesh that could be had.

A flowerbed ran along the bottom of the wall, a thick carpet of spreading junipers that stank of pine tainted with gin. English ivy vines snaked across the red brick wall like rope, their leaves gone. When the group reached the gate, it was locked just as Jody had said it might be.

Beyond the gate a concrete path edged with blue paving stones ran through an arch to a parking lot. As the path led away from the complex it turned sharply east, where it eventually met the road. The walking path led to the restaurants, bars, and other commercial buildings along Patchogue River. Ward took several deep breaths to settle his nerves. They were that close.

There was yelling and screaming and commotion ahead. Crics gathered on the field as if called by the echo of their mother's final call.

"Back up and take cover," Desmond said. "Hurry!"

Ward and Timmy took several steps back and laid the stretcher atop the spreading junipers at the base of the wall. His back muscles ached, but Ward felt no guilt putting down his unconscious wife. What better place for her to rest than atop a bed of evergreens?

Jody and Janet took up positions behind Ward and Timmy, and the crew watched as Desmond went to the closest oak tree trunk and used it as cover as he aimed his AR-15 at the gate's lock. Bullets twanged and cracked against the metal. Desmond fired five times before he was satisfied, and it still took several violent kicks to spring the gate open.

The parking lot beyond was an apocalyptic nightmare.

Crics of all sizes scuttled and hopped over cars, and many of them turned their attention toward the sound of the gunshots. The mutants gathered, a swarm forming, a knot of pincers, legs, and teeth focusing its collective rage on Ward and his companions as they swept through the gate, Desmond covering the team as he held the gate open with his butt.

Ward and Timmy did their best to hold the stretcher steady, but despite their efforts, Jenni was jostled around, and wrinkles of pain cut across her reddened face.

A scream pierced the day and Ward looked over his shoulder as he surged forward, the stretcher twisting in his hands.

Desmond stood silhouetted under the gateway arch, a dog-sized Cric sitting atop the red brick wall, its pincers and spikes striking at Desmond as he struggled to bring up his gun.

The gate slammed home with a clang, and Desmond was on the outside.

Ward felt a scream forming in his throat, but he made no sound.

Janet released her children and put the stock of the AR to her shoulder.

The Crics shrieked as one, and the horde forming up in the parking lot heaved forward like a breaking wave, a roiling fist of Crics leaking over the cars and blacktop and coming at the party.

Desmond took several unsteady steps as he raised his rifle. As he fired, he let loose with a battle cry that would've shattered crystal had there been any on hand. The gun spat bullets, and the large Cric atop the wall was blown from its perch, the bullet passing through the monster and plunking into a black pickup truck with four flat tires.

Ward turned his attention back to the swarm coming at him across the lot.

"No!" yelled Janet.

Timmy dropped his end of the stretcher and bolted toward his mother, who was running toward the closed gate.

Through the steel bars of the gate, Ward saw Desmond struggling with three cat-sized Crics. One was on his shoulder, the other two fighting to climb up his legs, tugging at his motorcycle pants with claws and teeth.

Ward put the stretcher down and swung the Benelli off his back. If his count was correct, there were only two bullets left in the gun, though Jenni still had shells in her jacket pocket.

A ray of sunlight broke through the thinning cloud cover like manna from heaven, and Desmond was illuminated in his struggle like a gladiator at the center of a vast colosseum.

Janet tried to open the gate, but when Timmy arrived at her side, he grabbed his mother's arm and tugged her away. The struggle didn't last long, and when Timmy succeeded in wrenching his mother's hand from the gate handle, they both fell to the ground in a tangle of arms, legs, and tears.

Beyond the closed gate, more Crics inched into view, and one of the beasts crawled up Desmond's leg and managed to clamp a claw on one of his gloved fingers. A screech of pain slowed the approaching swarm as it spilled across the parking lot, but the mutants were only fifty yards away.

Desmond twisted and thrashed, the AR firing into the air. A Cric pulled at Desmond's hair with one pincer, and with the other tore off the top of Desmond's left ear. Blood leaked down the side of Desmond's face as he stared through the closed gate at his sister's family.

A larger Cric bounced onto the scene, and Desmond was knocked to the ground. He crawled and fought and struggled as the Crics mounded over him, the AR barking.

Janet screamed, a gut-wrenching wail that tore Ward apart, his insides molten hot.

Desmond fell to his knees and crawled toward the gate.

Smaller Crics bounced and scuttled all around Ward.

"Run, you fools! Run!" Desmond yelled, and then he was gone.

31

Ward stood in stunned silence, his feet rooted to the ground, terror paralyzing him, sorrow sucking away what little energy he had left. He squeezed the Benelli's trigger, but the gun was empty, like him. His count had been wrong.

Gunshots, screaming, then silence from the other side of the wall.

"Come on, Mom! Come on!" Timmy had taken control, and he held the AR like a pro, no doubt copying what he'd watched his old man do many times.

The shotgun blasts had given the Cric's pause, but it didn't buy much time.

Ward had managed to drag the stretcher between two cars, and the approaching Crics had slowed, but hadn't stopped. The beasts surrounded Ward and Jenni, and it was Timmy, AR-15 blazing, bullets ricocheting around like deadly sparks flowing off a fire, that was pushing the monsters back.

Jody arrived at Ward's side like a ghost materializing out of the ether.

"Are you O.K.?" Ward asked, but somehow, he knew Jody would always find a way to be O.K. She had a steady calmness about her that he had originally taken for shyness or aloofness, but he'd come to discover that was only teenage angst.

Jody nodded as she stared at her mother and brother as they closed the distance between the gate and where Ward had hunkered down.

When Janet and Timmy arrived, Ward said, "Cover me so I can reload."

"Yeah," said Timmy as the boy let the magazine drop from the rifle as he held out his hand to his mother.

Janet watched her son with a mix of pleasure and worry. With her gas mask on, her features were hidden, but Ward still saw the pride welling in her eyes as she handed her son the spare loaded magazine.

Ward drew back the bolt, pressed the safety button, turned the M4 over, and fumbled in his wife's jacket pocket for shells. There were four shotgun shells left. He pumped them into the tube, hit the load button, and jacked a shell into the firing chamber.

When he looked up, he found Timmy holding out the AR. "There's seventeen bullets in the magazine," the kid said.

Four shells of #4 turkey, seventeen .45 MM rounds, and a quarter mile of Cric-infested territory was all the team had left.

"I don't know who's a better shot," Ward said, and he wasn't kidding. Knowing Bill, the boy had probably shot more rounds at the range than he had.

Sorrow consumed the party then, Crics pressing in around them. Janet wept openly, as did Jody, and though Timmy did his best to fight back the tears, his face growing red, he lost the battle and soon they were all weeping for the man who had given his life for theirs. Like Bill, Ward and Jenni would never have made it this far without Desmond's help. Hell, Ward and Jenni wouldn't have made it off their front lawn.

The Cric horde wasn't as respectful. With the fireworks over, the beasts surged into motion once more, their legs scraping on the blacktop, claws and spikes scratching metal.

Timmy handed the shotgun off to his mother and lifted one end of the stretcher.

Without having to be asked, Jody took up the other end.

Ward smiled at the teenagers. No orders were necessary. The team had been through too much, and they each knew what needed to be done.

Condominiums loomed on all sides of the parking lot except the northern border. Ward wanted to head east, and he saw no reason not to continue to use the brick wall as protection as they had before. He vaulted to his feet, put the stock of the AR to his shoulder, and looked east for targets.

Rat-sized Crics encroached on their position like ants circling a fallen ice cream cone, but Ward saw only two larger Crics. Desmond's words came back to him like a gut punch, "The things like to hide under cars."

Ward popped off three shots as he ran for the cover of the brick wall.

The two larger Crics disappeared in a mist of guts and legs. Ward pressed his back to the red brick as he'd done before. He watched with delight as the teenagers lugged his wife, Janet rotating like a combat veteran, the shotgun at the ready.

Several large mutants pushed out from their hiding places, the beasts crawling over cars and blocking the easterly path.

"Shit!" Ward yelled, his frustration boiling over as he stomped on the first wave of Crics, which made the other mutants pause.

A mutant hopped onto the wall, pulled itself atop the white stone coping, and pounced on Ward, knocking him to the ground.

Screaming and yelling as the kids dropped the stretcher and Janet fell back, aiming the shotgun but unable to fire due to the proximity of Ward and her children.

Ward flipped onto his back as he gripped the Cric's forelegs with both hands, holding the beast back as it straddled him, the beast's mouth flexing open as the mutant tried to take a bite out of him.

Gunshots, three fast cracks, and then Ward was covered in Cric goo, blood, and pieces of carapace as the monster exploded, the bullets tearing into the creature and smacking into the wall.

Ward sat up and looked at Janet, who stared at her gun as if it possessed some magic. She hadn't fired, and Ward hadn't fired, so who had?

A woman wearing a hunting outfit, and a green JETS football helmet with ski goggles jumped onto the hood of a car, a pistol in her hand. She also carried what looked like a giant flyswatter, and she hopped from car to car, crunching Crics. The woman stopped at the edge of the parking lot and stared.

Ward didn't need to see the woman's blue eyes or the tuft of blonde hair leaking out from under the JETS helmet to know it was the woman who had attacked him and taken his .45. She'd spared his life, and he reciprocated, and now she'd saved his ass with his grandfather's gun.

"Sorry about before, but I need to hold onto this a bit longer," she said as she held out the pistol, palm up, weapon pointed at the ground.

Ward said nothing. All guns were trained on the newcomer.

"I can take you to the line," she said. When nobody spoke, she added, "There's a line to get out. I can take you there."

The woman moved in closer, and Ward saw that her eyes had cleared. "What's your name?"

"Tess."

"You look better than when we first met, Tess."

"They pricked me." She jerked a thumb east.

"So why are you here?" Janet pressed, her eyes bouncing around wildly as Crics crept toward their position.

"I was kind of out of it this morning," she said. Her eyes locked on Ward. "I came back to…"

"What?" Ward said.

Tess was staring at Jenni. She said, "You need to get her the needle. She looks…"

"What?" screamed Ward.

"Like she don't have long!" Tess screamed. "She can hear us, you know."

Ward hadn't known.

"Take us out of here," Janet said.

Ward shouldered the AR with its thirteen bullets and watched the team's rear as Jody and Timmy carried Jenni. Tess used her flyswatter, and Ward popped the bigger Crics as the parking lot gave way to a thin border of grass that led to the condo buildings along the west side of River Avenue.

Jenni cried out, a terrible wail that sounded like skin being torn. She thrashed and heaved on the stretcher, the belts barely holding her in place as she snaked out an arm and freed her legs.

Jody and Timmy dropped the stretcher and both the teenagers screamed as they stared at Jenni, terror cutting across their faces.

Jenni's gas mask was long gone, and so it was that Ward saw the Cric larva ooze from her ear and plop onto the ground.

When Ward was eight, he saw his dog run over by a car. The young beagle bolted into the road chasing after an errant throw of his. The screech of rubber, the yelp, and the crunch of bone had stayed with him like an evil parrot on his shoulder, always reminding him it had been his fault. That feeling was the closest to what he felt now, a soul-sucking sorrow that threatened to break him. His wife was dead. He'd been too slow, and too late.

Jenni's back arched off the stretcher, her eyes going wide, her hands finding her neck.

Janet peeled away the hands, soothing Jenni with words and caressing her forehead with a gloved hand.

"Come on, we've got to go," Tess said.

Blood trickled from Jenni's ear and down her neck.

The party gaped at the Cric larva flopping around on the ground. Then the slug fell still and deflated.

"Come on," Tess said. "That's a good thing. The thing is dead. Same thing happened to me. She needs the needle. Let's go. Now!"

32

The sun began its descent to the horizon, the sky painted a deep purple-orange, sunlight fighting to get through the remnants of the storm clouds, which were nothing more than dirty stretched cotton. There were puddles along the walkway, and the strip of grass before the condo building was damp, but the Crics were still getting curious as daylight faded and dusk painted the land in shadowy grayness.

Tess headed north, intent on going around the building, her legs pumping, Ward's grandfather's .45 out before her in a doublehanded grip.

Through the breezeway that ran through the center of the condo building, Ward saw the reflection of spinning lights. The glass doors were smashed, but tall antennas and arched legs swayed in the tunnel of darkness. Many of the Crics had yet to venture out of their hiding places where they'd sheltered from the storm, but with a gentle breeze drawing away the moisture and darkness on the way, that would soon change.

Gunshots, helicopter blades pounding the air, screaming, and chaos filtered through the condos.

Tess reached the northwest corner of the building.

Janet was right behind her, the kids still heroically hauling Jenni, who was trying to sit up. Her chin was pressed to her chest, her head swinging around wildly as she tried to see what was happening.

Ward watched the team's rear flank as he turned a hundred and eighty degrees. He passed an emergency stairwell that led down into the building's basement, and a Cric launched at him from within the stairwell and landed on his back.

Two gunshots rang out and Ward was splattered with Cric goo as the bullets passed through the monster and plunked into the building. Ward slipped and fell to the ground, almost cracking his head on the steel railing that surrounded the stairwell.

The rest of the party continued running and didn't look back, and as they rounded the corner, Ward smiled. He felt so comfortable lying there on the ground staring at the patches of gray filtering through the dark clouds. He still had a few bullets left, but he didn't care anymore. What happened, happened. He had no energy left. No strength.

Jenni's face filtered through his mind's eye. She looked like she was going to be O.K. and would probably need him in the coming weeks and months.

33

Ward passed his superficial physical examination and was allowed to inch between two of the soldiers manning the border of the rescue area. Neither person looked at him, their faces hidden behind dark blast shields. Ward kept looking over his shoulder for Desmond, but he didn't see him.

The crowd parted and then Timmy was there, his young face stained with dirt, blood, and Cric goo, but he was smiling. "Ward, they need you."

Ward stopped walking and stared at the kid like he was speaking another language.

Timmy grabbed Ward's elbow and tugged him forward.

Having entered the womb of the United States military, people stood around like zombies, waiting to be checked and loaded onto ferries that would bring them to a quarantine camp on Fire Island. Ward knew this because a speaker blared instructions that informed all citizens that nobody would be released from what the bigheads had dubbed Protective Custody, until the powers that be were certain there was no contamination beyond the Containment Zone. That involved a physical examination and spraying for larva and eggs, which had proven to be the biggest challenge.

Timmy and Ward reached the others and found two EMTs hovering over Jenni. When they saw Ward a young blonde with crooked teeth asked, "Is this your wife?"

Ward nodded.

"Do you give us permission to—"

Ward's frustration boiled over. This was an extreme emergency, but protocol was protocol and what were human beings without it? A pack of wolves. "Yes. Help her. Please, do whatever you have to."

One of the EMTs stuck Jenni with a needle and she convulsed, white foam leaking through her lips, her body shaking violently.

Ward stepped forward but Janet put out an arm to stop him.

Jenni stopped shaking, and the medic undid the buckles holding the belts in place, freeing her. To Ward's astonishment and pleasure, Jenni sat up, rubbed her eyes, and said, "Where am I?"

Laughter, high fives, and as Jenni was taken away to the doctors, Ward slumped to the ground, his head in his hands. It all came out then; the sorrow, fear, angst, and determination. He cried for the first time in he didn't know how long, pain knifing down his back, his neck a superheated knot of agony. Ward laughed. He figured he'd lost ten pounds over the last few days, and now he planned to spend the next week eating.

Tess knelt, gave Ward his .45 back, and said, "Sorry again." She held out a hand and Ward shook it. Then Tess got up, waved to the others, and disappeared into the crowd. Ward never saw her again.

Timmy stood over him, and Ward took the boy's offered hand and got to his feet.

"Good news," the kid said. "My mom just got an emergency text on her phone."

"There's a cell signal?" Ward hadn't thought about cell service or the internet in what felt like years.

"Wireless internet," Timmy said. "Some rich dude parked one of his satellites over the area."

Ward padded his shirt absently. He had no idea where his phone had ended up. He recalled using its light app but beyond that… "What was the message?"

"Jazz texted," the kid said. "They were rescued a few hours ago. Her, Toby, and Muffin are fine. They're already at the holding center over at Davis Park."

Relief flooded through Ward, and then a bolt of pain stabbed his knotted neck muscles. "So it was all for nothing," he said.

The kid's eyebrows wrinkled.

Seeing his confusion, Ward said, "We should've stayed put, holed up, and waited for rescue. Had Lacy done that she'd still be alive."

"But Jenni wouldn't," the kid said, his tone a notch below his 'are you stupid' tone.

Ward asked, "What do you mean?"

"I heard the medics say that if Jenni hadn't gotten those meds, and a high dose of them at that, she wouldn't have made it. We saved her. You saved her."

Ward would come to learn in the days that followed that the antibiotics had been like the first line of an army, and while the drugs did nothing to cure the Cric sickness, they were effective at helping to keep the disease at bay until real treatment could be administered.

Timmy looped an arm around Ward's waist. "We did make it just in time, though."

Ward said nothing as he lifted an eyebrow and stared at the boy. He wanted to ask why but knew the kid was going to tell him.

"The flyboys are moving in with the gas," he said.

The survivors pushed forward and became two lines, and emergency workers in hazmat suits delivered water, crackers, and basic medical supplies to those waiting to be processed.

Helicopters whirled overhead, and gunshots cracked in the distance, but none of that was Ward's problem any longer. The ever-present scraping and clicking of the Crics was gone, replaced by the murmur of the crowd. With the adrenaline draining, Ward's muscles turned to concrete, and his many bumps, bruises, and lacerations tingled and prodded with jabs of pain.

Timmy and Ward caught up with Jody and Janet, who had stepped out of line and were waiting for them. Mother and daughter were drinking water, and munching crackers, and neither looked the worse for wear, though new carelines crisscrossed their faces, proof of past horrors and future mourning.

"Where's Jenni?" Ward asked.

Janet hiked a thumb toward a large white tent that sat at the edge of Patchogue River.

Ward nodded, and the companions got back in line, no further words necessary. Jenni was alive because of their help, and Ward saw Janet and the kids, Desmond, Jazz, and Toby as family, and were forever part of him. Wherever he went, no matter what he did from here on out, these people would always be in his thoughts, and he would do anything for them.

It would take months to count the dead, and not all would be accounted for. Surviving islanders would be relocated like so many other islanders before them. Some would come back, more over time, but in the end, the northern paradise that was Long Island would never be the same. He and Jenni would be forced to start a new life and rebuild things they'd considered set in stone.

Ward smiled at the thought. Maybe that was exactly what he needed.

CODA

Smithtown, Long Island, New York, 11:49 PM EST, *night prior to complete infestation*

Jake fought his way through the thick shrubs on the northern side of his house, sweat dripping down his back, fear and worry eating away at his stomach. He pressed his back to the white vinyl siding, staring back through the thick greenery that filled the flowerbed and rose to window height.

The spider-like creature that attacked him in the garage had backed off, but Jake saw the beast at the edge of the shrubbery, its bulbous wet eyes scanning the vegetation, sharp teeth glinting, arched rear legs casting long shadows over the lawn.

Evergreen needles poked his skin, the five-gallon gas can he carried heavy and awkward. Moonlight seeped through the thin clouds, and wavering cones of light cut across the swaying trees and whispering water reeds. To the east the Nissequogue River sparkled, the inky water undulating in the gentle breeze.

It had been five days since the strange smoke had pushed across Long Island, and Jake's mind spun with a full range of conspiracy theories. His father had literally smelled trouble from the start, and he along with Jake's mother and sister were at the family ski house in Vermont. He'd refused to go, but now he wanted nothing more than to get off the island. Unless he was the unluckiest person on Earth, there were more of these mutants that looked like oversized camel crickets but were half mouth and had front pincers.

Jake reached the corner of the house and peered around its edge. The front yard gave way to Riviera Street, which was still, the thin border of marsh grass and trees that separated the road from the river bathed in pale moonlight.

The jet ski sat on the shore, its trailer's large bulbous yellow wheels gray in the half-light. Jake patted his rear pocket with his free hand and felt his wallet, the scent of gasoline forcing out the deep smell of must that tickled his nose.

A single gunshot cracked in the distance, and it sent a surge of nervous energy pulsing to his extremities. Jake ran across the front lawn, the gas can swinging as his legs pumped, and though he fought the urge, he lost the battle and looked over his shoulder.

Bathed in the pale light the dog-sized camel cricket reared up, its pincers snapping as it jumped and landed on the lawn ten feet behind him.

Jake had no gun, no weapon at all except his wallet. If he could get to the jet ski, he would cross the sound, his dad could rent a car, and he would be in Vermont by breakfast. He hated the thought of abandoning the jet ski, but his father would understand. He'd predicted a lockdown, and Jake had laughed. He wasn't laughing anymore.

The mutant crawled behind Jake, watching him as he crossed the road to the grass, his feet sinking into the damp bog-like earth.

There was no time to gas up, so Jake tossed the gas can onto one of the ski's footwells, and began pushing the trailer toward the water, which was ten feet away.

Clicking, scraping, and faint titters. Crickets jumped in the grass all around him, the sound of... was he hearing the creatures chewing on the vegetation?

He gave the idea no further thought as he pushed the jet ski into the water, the oversized trailer wheels floating on the dark surface as the craft slid into the river.

The monster stood on the shoreline and didn't follow Jake as he waded out into the water.

Jake cradled the gas can as he mounted the ski. The keys were in the ignition where he'd left them, and the gas gauge read three-quarters full. With the extra gas he had plenty of fuel to make it to Black Rock Neck, and with a gentle wind out of the south, the waves would be almost nonexistent.

The ski roared to life, and when Jake looked back toward shore, he saw a pixelated shadowy wave gathering around the mutant as it stared at him.

Jake goosed the ski's throttle and tore upriver.

He passed Kings Park Bluff, the sea beyond shimmering silver. Jake encountered no one as he crossed the Long Island Sound. He stopped when there was an eighth of a tank of gas left, and he refilled the ski with the fuel he'd lugged before continuing.

It took forty-five minutes to cross the sound, sea spray biting his face. Jake's heart hammered in his chest as beams of light from the Fayerweather Island Lighthouse periodically cut through the darkness. Black Rock Channel was dark, and nothing moved on the spit of rock and sand that jutted a mile out into the sound.

The ski gurgled and popped as he backed off on the throttle. Lights sparkled in the darkness, the tall lampposts of Captain's Cove Marina aglow despite the late hour. His father had used the marina many times, but if he pulled up on the jet ski, he'd have to answer a thousand questions. His gut told him slipping away without notice would be best, so he beached the ski on the inner banks of Seaside Beach, where he abandoned it, though he took the craft's key.

A road led out to the lighthouse, and when he reached it, Jake hugged himself and started his trek north to South End. At first light, he'd call his father to arrange a car. With the sense that he'd dodged a bullet, Jake sucked in the clean air and patted himself on the back. Perhaps he should have listened to his father, but at least he'd done right in the end.

Hours later, with the faint purple-orange glow of sunrise blossoming on the horizon, a group of teenagers found the jet ski. There was no key in the ignition, so they broke open the seat storage compartment. When they found nothing, the boys urinated on the ski and moved on.

So it was that the boys didn't see the three strange crickets that crawled from the ski's storage compartment and hopped into the beachgrass. The mutants stayed together, the two tiny translucent creatures following their mother.

A sour sweet breeze rustled the beachgrass as the Crics reached the road that ran to the lighthouse, a streetlight creating a puddle of brightness. The mutants jumped and crawled toward the light, the largest Cric pausing at the edge of a sewer grate. Water sloshed, and the sound of shells being pulled over pebbles echoed on the wind as the lead Cric inched forward and hopped between the sewer grates, its two children following diligently.

The End

Other Severed Press novels by Edward J. McFadden III: Terror Lake, TRAGIC, Predators & Prey, Wolves of the Sea, Fortune's Cypher, Crimson Falls (#1 Amazon Bestseller Tag), Hell Creek, Barracuda Swarm, The Cryptid Club, Dinosaur Red, Drop Off (#1 Amazon Bestseller Tag), Jurassic Ark, Keepers of the Flame, Throwback, Sea Tremors, Primeval Valley, Shadow of the Abyss (#1 Amazon Bestseller Tag), Awake, and The Breach (#1 Amazon Bestseller Tag, Amazon #1 Hot New Audio Release Tag). His other novels include: Terror Peak (#1 Amazon Bestseller Tag), the Ellis Parker Adventure Thriller series: The Modern Pharoh, The Doomsday Deception, and The Sigils of Solomon, the Theo Ramage Thriller series: Quick Sands, Sandbagged, and Too Much Grit, and Dogs Get Ten Lives, The Black Death of Babylon, and HOAXERS. Ed lives on Long Island with his wife Dawn, their daughter Samantha, and their cats Snoop and Skittles.

Check out other great

Cryptid Novels!

C.G. Mosley

BAKER COUNTY BIGFOOT CHRONICLE

Marie Bledsoe only wants her missing brother Kurt back. She'll stop at nothing to make it happen and, with the help of Kurt's friend Tony, along with Sheriff Ray Cochran, Marie embarks on a terrifying journey deep into the belly of the mysterious Walker Laboratory to find him. However, what she and her companions find lurking in the laboratory basement is beyond comprehension. There are cryptids from the forest being held captive there and something...else. Enjoy this suspenseful tale from the mind of C.G. Mosley, author of Wood Ape. Welcome back to Baker County, a place where monsters do lurk in the night!

Hunter Shea

LOCH NESS REVENGE

Deep in the murky waters of Loch Ness, the creature known as Nessie has returned. Twins Natalie and Austin McQueen watched in horror as their parents were devoured by the world's most infamous lake monster. Two decades later, it's their turn to hunt the legend. But what lurks in the Loch is not what they expected. Nessie is devouring everything in and around the Loch, and it's not alone. Hell has come to the Scottish Highlands. In a fierce battle between man and monster, the world may never be the same. Praise for THEY RISE : "Outrageous, balls to the wall...made me yearn for 3D glasses and a tub of popcorn, extra butter!" – The Eyes of Madness "A fast-paced, gore-heavy splatter fest of sharksploitation." The Werd "A rocket paced horror story. I enjoyed the hell out of this book." Shotgun Logic Reviews

 SEVERED**PRESS**

CHECK OUT OTHER GREAT CRYPTID NOVELS

RETURN TO DYATLOV PASS
by **J.H. Moncrieff**

In 1959, nine Russian students set off on a skiing expedition in the Ural Mountains. Their mutilated bodies were discovered weeks later. Their bizarre and unexplained deaths are one of the most enduring true mysteries of our time. Nearly sixty years later, podcast host Nat McPherson ventures into the same mountains with her team, determined to finally solve the mystery of the Dyatlov Pass incident. Her plans are thwarted on the first night, when two trackers from her group are brutally slaughtered. The team's guide, a superstitious man from a neighboring village, blames the killings on yetis, but no one believes him. As members of Nat's team die one by one, she must figure out if there's a murderer in their midst—or something even worse—before history repeats itself and her group becomes another casualty of the infamous Dead Mountain.

DOVER DEMON
by **Hunter Shea**

The Dover Demon is real...and it has returned. In 1977, Sam Brogna and his friends came upon a terrifying, alien creature on a deserted country road. What they witnessed was so bizarre, so chilling, they swore their silence. But their lives were changed forever. Decades later. the town of Dover has been hit by a massive blizzard. Sam's son, Nicky, is drawn to search for the infamous cryptid, only to disappear into the bowels of a secret underground lair. The Dover Demon is far deadlier than anyone could have believed. And there are many of them. Can Sam and his reunited friends rescue Nicky and battle a race of creatures so powerful, so sinister, that history itself has been shaped by their secretive presence?

CHECK OUT OTHER GREAT CRYPTID NOVELS

BIGFOOT WAR
by **Eric S. Brown**

Now a feature film from Origin Releasing. For the first time ever, all three core books of the Bigfoot War series have been collected into a single tome of Sasquatch Apocalypse horror. Remastered and reedited this book chronicles the original war between man and beast from the initial battles in Babblecreek through the apocalypse to the wastelands of a dark future world where Sasquatch reigns supreme and mankind struggles to survive. If you think you've experienced Bigfoot Horror before, think again. Bigfoot War sets the bar for the genre and will leave you praying that you never have to go into the woods again.

CRYPTID ZOO
by **Gerry Griffiths**

As a child, rare and unusual animals, especially cryptid creatures, always fascinated Carter Wilde.

Now that he's an eccentric billionaire and runs the largest conglomerate of high-tech companies all over the world, he can finally achieve his wildest dream of building the most incredible theme park ever conceived on the planet...CRYPTID ZOO.

Even though there have been apparent problems with the project, Wilde still decides to send some of his marketing employees and their families on a forced vacation to assess the theme park in preparation for Opening Day.

Nick Wells and his family are some of those chosen and are about to embark on what will become the most terror-filled weekend of their lives—praying they survive.

STEP RIGHT UP AND GET YOUR FREE PASS...

TO CRYPTID ZOO